HER WILD HIGHLANDER

Books by Emma Prince

Highland Bodyguards Series:

The Lady's Protector (Book 1)

Heart's Thief (Book 2)

A Warrior's Pledge (Book 3)

Claimed by the Bounty Hunter (Book 4)

A Highland Betrothal (Novella, Book 4.5)

The Promise of a Highlander (Book 5)

The Bastard Laird's Bride (Book 6)

Surrender to the Scot (Book 7)

Her Wild Highlander (Book 8)

Book 9 coming Fall 2018!

The Sinclair Brothers Trilogy:

Highlander's Ransom (Book 1)

Highlander's Redemption (Book 2)

Highlander's Return (Bonus Novella, Book 2.5)

Highlander's Reckoning (Book 3)

Viking Lore Series:

Enthralled (Viking Lore, Book 1)

Shieldmaiden's Revenge (Viking Lore, Book 2)

The Bride Prize (Viking Lore, Book 2.5)

Desire's Hostage (Viking Lore, Book 3)

Thor's Wolf (Viking Lore, Book 3.5)—a Kindle Worlds novella

Other Books:

Wish upon a Winter Solstice (A Highland Holiday Novella)

To Kiss a Governess (A Highland Christmas Novella)

HER WILD HIGHLANDER

Highland Bodyguards, Book 8

EMMA PRINCE

For Scott. Always.

Chapter One

Late August, 1320
Scone Palace, Scotland

Today was as good a day as any for an execution.
Kieran MacAdams planted his feet and clasped his hands behind his back. Judging by the yellowish tint to the air, dawn was only a few minutes away.

"It is time," Robert the Bruce, King of Scotland, said beside Kieran. His somber, serious voice boomed over the silent crowd gathered in the palace courtyard.

The palace's double doors creaked open, and a string of guards leading three prisoners emerged into the yard.

Even though the sun still had not risen, the prisoners blinked at the comparative brightness after spending nigh a month in Scone's dungeon. Once finely clad nobles, the three men now huddled in rags, their shoulders hunched against the mute stares of those in the courtyard.

They were led to the wooden gallows that had been constructed after the King had passed down his judgment at the Black Parliament less than a sennight past. Though Kieran wasn't normally one for sensationalism, Black Parliament was a fitting name for what it had been.

Three death sentences for three traitors.

Each man was positioned on a wooden box beneath a length of rope. Then the executioner, dressed in black and with a low-drooping cowl to hide his face, slowly fitted the noose around each man's neck in turn.

But the King held up his hand to stay the executioner, then motioned toward the palace doors once more.

The Countess Agnes of Strathearn appeared, sagging against her guard and weeping into a kerchief. Kieran nearly grunted at her overdone display. The countess was not to be executed today—or any day, assuming the Bruce didn't change his mind. She had been found guilty of participating in a treasonous plot to assassinate the King, just like the others, yet because she'd broken down and confessed the names of her co-conspirators within moments of being found out, the Bruce had shown leniency.

Still, the Bruce meant for her to witness a demonstration she was not likely to forget this morn. Her allies would hang, and she would be made to watch.

When the final prisoner emerged into the yard, Kieran clutched his hands so tightly behind him that his knuckles were no doubt as white as the countess's kerchief.

William de Soules.

Unlike the countess, the scheming Lowland bastard did not cry or lean against the guard holding him. Instead, he strode with surprising calm through the yard. His gaze landed on the Bruce, snagging only a hair's breadth before traveling coolly over the members of the Bodyguard Corps flanking the King.

When de Soules's dark eyes settled on him, Kieran actually drew back his lips and gave the man a silent snarl. Hot hatred flashed in de Soules's gaze before his icy control snapped back into place once more.

De Soules clearly still despised the Bruce for the perceived slight against him when titles and lands had been distributed among the King's nobles. That had prompted de Soules to launch an attempted coup against the Bruce, landing him here among his fellow traitors.

Yet the Lowlander also seemed to hold a special loathing for Kieran. After all, Kieran had been the one to drag de Soules's sorry arse to the King for judgment after his conspiracy had been uncovered.

The guard drew de Soules to the countess's side before the gallows. Though de Soules had been the clear mastermind behind the scheme to assassinate the Bruce, he had been granted a life of imprisonment rather than the drawing and quartering he deserved. But the King believed de Soules would serve as an example—and a deterrent—in life better than in death.

Kieran wasn't so sure. He stared hard at the bastard who had plotted to kill the King.

Thanks to Jerome Munro and Elaine Beaumore—soon to be Munro as well—who stood on the King's other side, the scheme had been unraveled just in time and the major conspirators rounded up and imprisoned until punishment could be meted out. At last, those guilty would pay for their betrayal. Except for de Soules, the guiltiest of all, who would live to see another day, albeit from within the bowels of Scone Palace.

Just then, the sun crested the eastern horizon, sending rays of orange light over the silent gathering. The Bruce cleared his throat.

"John Logie, Gilbert Malherbe, Richard Broun," the King intoned. "Ye have been found guilty of treasonous conspiracy against yer sovereign and country. The punishment for such a crime is drawing, quartering, hanging, and beheading. Yet I dinnae take pleasure in the deaths of my countrymen, men I have broken bread with countless times. Therefore ye are to be hanged by the neck until ye are pronounced dead."

Kieran barely resisted the urge to spit on the ground. These bastards didn't deserve leniency. But it wasn't Kieran's place to pass judgment. The King had also granted them the right to a Christian burial, another mercy Kieran wouldn't have had the grace to grant.

Just as well that Kieran didn't bear the burden of leadership. He was only a warrior, a soldier who did the Bruce's bidding. Aye, he was a member of the King's Bodyguard Corps, an elite group of warriors who protected those most vulnerable to the attacks of Scotland's enemies. But he knew his place. He was a weapon, the King's sword and shield, to be wielded as the Bruce saw fit.

A white-robed bishop emerged from the abbey attached to the palace, gliding toward the gallows with a somber expression. He mounted the wooden steps and moved to each man in turn, murmuring a prayer for their souls and making the sign of the cross before them. Then he turned to the King and tilted his head.

Those gathered in the yard seemed to hold their breath then. Only the sound of the countess's soft weeping and the rattling of wood against wood broke the thick silence. John Logie, the first of the prisoners, was shaking so badly that the box he stood on clattered hollowly against the gallows.

The King gave the executioner a single nod. The black-clad man moved to Logie and kicked away the box, silencing the clattering. The traitor dropped like a stone, a single gurgling noise rising from his throat before his life was extinguished.

The executioner moved silently to the second man, who had urinated himself in fear. Befitting the somber mood, the executioner did not pause for dramatic effect or to extend the man's terror. Instead, his boot moved swiftly, kicking away the box. With a hard jerk and three twitches, the man was dead.

Yet when the executioner reached Richard Broun, the traitor dared to spit in the black-clad man's face. A gasp of surprise rose from those gathered. Broun's gaze flicked to de Soules before latching onto the King.

"Ye think this is over, ye bastard?" the man hissed. "There are more of us. There will always be more of us. And we willnae stop hunting ye and yer allies until we get our just rewar—"

The executioner unceremoniously knocked the prisoner's box away, cutting off his diatribe. But the man did not die easily. He thrashed and gurgled, his legs seeking purchase on naught but air. His face turned red, then purple, his tongue swelling and lolling from his mouth until at last his struggles ceased and he swung lifeless in the bright morning sun.

Kieran's gaze shot to de Soules. The man stood in profile to him, but even still, Kieran could make out the faint smile curving his lips.

Hell and damnation. Cold trepidation seeped into Kieran's bones despite the mild summer morn. It was just as he feared. De Soules still had allies in his mad scheme against the Bruce, despite his seeming lack of power as a prisoner.

The guards pulled the countess and de Soules away from the gallows, the countess still crying into her kerchief. De Soules kept his brown head modestly dipped as he was drawn past the King and his bodyguards, yet the ghost of a smile still played around his lips.

When the prisoners were inside once more, Kieran spun on his heels and faced the Bruce. "Robert," he said, keeping his voice low. The King had granted Kieran such familiarity in private now that he was a member of the Corps, but the yard was still crowded with onlookers. "Ye cannae doubt now that de Soules still schemes something."

The Bruce kept his weathered features smooth, yet Kieran didn't miss the flicker of concern in the man's keen brown eyes. "We will discuss this matter further inside—all of ye," he replied curtly to Kieran and the other members of the Corps surrounding him.

They fell in behind the Bruce as he strode toward the palace. They crossed the great hall and made their way down one of the many corridors leading to the palace's private chambers. The Bruce halted in front of one of his meeting rooms and shoved inside.

Only when the door was tightly shut behind them did the King mutter a curse under his breath.

Kieran planted himself in front of the door, letting his gaze travel over those inside. It was one of the oddest assortments of people he'd ever shared a chamber with, yet they were all members of the same small, select group whom the King trusted most.

There were eight of them all together, not including the Bruce. Apparently this wasn't the entire Bodyguard Corps, for the King had sent many of his best warriors to the far-flung corners of Scotland and the Borderlands. Yet once the assassination attempt had been thwarted a month past, the Bruce had called down several members of the Corps who'd been training at a camp somewhere in the Highlands.

Jerome and Elaine, who stood to Kieran's right, were the only ones he'd known until a fortnight past.

He'd been introduced to Colin MacKay and his wife Sabine, who stood to the left of the King, once the

Bruce had made Kieran a member of the Corps. Colin, blond and sharp-eyed, was apparently one of the founding members of the Corps. Sabine, who never seemed far from Colin's side, ran the King's network of spies and messengers.

Will Sinclair, the one with the eye patch and the constant scowl standing on the King's other side, was an obvious choice for the Corps. The man had the tall, strong build of a warrior. But the remaining two, Niall Beaumore and Mairin Mackenzie, were strange additions indeed.

Niall was Elaine's older brother, and though the russet-haired English lad had a fighter's frame, he looked to be a few years before his prime.

And Mairin... The lass was as thin as a wisp, her dove-gray eyes ever watchful. Elaine and Sabine, while members of the King's inner circle, weren't technically part of his elite fighting force. But Mairin, with her short sword belted to her hip and more often than not a bow and quiver slung over her back, most certainly was. What on earth was a wee thing like her doing in the King's Bodyguard Corps?

For Kieran's part, he towered over all the others, even the other men born and bred in the Highlands. He was used to being the biggest, strongest man in any given room, yet he was the newest member of the Corps. Though he had a few choice words to spew about de Soules, he held his tongue.

Jerome was the first to speak, saying what they were all no doubt thinking. "We all heard what Broun said. De Soules may still be scheming even from his cell."

"There should be more of us here to watch yer back, Robert," Colin said quietly.

The King shook his head slightly. "Garrick is never far, and we could easily call upon Ansel, or even Kirk or Logan, if the need truly arose."

"And ye dinnae think it already has?" Colin asked. "Broun used his last breath to threaten ye, Robert, and de Soules looked like a cat who swallowed a canary out there. This matter could be easily remedied if ye would—"

"Enough," the King snapped.

Apparently Kieran wasn't the only one who thought de Soules should have been given a traitor's death, but the Bruce wouldn't be swayed.

The King smoothed his red and gray beard to regain his composure. "I willnae make a martyr of de Soules, for it will only embolden his allies—if he truly has any. I am loath to put much faith in the words of lying scum like Richard Broun."

"Fair enough," Elaine said, tilting her coppery head. "It is your decision, sire. And truly, I cannot see how de Soules or anyone still loyal to him could possibly strike against you—not with so many members of the Corps here. But what of the threat against your allies?"

"Like Lady Vivienne."

Everyone in the chamber turned to Kieran at his gruff interjection.

Kieran crossed his arms over his chest. "Ye granted me permission to fetch her from the French court nigh on a month past, Robert. Yet here I am, listening to de

Soules's crony make threats even with a noose around his neck."

The air crackled with tension for a long moment. Though the King granted a certain informality amongst the members of the Corps, Kieran had just bluntly called the Bruce to task before the others. He didn't give a damn, though. He wasn't one to soften his words, even for a King.

"I wished for the Black Parliament to be over and done with before sending ye on an assignment," the Bruce replied tightly. "And what's more, I believe ye should be more fully integrated into the Corps before ye are turned loose in France."

Sabine cleared her throat, breaking the tension somewhat. "Who is Lady Vivienne?"

The Bruce waved at Kieran. "Ye can explain."

"Ye all ken that Jerome and I—along with de Soules —were selected to deliver the King's Declaration of Arbroath to the Pope, aye?" At the nods, Kieran continued. "By the time we'd reached King Philip's palace in Paris, Jerome and Elaine suspected de Soules of some nefarious scheme, yet they assumed it had something to do with thwarting the delivery of the declaration. But one of the Queen's ladies-in-waiting, Vivienne, alerted them to the fact that de Soules had been seen visiting Edward Balliol's estate in Picardy."

Thanks to that discovery, Jerome and Elaine had realized that de Soules had no interest in the King's declaration proclaiming Scotland's independence and petitioning the Pope to recognize the Bruce as King. Nay, de Soules had in fact been plotting with Edward

Balliol, the son of the former King of Scotland, to assassinate the Bruce and usurp the throne for Balliol. The other members of the Corps had been apprised of the plot against the Bruce when they'd been called to Scone, but not of Lady Vivienne's involvement in helping thwart the scheme.

"Jerome sent me on to Avignon to deliver the declaration, but we didnae ken what to do with de Soules. We couldnae openly accuse him, as we didnae have proof yet, but nor could we allow him to catch wind that we were on to his scheme," Kieran continued. "Lady Vivienne slipped de Soules a draught to incapacitate him—and kept him dosed for nigh on a fortnight until I returned from Avignon to drag his arse back to Scone to face charges of treason."

Elaine, who had befriended Vivienne in the short time they'd spent at the French court earlier that summer, jumped in. "Lady Vivienne's actions against de Soules are now apparently common knowledge in France. If de Soules has any allies at all, Vivienne would certainly be a target for her part in his downfall."

"And he likely does have at least a few lackeys in France," Jerome added, his features grim. "After all, he fomented his would-be uprising no' only on Scottish soil, but in France as well."

Sabine's brows drew together. "I haven't heard aught from our network of eyes and ears, but we do not have much of a presence in France. Besides, word travels slowly with the North Sea between us."

Will Sinclair spoke for the first time. "Then ye plan to send MacAdams to France, Robert?"

Kieran tensed as he waited for the Bruce's response. Of course, the King had already agreed nearly a month ago to allow Kieran to remove Vivienne from court and take her somewhere safe until the danger had passed. Though some rational sliver of Kieran's brain understood the King's reasoning for wanting to keep Kieran and the rest of the Corps close until punishments could be meted out, every time he thought of Vivienne being in danger, his stomach twisted in rage.

From the moment he'd laid eyes on her earlier that summer, he'd understood that she was never meant to be a part of the violent, dangerous, and harsh world Kieran inhabited. She was a creature of light and air, a beauty so rare and delicate that she might as well have been made of hand-painted porcelain.

And the second she'd glanced at him with blue eyes as dark and cold as a midnight sky in winter and tilted her head in that infuriatingly imperious way, he'd known that he'd just as soon be driven mad by her haughtiness as kiss that perfect mouth of hers.

Aye, she was a frosty one, yet she somehow managed to fan his ire to red-hot flames with her polished superiority. Still, he couldn't ignore the obvious danger she was in—thanks in part to him.

The Bruce tugged on his beard. "Aye," he said at last. "Even if de Soules doesnae have the power to strike directly anymore, he cannae be allowed to harm our allies. Those who have aided Scotland must be kept safe."

He turned to Kieran, his dark eyes hard. "But if the

12

threat is as grave as ye fear, MacAdams, I dinnae like the thought of sending ye alone."

"I work better on my own." All eight sets of eyes snapped to Kieran then, some widening at his sharp tone.

But Kieran wouldn't apologize for it. Aye, he was blunt, and crass, and downright rude at times, too, even to his King. But he hadn't been brought into the Bruce's inner circle for his manners. He'd been brought in because he was a damn good warrior, loyal and unrelenting. And he wouldn't waste time on flowery words when there was a task at hand.

"I'll be able to move faster," he added when the Bruce continued to eye him. "And it willnae cause as much of a kerfuffle in the French court if I go alone. Besides, ye're better off keeping as many of the Corps as ye can close at hand, though I agree with Elaine that de Soules doesnae have the power to mount a direct attack against ye."

The Bruce's russet brows lifted. "I dinnae ken about ye avoiding a kerfuffle in France. Ye are like a raging bull tearing through a market square, man. Ye cannae help but cause a commotion wherever ye go. But," he added, giving him a grudging nod. "Ye are right that I would prefer to keep the rest of the Corps close for the time being."

"Then it is settled," Kieran replied. "I'll depart for Paris within the hour."

"And after ye reach King Philip's palace, where will ye take this Lady Vivienne?" Colin asked.

Kieran leveled him with an assessing look. Though

he knew all the members of the Corps were honorable, loyal warriors, he was not inclined to trust so easily—especially when it came to Lady Vivienne's safety. "Scotland," he said noncommittally. "I have a place in mind, but there isnae reason to make it known."

Colin's eyes narrowed on him, but the Bruce spoke before the exchange could grow more tense.

"Verra well, but I want ye to return to Scone before ye tuck the lass away in some remote corner of the country," the Bruce said. "I'll want an appraisal of matters in Paris—and I'd like to thank Lady Vivienne in person for her aid, as well."

Kieran responded with a curt nod.

The matter decided, the others began to file out of the meeting room. Kieran waited for the King to pass through the door, then moved after him, his mind already full with his task, but Jerome's hand on his arm halted him.

"Give our best to Vivienne," Jerome said. A knowing smile curled the corners of his mouth. "That is, if ye can remember our names—or yer own, for that matter —when ye lay eyes on her again."

"What the bloody hell is that supposed to mean?" Kieran snapped, shifting a glare between Jerome and Elaine, who had lingered in the chamber as well.

"Naught," Elaine said, lightly swatting Jerome. "He's only teasing you."

Kieran grunted. "Ye damned lovebirds see romance and ardor everywhere ye look. Ye're mad, the both of ye, if ye think Lady Vivienne and I—"

"Peace, man," Jerome cut in. "Ye dinnae need to explain yerself to us."

Aye, he didn't, yet Kieran found himself doing just that. "Ye cannae fault a man for resting his eyes on a beautiful woman, but it doesnae mean aught. Ye think I want to get tangled up with a spoiled French noble-woman? No' bloody likely. But she is in danger in part thanks to me. It is my duty to protect her. If she were anyone else, I'd do the same."

Elaine blinked at the sudden outpouring of words. Jerome lifted his dark eyebrows. Hell and damnation, Kieran was making a fool of himself.

He clamped his lips shut and locked his features into a scowl. He'd promised himself ten years past not to grow soft in the head over a lass again, and he sure as hell wasn't going to break that vow over a damned self-important French chit.

With only the faintest nod of farewell, Kieran strode from the chamber without a backward glance. The sooner he reached France, the sooner he could ensure Lady Vivienne's safety. He was only doing his duty—naught more.

Chapter Two

◆◆◆

Vivienne carefully laid a strand of rubies against the Queen of France's neck. The Queen regarded herself in the rare and expensive mirror propped upright on her dressing table. She cocked her dark head in consideration, then nodded to Vivienne's reflection.

"These will go nicely with your burgundy silks, *ma reine*," Vivienne commented as she fastened the necklace's clasp. She adjusted the strand so that the rubies, each the size of her thumbnail, lay in perfect symmetry across the Queen's décolletage.

The Queen smiled at her in the mirror. "An excellent idea, *ma chère*."

As the Queen turned and spoke to another one of her ladies-in-waiting, warm pride filled Vivienne's chest. The Queen called many of the other ladies her dear, or her sweet, yet the endearment still touched her heart.

She stepped aside so that the others could attend to the Queen's hair and veil, which would be deep red to match the gown Vivienne had suggested.

Like the other ladies, Vivienne was already dressed in one of the pastel gowns the Queen favored for her attendants. This eve she wore light yellow, which didn't suit her flaxen hair or pale skin, but it wasn't her place to question the Queen's wishes. Vivienne preferred rich, dark colors. But on such evenings as tonight, when the King was hosting a feast for several of his nobles, the Queen liked for her ladies to look like a bouquet of spring flowers as they fluttered around her.

As the Queen was helped into the burgundy silk gown by two ladies, Vivienne dabbed the Queen's favorite rose water on her throat and adjusted the veil, which was more modestly opaque than the ladies-in-waiting wore.

When at last their preparations were complete, Vivienne fell into place with the other seven ladies-in-waiting around the Queen. Vivienne didn't even have to consciously adopt the air of grace and poise that she'd once had to practice when she'd first arrived at the palace. Now it was as natural as breathing.

She glided with the others down the wide flight of stairs that led from the Queen's private chambers to the most opulent of the King's great halls. Even before they reached the hall, strains of chatter and music drifted to them. The feast was already well underway. Though ever the perfectly decorous monarch, the Queen did like to make an entrance.

The guards outside the hall stiffened to attention as the women approached in a cloud of colorful silks, delicate scents, and feminine murmurs. They drew open the hall's double doors, bowing as the Queen and her ladies passed.

Vivienne dipped her head in demure modesty as they entered, but even with her eyes lowered, she knew what lay inside. She'd faced countless feasts and celebrations in her seven years at court.

She felt more than saw all eyes turn to them. Several gasps and murmurs of awe rose from those gathered inside. As they glided toward the raised dais where the King sat, the crowd of nobles bowed or dipped into deep curtsies for the Queen.

Vivienne and the other ladies parted, allowing the Queen to take the lead. They fell in behind her like a rippling wake of flower petals.

The Queen mounted the dais and curtsied to the King, who had risen to his feet. And in a show of devotion and courtly love, the King took her hand and lowered his head to kiss it.

The nobles clapped and murmured their pleasure at the gesture. It was proof that their monarchs—and therefore all of France—were strong and united.

As the applause died down and the guests returned their attention to their own conversations, Vivienne took her place at one of the tables just below the dais.

It seemed they had been so fashionably late that they'd missed much of the actual feast. Servants in the King's blue and gold livery were already clearing trenchers and platters of meats, vegetables, and pastries from the other tables. Musicians had struck up a song at the other end of the hall, and several nobles were beginning to dance.

A few platters of food still remained on the table for the ladies-in-waiting, but Vivienne had scarcely taken two bites when someone behind her interrupted with a clearing of his throat.

"Might I claim a dance with you this eve, Lady Vivienne?"

Vivienne turned to find Thierry de Pontier hovering over her. He bore a practiced smile on his smooth-cheeked face, his hand extended expectantly toward her.

Vivienne matched his smile, pretending as though she didn't wish to continue eating. One did not turn down the attentions of a rich and well-established nobleman just because one was hungry. Especially not when said nobleman had so assiduously pursued Lady Vivienne for nearly a year now.

She accepted his hand and allowed him to draw her up from the table. When she faced him, she took in his yellow silk cotehardie and matching breeches.

"A little birdie told me that a particular lady would be wearing yellow this evening," he said with a dazzling grin.

Vivienne felt heat creep up her neck. It was a clear sign. He wished to show all those at the feast that they were a couple. She was closer than ever to securing an excellent match.

Then why had her stomach suddenly turned into a

pit of writhing snakes? Thierry was wealthy and well-positioned—he owned a large estate near Orléans, and everyone at court agreed that he was amiable and perfectly mannered.

Vivienne was already four and twenty—far older than any unmarried lady-in-waiting should be. She'd followed along with every step of the carefully orches-trated dance of courtship Thierry had begun a year past when he'd first shown interest in her. There had been the requisite witty and extravagant praise of Vivienne's beauty, several perfumed missives exchanged, and even a few kisses at feasts like this one.

And his attempt to claim her publicly by wearing the same color was yet another maneuver in the game. This was what she wanted, she reminded herself firmly. A safe match. A secure position in life.

Yet her face ached with a forced smile as she allowed Thierry to lead her toward the other dancing couples.

Thierry picked up the steps elegantly, gliding with Vivienne in the controlled dance. He never touched her, as was appropriate given her position as one of the Queen's ladies, but his gaze remained fixed on her as they wove through the other dancers, an appreciative light in his brown eyes.

Vivienne was used to men looking at her. Her father had always told her she took after her mother, who was said to be a great beauty. And just as she wanted the stability and security a union with Thierry could give her, he had no doubt calculated the value of a beautiful wife who was a favorite of the Queen for his own wealth and position. They could both get what they wanted if Vivienne would allow the game to continue.

As one dance bled into another, Vivienne let her gaze wander from Thierry to the rest of the great hall. As always, the hall was filled with glittering jewels, shimmering silks, and rich brocades. Thousands of candles made the marble floors seem to glow and filled the air with gilded light. Yet her gaze snagged on the deep shadows in the vestibule leading from the hall to the entrance of the palace.

Sometime during her and Thierry's dance, the King had moved from the dais into the dimly lit vestibule. Vivienne could just make out his blue, ermine-trimmed cape where he stood amongst his guards.

She squinted at a particularly large shadow that had seemed to move in front of the King. Her skin prickled as if her body knew something before her mind could make sense of it.

Non. It couldn't be. It was just a trick of her eyes, a combination of boredom with this particular dance and the darkness of the vestibule.

Yet to her disbelief, the King was nodding to the looming shadow, saying something and then pointing to her. The shadow moved forward and became the shape of a man. A giant man.

And not just any giant.

Kieran MacAdams.

Vivienne stumbled, her feet tangling in her silk skirts. She staggered ungracefully into Thierry's arms.

"Are you all right, *mademoiselle?*" Thierry asked as he helped her right herself.

"*Oui*, forgive me," Vivienne replied, her voice weak.

"Are you sure, *ma petite*?"

Vivienne was vaguely aware of Thierry's gaze—and hands—lingering on her, but she couldn't tear her eyes away from the man now barreling across the great hall like a bull in a rage.

Just as he had when she'd first laid eyes on him a month and a half ago, Kieran MacAdams wore a red-checked plaid belted around his waist, with an extra length of material thrown over one broad shoulder. His plain linen shirt looked to have seen some abuse, as had his dust-covered boots.

His unbound hair curled in brown waves around his shoulders, his mouth set in a familiar grim line. And even from halfway across the hall, she could feel the cold intensity of his pale blue eyes, which did not falter from her even as he plowed through several groups of flabbergasted nobles.

Vivienne's heart lurched against her ribs nigh painfully. The man looked like a granite boulder tumbling through a sea of polished gemstones. He was so different from anyone at court—big, bold, and more than a little rough around the edges. Unlike the carefully controlled and immaculately graceful nobles all around, he carried his powerful, heavily muscled frame with undeniable determination.

And it seemed he was determined to reach *her*.

He cut the most direct line across the hall straight toward her, uncaring of the mutters of shock and confusion rippling in his wake.

When he was only a few paces away, his gaze

dropped from her face to Thierry's hands, which still rested on Vivienne's arms. His brows lowered in a severe line over his faintly crooked nose.

Thierry must have noticed the fierce Scotsman's glare on his hands, for he quickly snatched them back. With one pace, Kieran had closed the remaining distance between them. But instead of bowing or introducing himself to Thierry, he simply wedged himself between the nobleman and Vivienne, actually shouldering Thierry out of the way.

Ah, *oui*, there it was. In the commotion of his arrival and the strange thrall his imposing presence had on her as she'd watched him approach, Vivienne had forgotten what an unrepentant brute Kieran was.

She had likely been about to make a fool of herself by continuing to gaze wide-eyed at him or murmuring some breathless greeting in her state of shock. But at his show of boorishness, she remembered herself.

She drew herself up and lifted her chin, managing to look down on him despite the fact that she only came up to his shoulder. Leveling him with a cool stare, she squared off with him.

"I thought you'd returned to Scotland, Monsieur MacAdams."

"I did."

She arched one brow ever so slightly. "And yet here you stand, causing a scene in King Philip's palace."

"I dinnae care a single flea's arse if I'm causing a scene or no'," he replied in that unapologetically coarse brogue of his.

"Then why are you here?" she asked, struggling now

to keep her voice even and pleasant in the face of his brashness.

His pale blue eyes flashed with something she couldn't quite name, but another foreboding ripple of awareness stole over her.

"Ye are in danger. I'm here to protect ye."

Chapter Three

Lady Vivienne blinked those depthless midnight-blue eyes at him.

"What?"

At last, Kieran had managed to catch the imperious chit off-guard. Though there was naught humorous about the threat facing her, he couldn't help feeling the itch of a smile on his lips at the small victory.

"Ye are in danger," he repeated. "I'm here to protect ye."

She seemed to regain some of her composure then. "I have no idea what you are talking about, Monsieur MacAdams, but—"

"I told ye before," he interjected. "I'm no' 'Monsieur.' Call me Kieran." When he'd been in Paris earlier that summer, the lass had willfully ignored his instructions to simply use his given name, and she was apparently at it again.

"—but you are disrupting an otherwise pleasant

evening," she continued as if he hadn't spoken. "And what is more, you have been unforgivably rude to Seigneur de Pontier."

He glanced over her shoulder at the man he'd butted out of the way to reach her. "Ye mean the fop in yellow silks?"

Offense flashed across the man's smooth features, yet instead of stepping forward to challenge Kieran over his words, he melted back a step into the gathering onlookers.

"He is not a fop, he is a lord," Vivienne replied tightly. Her gaze darted over the crowd forming around them, her mouth compressing.

Of course. He was embarrassing her. He didn't give a damn what these pompous nobles thought of him, but if he wanted Lady Vivienne to listen while he explained why he was here, he'd have to get her away from all the sharp, disapproving gazes surrounding them.

Without asking permission, he tucked her arm under his and pulled her toward one of the alcoves lining the great hall's back wall.

He realized belatedly that he was practically dragging her across the hall, for his long strides covered more than double the distance of her dainty steps. No doubt all at the feast now took him for a barbarian not only in looks but in actions as well. He didn't care a whit about that either, but he slowed his pace to allow Lady Vivienne to keep up.

When they stepped into one of the empty alcoves, he released her arm from under his and deftly yanked the blue velvet curtains on either side free from their ties.

With the curtains shut against the hubbub of the feast, the alcove suddenly seemed far too small for his large frame. Muted chatter and a sliver of candlelight still filtered in through the crack in the velvet drapes, but otherwise the space was dim and quiet—and cramped. He could hardly take a lungful of air without brushing up against Lady Vivienne.

Best to get this over with as quickly as possible.

"The Bruce sent me," he said without preamble. "We believe William de Soules still poses a threat."

At that, she stilled. "But…but you took de Soules to Scotland for judgment."

Hell and damnation, he didn't like the faint edge of distress in her voice. He had never wanted to involve her in de Soules's detainment, but Jerome and Elaine had brought her into their plan before he could stop them.

When they'd proposed that Lady Vivienne give de Soules a draught to lay him low long enough for his conspiracy to be unraveled, Kieran had railed against them, insisting that such a dangerous and precarious position was no place for a high-born lady.

But Lady Vivienne herself had insisted that she wanted to help, for apparently she believed, as Kieran did, that spineless bastards like de Soules could not be allowed to threaten the peace that had been forged in both France and Scotland alike.

Much to Kieran's displeasure, Vivienne had not only drugged de Soules the night before their envoy had been set to depart for Avignon, but she had continued to keep him dosed for nigh on a fortnight while Kieran had delivered the Bruce's Declaration of

Arbroath and returned to collect de Soules for punishment.

That should have been the last time he'd ever laid eyes on Lady Vivienne, yet here he was, standing only inches away from her.

"De Soules is still being held in Scone's dungeon. He isnae going anywhere," he said in an attempt to offer what reassurance he could. "But there may still be others on the outside working for him."

She straightened, and even in the dim light he could see that she had plastered on that serene, elegant mask of unconcern.

"There has been nothing to indicate that I am in any danger. Once you removed de Soules from court, all returned to normal."

Kieran clenched his teeth. He didn't want to scare her, but he would if she insisted on being unreasonable.

"A little over a sennight ago, three of de Soules's co-conspirators were hanged. One of them, Richard Broun, used his dying breath to tell the Bruce that there were more like him, and that they would stop at naught to seek retribution against the Bruce and his allies—that's *ye*, lass."

Her delicate brows drew together. "I am no one."

"Nay, ye are the woman who helped bring William de Soules and his traitorous plot down. What's more, ye are a close confidante of the Queen of France, whose King is an open supporter of the Bruce's reign in Scotland. If someone wanted to avenge de Soules and hurt the Bruce in one fell swoop, ye'd be the most obvious target."

She hesitated then—a rare crack in her normally controlled façade. *Good*. Mayhap he was getting through to her.

"Even if that is the case, whom do you expect to come after me?" she asked. "De Soules is imprisoned, as you say, and his allies have been executed."

"I said *three* of his allies were executed. One was given leniency, and another died in the dungeon before the Bruce passed judgment. But that doesnae mean all of his allies have been weeded out. Likely a few slipped into the woodwork when de Soules was captured. And he plotted on French soil as well as Scottish. Any number of cowards could be waiting to strike."

Though his words had been meant to frighten some sense into her, foreboding snaked up his own spine at the picture he painted.

But it was the truth. When de Soules had been passed over for land and titles he thought he deserved, he'd quietly begun to gather other similarly disgruntled nobles, mainly in the Lowlands, to plot the Bruce's assassination.

Yet it hadn't been enough for them to simply rid themselves of the King they believed was overlooking them. Nay, de Soules had spent time in France, presumably to visit his small holding in the Picardy region to the north, but in truth he'd been meeting with Edward Balliol, the exiled son of the Bruce's predecessor, King John Balliol.

John Balliol had been little more than a puppet King, placed on the Scottish throne by the English to do their bidding. Apparently de Soules and his cronies had believed that Edward Balliol would follow in his father's footsteps if they placed him on Scotland's throne. They'd sought their own puppet King to fill their coffers and lavish land and titles upon them.

Thank God Lady Vivienne had told Jerome and Elaine that de Soules had not merely been visiting his own holding, but instead had been sniffing around Balliol's estate in Picardy. Otherwise, Balliol might be wearing the Scottish crown right now, and the Bruce's head would likely be rotting on a pike.

Horrified at the plot against his Scottish ally, King Philip had stripped not only de Soules but also Edward Balliol of all their French lands. Yet Kieran had learned from years of underhanded warfare against the English that one's enemies were rarely so easily vanquished. Like weeds, men with grudges to settle could pop up anywhere.

And Kieran would be damned if Lady Vivienne came to harm in the process.

She shifted, the silk folds of her gown whispering in the darkened alcove. "I still do not understand why you are here," she said. "Your King sent you to—what? Follow me through the palace? You know we already have guards, do you not?"

Before he could growl a response, she went on. "Or would you like to help me pick the Queen's jewels and gowns? Or perhaps you would prefer to work on your embroidery skills with me and the other ladies-in waiting."

He moved forward, forcing Lady Vivienne to back

up or be flattened into his chest. "This isnae a game, lass."

In one step, her retreat came to an end, for she bumped against the alcove's back wall. Yet despite the fact that he had her pinned and was looming over her in the darkness, her voice was surprisingly calm.

"Even if there is a threat—which I still question, as there has been no indication that I am in danger—I am surrounded by guards at all times," she countered. "As one of the Queen's ladies-in-waiting, I am one of the most watched women in all of Paris."

"Yer role in thwarting de Soules is public knowledge at court," he shot back.

"*Oui*, and yet in the month and a half since I poisoned de Soules, no harm has befallen me. Your services are not needed, Monsieur MacAdams, for I am perfectly safe at court."

He lowered his head so that his breath fanned close to her ear. "Och, but ye arenae staying at court, lass. I'm taking ye away."

She jerked in surprise at that, but there was nowhere for her to go—unless she chose to move forward and close the last inch of space separating them.

This near, he could smell her skin. She wore the same flowery fragrance that she had earlier that summer—violets, he thought. The scent was subtle and ethereal. Fitting for her.

For his part, Kieran likely smelled of sweat and horseflesh, for after the five-day sea crossing from Scone to Calais, he'd immediately secured a horse and ridden hard for three days to Paris. What did he care if his scent offended her delicate sensibilities, though? His job was to protect her, not court her.

"I am not leaving the palace," she stated, tilting her head up to meet his gaze with defiant eyes.

"Oh aye, ye are. Ye are to be placed somewhere safe until the Bruce can be sure the threat has passed."

"I am safe *here*."

A lazy grin tugged at the corners of his mouth. Damn, but it was satisfying to get under the wee chit's skin.

"Luckily it isnae up to ye," he replied, straightening. "I've already spoken with King Philip. In the interest of maintaining his strong friendship with the Bruce, Philip is eager to acquiesce to the Bruce's request that ye be removed from court—for yer own safety, of course."

She waved her hand, nearly brushing his chest. "Ah, but my position at court does not fall under the King's purview. I am the *Queen's* lady-in-waiting, here by her invitation and at her pleasure alone. The King would never cross his Queen's wishes on such a matter."

Kieran lifted one shoulder. "Mayhap I should take the matter up with the Queen then. Either way, ye are coming with me, lass."

"Don't call me *lass*, Monsieur MacAdams. And I am staying."

"Dinnae call me *Monsieur*, lass, and nay, ye arenae."

She huffed an annoyed breath and muttered something in French. Kieran caught the word *brute* and could surmise the general gist of her mood.

His barely leashed temper broke free at last. "Bloody hell, woman, why are ye fighting me on this? Ye ken the extent of de Soules's scheme. He meant to assassinate a bloody *King*. Ye think he cannae find a way, even from a cell, to have a wee French chit killed?"

"I have duties here," she retorted. "And a position to uphold."

"What, ye mean dancing with bairn-faced fops and trussing yerself up for some feast or other every night? I ken ye must like all the finery and games of etiquette at court, but are they worth yer damned life?"

Vivienne stiffened, and the air around them crackled with tension.

"You know nothing of my life, Monsieur," she replied at last, her rigid voice betraying an edge of pain.

Hell and damnation, he was losing sight of his mission. He wasn't here to verbally spar with Lady Vivienne, and he damn well wasn't here to corner her in alcoves that were no doubt meant for lovers' trysts.

He had one job—to protect her. And whether she liked it or not, he would get his way.

"As I said," he muttered, forcing himself to keep his voice even, "I'll take the matter up with the Queen."

"She has no doubt retired for the evening," Lady Vivienne said, suddenly sounding weary. "I need to attend to her."

She slipped past him with surprising agility and pulled back the blue velvet curtains. The feast continued as before, with the nobles dancing and chattering and the servants flitting about to refill wine goblets.

King Philip was engaged in deep conversation with one of his nobles on the raised dais. Since Kieran had already explained his presence and the Bruce's wishes, he felt no need to speak with the King again this eve. But just as Lady Vivienne had said, the Queen was no longer beside the King. The gaggle of ladies-in-waiting who had been seated below the dais were gone as well.

"I must go to the Queen," Lady Vivienne muttered, starting off across the great hall.

With two strides, Kieran caught her arm and halted her. "How many ladies does the Queen have to attend her?"

She blinked at him. "Eight, including me."

"Then let the other seven earn their keep tonight. Ye are tired."

"What does that matter?"

He fixed her with a firm look. "Because I am no' through with ye just yet."

Chapter Four

The space between Vivienne's shoulder blades tingled with awareness as she walked down one of the palace's many winding corridors.

She wished she could say it was caused by a draft, or a loose lock of hair tickling her back, but the true source of the tingle was obvious.

Kieran walked close behind her, his boots tapping softly on the stone floor and his large form casting a shadow over her every time they passed a lit wall sconce.

After insisting that she neglect her duties to the Queen this eve, he'd then informed her that he would be doing a thorough sweep of her bedchamber before allowing her to retire for the night.

Instead of causing a scene in the great hall with yet another round of verbal jousting, Vivienne had pressed her lips together and given him the barest of nods in assent.

There was nothing she could do about his presence

at the moment. He'd apparently already gotten permission from the King to act as her bodyguard. Vivienne trusted that the Queen would never agree to allow the giant Scotsman to whisk her away to some undisclosed location, but the Queen was no doubt already abed and could not be disturbed until morning.

That meant Vivienne was stuck with the blasted giant for the night. For some reason, that thought sent heat up the back of her neck and into her cheeks. Thank God he could not see her face at the moment.

She mounted the stairs leading to the Queen's suite of chambers, which included rooms for each of her ladies-in-waiting. After a few more moments spent winding down yet another corridor, she arrived at her chamber door and reached for the handle.

But to her shock, Kieran darted forward and lifted her hand away.

Non, not just her hand—he lifted her entire body. He plucked her up as if she were no more than a feather and spun her away from the door.

"What in—"

Just as abruptly as he'd scooped her up, he set her down, leveling her with a scowl.

"From now on, dinnae go into—or out of—chambers unless I have checked them first. Understand?"

Non, she didn't, not in the least. He expected her to wait and, what, twiddle her thumbs while he searched every single chamber she entered or exited while going about her life?

Before she could form a reply, he'd turned his attention back to her bedchamber door and slowly pushed it open.

Inside, everything was as she'd left it. Her bed was neatly made, her dressing table meticulously ordered. Her clothes were all latched away in the armoire opposite the table. A low fire gave off a warm orange light.

Kieran's sharp eyes swept the chamber before motioning her inside, but apparently he wasn't done yet. He closed the door after her, then began to stalk slowly around the space.

Pretending to ignore him, Vivienne went to her dressing table to begin her nightly ablutions. She lifted the sheer, buttery-yellow veil from her head and set it aside, then poured water from the pitcher on the dressing table into the matching basin.

But before she could splash the water on her face, Kieran was by her side, sniffing first the pitcher and then the basin.

"*Mon Dieu*," she muttered. "It is only water."

"And these?" he demanded, waving at the neat row of glass bottles and vials arranged on the table. He lifted one, pulled out the stopper, and inhaled.

"Orange blossom perfume," she said dryly. "And that one is rose water. I should think you might prefer the less floral scents for yourself, Monsieur MacAdams. That one over there is sandalwood oil—decidedly more manly than the orange blossom."

He didn't react to her droll comment, but instead examined each vial and bottle in turn. When he reached her favorite, a bottle of violet oil that had been a gift from the Queen, he froze.

"This is what ye wear most often, is it no'?"

Vivienne's pulse jumped. He had noticed? "*Oui*," she managed.

His rugged features were unreadable in the low firelight, but his eyes flickered with intensity before he returned his attention to the other vials on the table.

She took the opportunity to dab some of the rosemary and wine mixture—which he'd already examined—into her palms, then swiped it over her face, as was her routine every evening.

"No one is going to poison me through my perfumes and flower waters, Monsieur MacAdams," she said as she wiped away the beauty concoction.

Again, he ignored her, moving toward her armoire. He flicked open the latch and spread the double doors, exposing all her tidily hung silks and brocades.

She watched as he thumbed through the garments, her insides beginning to flutter despite her best efforts to remain calm. It was not that she expected some knife-wielding rogue to leap forth from the armoire. *Non*, she seriously doubted she was in any danger from de Soules or any of his cronies at all.

At the moment, the only danger seemed to be coming from Kieran MacAdams.

It had felt far too intimate to be tucked away in one of the great hall's alcoves earlier that night. No doubt she would have a great deal of work ahead of her to undo the gossip those few minutes would inspire. Thierry would expect an explanation as well. In less than an hour, Kieran had managed to undo years of Vivienne's careful efforts to position herself at court.

And now he was in her bedchamber. Alone. And rifling through her clothes.

To give her hands something to do, she busied herself with removing the pins from her hair. But she watched him in the polished plate of silver that served as her mirror.

He'd reached the end of the multi-colored gowns and found her carefully hung silk and linen chemises. When his hand glided down a particularly sheer one, he cleared his throat and abruptly closed the armoire doors.

Vivienne thought this torture was over at last, but instead of moving to the door, he strode toward her bed.

This was quite enough. She rose from the dressing table, her hair hanging partially loose, and moved to intercept him.

"What can you possibly expect to find there, Monsieur MacAdams?" she demanded.

His only reply was a grunt, then he lowered himself to the floor and peered under the bedframe. Seemingly satisfied, he stood, then unceremoniously yanked back her coverlet.

Heaven help her. Now he was looking *in* her bed?

Blessedly, his examination was short-lived, as there was nothing to see but her clean bed linens.

"Satisfied?" she said tartly, yet when his piercing blue eyes met hers, the word seemed to hang in the air between them, lingering like the subtle violet fragrance she loved so much.

When he didn't speak for a long moment, Vivienne began to feel her face heat.

"I wouldnae exactly say that, nay," he muttered
at last.

Vivienne silently cursed herself up and down for the
flush that no doubt clung to her cheeks. She was a lady,
a woman in the Queen of France's inner circle. She was
not some tawdry wench to be blushing at a man's double
entendres.

She needed to get him out of her bedchamber. *Now.*

"I'm sure you can sleep with the men-at-arms in the
lower hall," she said, grasping for the composure that
normally came so easily to her. "Or perhaps the King
will wish to assign you to a proper guest's chamber."

"Oh, I'm staying right here."

Her eyes rounded, and before she could regain
control over her features, a slow, arrogant smile began
lifting the corners of his mouth. Curse the man for
enjoying her embarrassment!

"That is, I will sleep directly outside yer door," he
clarified at last.

Vivienne drew in a steadying breath. "Very well,"
she said airily. "I will try not to step on you in the morning, then."

He leveled her with one of those fearsome looks she
imagined was meant to intimidate her, but instead only
raised her ire. "Ye dinnae seem to understand how seriously I take this assignment, lass," he said softly. "But ye
will soon enough."

With that, he spun on his heels and stomped out of
her chamber, closing the door firmly behind him.

Vivienne released a breath she hadn't realized she'd
been holding. The blasted giant's presence was so over-

powering that she could scarcely think with him nearby. Now that he was gone, she hurriedly unlaced her gown and hung it with the others, her mind tumbling over all that had transpired that night.

Kieran—and apparently also the King of Scotland believed her to be in danger. She still hesitated to put much stock into the idea, yet she could not deny that a seed of unease had taken root in her belly when Kieran had detailed Richard Broun's last words and de Soules's potential reach even from within a dungeon cell.

She was not normally one to brush off danger. In fact, her whole life ever since coming to court at the age of seventeen had been a series of careful, cautious calculations to avoid any risk whatsoever. Her father was counting on her. Besides, she'd learned long ago—the hard way—just how precarious even a noblewoman's position could be. One slipup and she could be back where she'd been before the Queen had taken her on as a lady-in-waiting.

Yet some part of her resisted the idea of a threat to her life. As she'd told Kieran, there was no evidence to suggest she was in danger. Life at court had been relatively quiet—well, if not quiet, then the normal amount of busy—since Kieran had passed through to collect de Soules.

Perhaps what she truly resisted was not the idea that her role in thwarting de Soules had put her at risk, but rather the fact that Kieran's sudden appearance would throw her carefully ordered life into a shambles.

Her days were a series of subtle, delicate maneuvers between etiquette, grace, and decorum. But there was

EMMA PRINCE

nothing subtle or delicate about Kieran MacAdams. *Non*, he was like a landslide, a driving force of unstoppable granite.

Vivienne eased herself into her bed, which was rumpled where Kieran's big hands had hauled back the coverlet. Heaven help her, she couldn't seem to stop herself from imagining his hands were still there, in her bed linens. On her skin.

She roughly yanked the coverlet up to her chin and squeezed her eyes shut, willing sleep to overtake her and wash away the memories of his piercing blue eyes burning into her. But sleep was a long way off that night.

Chapter Five

Kieran woke with a stiff neck from sleeping on the stone floor before Lady Vivienne's door. And a stiff cock from dreaming of the blasted chit.

Hell and damnation.

On the sennight-long journey from Scotland to the French court, he'd tried to steel himself against the thought of being in close proximity with Vivienne once again. A month and a half past, he'd been struck dumb by her ethereal beauty, yet riled by her knife-sharp tongue and imperious pride. He'd focused on his annoyance, reminding himself of her stubbornness, her upturned chin, how she'd gone against his wishes and involved herself with de Soules.

Yet the moment he'd laid eyes on her in the great hall last eve, he'd come damn close to forgetting it all and going all dunderheaded over her like some green lad.

Luckily, she'd been just as mulish and haughty as

before, questioning his presence and even the very idea that she was in danger. But her cool, controlled demeanor hadn't done nearly enough to quell his lust. Bloody hell, he'd almost kissed her in the alcove, and when his hand had grazed one of her flimsy, delicate wee undergarments—

Kieran jerked up from the ground, repositioning the extra length of plaid he'd used as a blanket back over his shoulder. He also straightened his kilt over his erection, willing it down with a muttered curse.

He'd scrubbed his hands in fresh water at the palace stables last night before speaking with King Philip, but he hadn't had a moment since then to wash more thoroughly or change his shirt. He eyed Lady Vivienne's door. It was hard to tell in the dim corridor what time it was, but Kieran had no doubt the sun hadn't risen yet. A lifetime of waking before dawn made him certain of that.

Though he was loath to leave lest she slip out of her chamber, he doubted she would rise anytime soon. He'd found himself unconsciously keeping track of her whereabouts when he'd been at court earlier that summer and had noticed that she often didn't appear until the sun was well above the horizon.

The decision made, Kieran wound his way from the Queen's wing of the palace back toward the stables, where he'd left his saddlebags the night before. The stable lads were just beginning to stir and start their chores when he arrived.

A cold wash out of a bucket and a clean shirt had him thinking clearer not long after. He retraced his steps to Lady Vivienne's chamber and propped himself against the corridor's opposite wall to wait.

A couple of hours later, his guess was confirmed when she at last pulled open her door.

She wore a forest-green brocade gown with delicate gold stitching in the shape of leaves and flowers on the bodice and skirts.

Her head was uncovered, but her hair was carefully arranged and pinned up in an intricate pattern of plaits and curls. He'd liked it better when her flaxen locks had been unbound last night as she'd prepared for bed, but at least she wasn't wearing a veil that obscured her slim, creamy neck anymore.

She assessed him with those cool, midnight-blue eyes for a moment.

"The Queen will be rising now," she said without preamble. "I am eager for her to settle this matter."

As if his presence—and her safety—were naught more than a mild annoyance. Kieran pushed off the wall, narrowing his gaze on her but refusing to acknowledge her comment.

She glided past him as if her feet were made of clouds, the only sound the faint rustle of brocade as she walked. He fell in behind her, clenching his teeth against a few choice words about uppity French chits.

She made her way up another flight of stairs and halted before two wide double doors. When she reached for the handles, he caught her slim wrists. He resisted the urge to scoop her off her feet completely as he had last night and instead settled for leveling her with a glare.

45

"I told ye before—dinnae do that."

He released her and yanked open the doors, only to find a small vestibule with two more double doors—and two guards.

She gave him a droll look that silently said *You are making a fool of yourself*, then glided toward the guards with a nod.

The men clearly knew her, for they returned the nod, but they both eyed Kieran suspiciously.

"Monsieur MacAdams is a…guest of the King," she said carefully. "He wishes to have an audience with the Queen."

One of the guards frowned. "Do you bear any weapons, Monsieur MacAdams?"

Knowing he wouldn't be permitted into the palace with his sword, he'd left it in the stables with his saddlebags. Of course, he had a dagger in his boot, but they didn't need to know that.

"Nay."

The guards exchanged a wary look, but apparently Lady Vivienne's standing as a member of the Queen's inner circle trumped their worries, and they pulled the double doors open.

Inside, Kieran found what could only be described as a feminine sanctuary. The Queen's chamber was filled with warm sunlight from several high, glassed windows. Dozens of candles also brightened the space, along with a cheery fire in the large hearth on one wall.

Intricately woven tapestries depicting fair maidens, mythical beasts, and grand celebrations tempered the stone walls. Several pieces of furniture were scattered throughout, including chairs, benches, and a dressing table that looked similar to Vivienne's except that it contained three times as many vials and colored glass bottles as hers had. Pillows upholstered in gold and purple silks softened every surface.

Kieran stepped inside and was enveloped in the sweet smell of dried herbs and flowers. Though no one was in the room, he could hear voices nearby.

Just then, a door at the back of the room—which Kieran assumed led to the Queen's private sleeping chamber—swung open and the Queen, followed by two ladies, stepped inside.

The Queen, who wore royal blue silks this morning, halted abruptly when her eyes landed on Kieran. Her gaze flicked to Vivienne, who'd moved to his side.

"Ah, there you are, *ma chère*. And you have brought your Scotsman."

Her Scotsman? Kieran nearly muttered a curse but then remembered he was in the presence of a Queen.

He bowed stiffly. "Majesty."

The Queen tilted her head in acknowledgement. "I was surprised to see you last night, Monsieur MacAdams. My husband mentioned something about your King Robert sending you, but he was too busy with other matters to explain further."

"That is why I brought him here, *ma reine*," Vivienne interjected. "There seems to be a...misunderstanding that I believe should fall to you to settle."

The Queen lowered herself on the cushioned chair before the dressing table. "Please, sit, Monsieur MacAdams," she said over her shoulder. "You can explain while Lady Vivienne helps me pick out my jewelry."

"Nay, I'd rather stand."

The Queen blinked at him, her brown eyes surprised at his gruff refusal, but she let the moment pass without comment.

Just as Kieran was about to launch into everything he'd told the King and Vivienne the night before, the double doors behind him opened once more and a string of the Queen's remaining ladies-in-waiting entered.

They nearly plowed into each other when the one in the front's gaze landed on Kieran. Several pairs of eyes widened on him, and then a giggle rose from somewhere in the middle of the cluster of ladies.

"*Bonjour, monsieur,*" one of the bolder ones said.

Unsure of what to do in the face of so many staring sets of eyes, Kieran simply frowned. That elicited another giggle and a few batted eyelashes before the Queen finally took pity on him.

"You may sit, ladies," the Queen said, her voice calm yet authoritative.

The ladies-in-waiting filtered throughout the chamber, taking up seats on chairs and benches and carefully arranging their skirts, but their eyes never left Kieran. He cleared his throat, feeling ridiculously out of place surrounded by trussed-up females in the Queen of France's personal chambers.

"As I was saying," he said, beginning again.

Under the curious stares of the ladies-in-waiting, Kieran explained the Bruce's decision to send him back to the French court to guard Lady Vivienne. He described the nature of the threat, doing his best to impress upon the Queen just how serious it was without shocking the ladies by describing the public execution.

The Queen listened as Lady Vivienne adorned her with gold and sapphire jewels, her face impassive in the mirror before her.

When he concluded, she shifted her gaze to Lady Vivienne. "What is the misunderstanding, then, *ma chère*?"

Vivienne's lips thinned slightly. "There has been no indication of a threat against me."

"Other than the words of William de Soules's co-conspirator, Richard Broun," Kieran cut it.

The Queen tilted her head. "*Touché, monsieur.* Although I agree that it is not enough evidence to warrant alarm, Vivienne, it is better to be on the safe side." Now the Queen pursed her lips, and Kieran had the impression she was trying to repress a smile. "Besides, there is no harm in keeping your Scottish protector close, is there?"

A few of the ladies tittered behind their hands, their gazes once again sliding flirtatiously over Kieran. He shot them a glower that wiped the grins off their faces.

"Monsieur MacAdams has omitted explaining that he does not simply intend to serve as my bodyguard here at court," Lady Vivienne replied, her voice tight. "He means to take me away to God knows where."

At that, the Queen arched her brows at Kieran. "Is that so?"

He met her gaze steadily. "Aye."

Now the Queen frowned. "*Non*, that will not do. Vivienne is most dear to me. I cannot simply let her go."

Lady Vivienne shot him a triumphant look. "I told him as much, *ma reine*. I do not wish to leave your side."

Kieran crossed his arms over his chest. "Apologies, Majesty, but I willnae be deterred. I have orders from my King." He left out the fact that there was no way in hell he'd leave Vivienne vulnerable if he had even the slightest doubt about her safety, which he did. He need not give the ladies more to gossip about.

The Queen tilted her brown head, assessing him with intelligent eyes. She was likely of an age with Kieran, yet she exuded the regal authority of her station.

"I gather that you are not a man easily dissuaded, *monsieur*. However, as I have said, I am loath to let Vivienne go. Perhaps we can reach a compromise."

"What do ye have in mind?"

She tapped a finger to her lips. "You and your King believe Vivienne is in danger. I observed you speaking to my husband last eve and it seems he is in agreement. Yet I see no need to remove Vivienne from court."

Kieran began to object, but the Queen simply flicked her wrist to cut him off. "Therefore it seems wise that you should remain here to look after our dear Vivienne—within the protected walls of the palace."

"The palace is vast, Majesty," Kieran said. "Many people come and go, and there are—"

"Then I suppose, Monsieur MacAdams," the Queen interjected smoothly, "you will simply have to stay *very* close to Lady Vivienne until you determine that the threat has passed."

The Queen glanced between Kieran and Vivienne, a pleased, knowing smile on her face. Bloody hell. First Jerome and Elaine, and now the damned Queen of France thought to jest about some imagined sentimental connection between him and Lady Vivienne.

Aye, Kieran couldn't deny that she was undoubtedly the bonniest woman he'd ever laid eyes on. Something about her pale gold hair and fair skin, those midnight eyes and pouty, petal-colored lips made him feel like he could never look his fill of her. And damn if her lithe, slim body, all elegance and grace and gentle curves, didn't snag his eye and stir his blood as well.

But he was only a man. From the possessive touch of that fop de Pontier last eve, Kieran wasn't the only one affected by Vivienne's beauty. Hell, nearly every man in the hall had gazed appreciatively at her when they'd taken their leave for the night. It didn't signify aught.

He glanced at Lady Vivienne to see how she had taken the Queen's insinuation. Her normally serene countenance had slipped and her brows creased with worry. No doubt she wasn't pleased that the Queen hadn't simply sent him packing. But nor did he like the idea of her remaining visible and unrestricted at court.

He grunted, crossing his arms over his chest once more. "Ye drive a hard bargain, Majesty. I am no' happy about it, but I damn well plan on seeing my job done, even if that means I must remain at court—begging yer pardon," he added belatedly.

Luckily, the Queen only smiled faintly, apparently amused by his blunt talk and coarse language.

"And this is only a trial," he went on. "If I catch even the faintest whiff of danger, I will remove Lady Vivienne whether ye like it or no'."

The Queen nodded placidly. Lady Vivienne, on the other hand, frowned even deeper. Her hand drifted toward her mouth and she began chewing on one of her fingernails. Abruptly, she seemed to realize what she was doing and yanked her hand away.

"*Bien,*" the Queen said briskly. "Now that the matter is settled, I suppose you should make yourself comfortable, Monsieur MacAdams. We have quite a bit of embroidery to do today, do we not, ladies?"

Another ripple of giggles moved through the ladies-in-waiting as Kieran awkwardly wedged himself into a chair that was clearly not built with a Highland warrior in mind. The dainty thing groaned under his weight as he shifted several unnecessary pillows out of his way.

Hell and damnation. He'd thought this mission would test his resolve against de Soules's underhanded schemes, but it seemed instead of fighting the traitor's cronies, he would be fighting off boredom in the Queen of France's private chambers.

Crossing his arms and dropping his features into a scowl, he hunkered down for what would undoubtedly be a long bloody day.

Chapter Six

Kieran barely managed to repress a grunt as he shifted in the wee chair that had apparently become his over the past sennight.

His arse hurt. And his back hurt. Never had he imagined sitting could be so draining. Yet after seven days spent doing little more than wiling away the hours in the Queen's front chamber, he was utterly exhausted.

He longed to feel the weight of his sword in his hands once more, to push his body to its limits on the practice field. Instead, he'd watched Lady Vivienne embroider, arrange hair, select jewels, and read aloud to the other ladies from various volumes of poetry and courtly romances.

Reading seemed to be the activity she did the most in the presence of the Queen. In fact, she currently sat on one of the cushioned benches, her legs tucked demurely beneath her and a leather-bound, gold leaf-edged book open before her.

He hadn't really been listening to the story—today it was a tale about a chivalric knight going off to battle, he thought—but damn it all if he hadn't been watching her surreptitiously out of the corner of his vision.

And it wasn't as though he had to keep his eyes on her for her safety. She was in more danger of getting a paper cut or a hoarse voice from all her recitations than anything else. Yet with naught else to do but sit in his damned wee chair and scowl at the walls, he found his attention repeatedly drifting to her.

She wore a pale blue silk gown today that made her creamy complexion look like porcelain. The day was overcast, so the chamber was filled with the warm glow of candlelight to aid her reading. It seemed to soften her normally controlled, cool exterior. Or mayhap she was more at ease because she was losing herself in the telling of the tale.

She was without a veil again—he'd noted that she only seemed to wear them in the evenings when she was expected to attend the Queen at various feasts and cere-monies, which apparently occurred nearly every night at court.

Kieran eyed her slim, swan-like neck. He hadn't been able to see that delicate neck last night. There had been a celebration to honor the return of a few of King Philip's ambassadors to Flanders, where they'd been negotiating a peace.

As usual, there had been feasting, toasts, and danc-ing. He'd managed to keep most of the men at bay with little more than a glower of warning, but the damned fop Thierry de Pontier had been bold enough to approach and ask Lady Vivienne for a dance.

When Kieran had given the man a firm nay before Vivienne could respond, de Pontier had persisted. Judging from the way the lass's cheeks had turned rosy and her mouth had thinned, Kieran's decision to simply bodily move the fop aside was not appreciated.

Though his brash—or nonexistent manners seemed to displease her, Lady Vivienne's behavior toward de Pontier and the other men at court didn't quite square. Kieran had been watching her closely for the past sennight. In every interaction, every social situation or conversation, she was perfect.

Too perfect.

She treated de Pontier with the same cool, formal regard as she did the palace guards. Though she was attentive and agreeable with the Queen and the other ladies-in-waiting, she never had so much as a hair out of place when she stepped foot into the Queen's quarters. Nor did she giggle or blush with the others at Kieran's obvious discomfort at being surrounded by so many feminine activities and fripperies.

After observing her so closely, following her every move, he couldn't help but wonder what lay under that perfectly coifed and controlled exterior. Judging by her sharp tongue—which she seemed only to direct at Kieran—passion in some form or other brewed beneath her careful façade.

In fact, with so little to do, Kieran's only sport had become seeing just how deep he could wriggle under her skin to draw forth more than just her usual haughty head-tilts or cool stares. So far he had managed to make her flush crimson a few times, and had even caught her gnawing on her fingernails after he'd embarrassed her in front of de Pontier last eve.

Of course, there was another activity that would alleviate not only his boredom but also his itch to know just what kind of woman truly lay under Vivienne's measured exterior. Would a thorough, commanding kiss be enough to ruffle her feathers, or would Kieran have to strip her naked and lick every inch of her until she screamed in unladylike pleasure?

For the thousandth time since arriving at the palace, Kieran jerked his thoughts away from that line of musings. Though carnal flirtations and even liaisons were apparently an open secret in the French court, Vivienne seemed the last woman to indulge in a dalliance if it meant risking public scrutiny.

Besides, he was there to protect her, not take a tumble with her, damn it. Yet torn between utter boredom and raging lust, Kieran's mission seemed a fool's errand now.

He forced himself to return his attention to his surroundings. Aye, this assignment might prove point-less, but he still believed there was a chance Vivienne was in danger.

His gaze swept over the other ladies-in-waiting, who were carefully arranged throughout the chamber like vases of cut flowers. The Queen sat picking at a piece of embroidery, occasionally looking up to smile at Vivienne as she read on.

And for her part, Vivienne leaned over her book, her

voice soft and lilting as she imbued the tale with emotion. Two of the men in the story seemed to be quarrelling, though Kieran hadn't been paying enough attention to know about what.

Vivienne looked up from the book, her eyes bright and her cheeks faintly pink as if she'd been running out of doors. She blinked and cleared her throat, coming back to herself.

"That was lovely, as always, *ma chère*," the Queen said warmly. "Let us continue tomorrow. For now, we had best prepare for the evening's events."

"*Oui, ma reine*," the ladies-in-waiting said in unison, rising.

Kieran pried himself out of his chair. He was familiar enough with the ladies' schedule to know that they each went to their own chambers to prepare themselves, then returned and all assisted the Queen.

Like a shadow, he fell in behind Lady Vivienne as the others filed out of the chamber and fluttered off to their private rooms. Her steps were slow and measured, as if she were still waking from the dream cast by the tale she'd been reading.

He noticed that she held the volume to her chest as if it were made of glass. Of course, books were rare and expensive, especially ones with stamped, dyed leather covers and gilt pages like the one she carried.

Despite himself, curiosity tugged at him. What was it about this particular book that had her so enchanted?

When they reached her chamber, he pulled open the door and quickly scanned the space, as was now his habit. But when he stepped aside to allow her to enter, instead of moving back into the corridor and closing the door, he lingered.

He cleared his throat, suddenly feeling awkward. Though he'd been in close proximity to her for the last sennight, he'd avoided doing aught outside the scope of serving as her bodyguard, lest he give the court gossips more to whisper about. But his interest got the better of him.

"What was that one called?" he asked brusquely, nodding at the book.

Her eyes widened in surprise for a fraction of a second before her composure returned.

"*The Song of Roland.* It is a most beloved poem here in France."

"Those men who were fighting…"

"Roland and Olivier?"

"Aye," he cleared his throat again. "What were they fighting about?"

At his interest, a pleased smile played around her mouth. "In the tale, they are leaders of the Frankish army under Charlemagne—and best friends. When they are outflanked and in danger of failing against their enemies, Olivier urges Roland to blow his horn, thus signaling to Charlemagne and the rest of the army that they need help. But Roland refuses."

"Oh? Why?"

"Because Roland believes it would be an act of cowardice." Now Lady Vivienne's gaze drifted, her eyes warming. "But Olivier swears that if Roland does not blow the horn, Roland will never again see Alde, Roland's betrothed and Olivier's sister."

Kieran couldn't help himself. He snorted in disbelief. "That is preposterous."

Vivienne blinked and drew back her chin. "I beg your pardon?"

"A man doesnae make decisions in the heat of battle based on love. And a true friend wouldnae attempt to sway a man's sense of honor with threats of no' letting him see his sister again."

She straightened, tilting her head in that infuriating way so that she seemed to look down on him with suddenly frosty eyes.

"Just because *you* cannot imagine acting for love doesn't mean it is preposterous."

"I never took ye for a romantic, lass."

"Don't call me lass, Monsieur MacAdams."

Och, they were back to this again? "Dinnae call me Monsieur, *lass*," he countered. "And aye, I wouldnae risk other men's lives for some flowery notion of courtly love. But by all means, tell me more about how men should act on the battlefield, since I assume ye have some great wealth of knowledge on the topic."

His words had the intended effect. She faltered for a moment, at a loss. A flush crept up her neck and into her cheeks.

He glanced down to find that she clutched the book with a defensive fierceness he had yet to see in her. She held it tightly against her chest as if he would attempt to rip it from her grasp.

Guilt suddenly struck him as surely as a punch. One moment he'd been so intrigued by her clear enchantment with the book that he couldn't keep from asking her about it, and the next he was berating her for sharing her—albeit misguided—sentiments.

"How does it end?" he blurted.

She eyed him warily for a moment. "Why are you so interested?"

He lifted one shoulder in an attempt at indifference. "Mayhap I wish to ken if Roland will prove himself a fool or no'."

Her lips thinned, but at last she relented.

"Olivier's plea turns out to be moot. They learn that there is no hope for them, for their army is sure to be overpowered. Knowing that reinforcements won't come in time, Roland blows the horn anyway so that Charlemagne's forces will hear and come to avenge them after they are slaughtered." She sniffed, smoothing her skirts. "Roland blows the horn so hard that his temples explode and he dies."

Kieran nodded thoughtfully. "Aye, that's much better. Far more realistic."

Vivienne's eyes widened with annoyance. "*That* is more realistic than Roland acting out of love for Alde? The entire army dying and his head exploding?"

"Aye," he replied evenly. "Warfare is messy and far less noble than they'd have ye believe in these chivalric tales. And a man losing his head for love is damn foolish."

He clamped his teeth together, suddenly fearing he was no longer talking about some silly poem. The old ache returned to his chest for a fleeting moment before he shoved the sentiment—and the memories—aside.

She bristled again, but instead of her usual tightly-reined anger, he thought he saw a ghost of pain in her eyes. "It is a story, *monsieur*. *Oui*, no doubt an embellished one meant to set ladies' hearts aflutter, but also one to inspire the best in us, the most noble and hopeful impulses."

Vivienne swallowed, clearly attempting to make her voice light, yet it came out forced. "I for one greatly enjoy the diversion of reading such tales. This one is a particular favorite of mine. My father gave me this volume when I was but a girl."

Now it was her turn to snap her mouth closed as if she'd said more than she had planned. Her hand drifted toward her lips and she had a fingernail between her teeth without seeming to realize what she was doing.

"Why do ye do that?" Kieran asked, pointing at her mouth.

She snatched her hand away as if she'd been burned. "It is an old habit from my childhood. I do it when I'm—it doesn't matter. It is most unbecoming."

Kieran tried to imagine what her childhood must have been like. No doubt she'd been born with a silver spoon in her mouth. She was nobility, after all. And the book alone must have cost a small fortune. He'd always assumed she'd led a spoiled, charmed life, but the sadness that lingered in her eyes and the embarrassment in her voice for chewing her nails told him there was more to the story than that.

He suddenly felt like a dunderhead to be standing awkwardly in her chamber, lingering after their surprisingly intimate exchange.

"Well then," he said, his voice coming out gruffer than he'd intended. "I'll let ye ready yerself."

He beat a hasty retreat to the door and shut it firmly behind him, releasing a breath once he was alone in the corridor.

Hell and damnation. This assignment was spinning out of his control. Being forced to stay at court instead of removing Vivienne had been bad enough, but he was beginning to fear that the potential threat to her safety here at the palace was the least of his worries.

Something about the wee chit had his insides in a knot and his heart hammering against his chest.

It was only because her words about love had stirred those dark memories from his past, he told himself. All the more reason to keep his interactions with Vivienne strictly limited.

The only trouble was, he couldn't seem to get enough of her.

Chapter Seven

Vivienne stepped into the September sun and released a long breath. These waning days of summer made her long for the open fields and fresh air of home, but even here inside the palace walls, it was a relief to be out of doors and to feel the sun on her face.

She and the other ladies-in-waiting had been sent by the Queen to cut the last roses of the season from the King's private, walled garden. They streamed around her where she'd stopped just outside the palace doors to savor the warm rays of sunshine. Dressed in their usual assortment of pastel silks, they looked like flowers themselves as they chatted and filtered toward the garden.

Vivienne lingered near the doorway, eager to reach the garden yet longing for the solitude and freedom she'd grown up with on her family's estate in Picardy.

"What's the matter, lass? Are ye frightened to set foot in the great wilderness that is the King's garden?"

Curse that all-too-familiar voice, low and gruff and

curling with a Scottish brogue. She might snatch a moment away from the other ladies, but it seemed she would never be rid of Kieran MacAdams.

It had been a sennight since their conversation—argument, really—about her beloved copy of *The Song of Roland*.

She'd embarrassed herself by chewing on her nails, a dreadful habit she'd thought herself rid of long before coming to court. What was worse, she'd allowed her emotions to rise at his flippant critique of the story. She'd no doubt looked doubly foolish when she'd defended the idea of love as a noble impulse. If Kieran knew the truth of her past, he would likely think her the greatest idiot of all for that.

Thank heaven he didn't. She spun on her heels to find him leaning in the palace's doorway, his large frame cast in shadow and his arms crossed casually over his chest. Ignoring his barb about the King's garden being some grand wilderness, she leveled him with an imperious look.

"How many times must I insist that you refrain from calling me lass, Monsieur MacAdams?"

He pushed himself from the doorframe and stepped into the sunlight so that he towered over her. Only the width of the basket she clasped in front of her separated them. Despite her instinct to step back, she held her ground, though she had to crane her head to hold their stare.

His brown hair shone like a polished chestnut and he was close enough that his scent, of soap and leather and something distinctly masculine, enveloped her. He pinned her with eyes that flashed with blue fire.

"I could ask ye the same thing."

Vivienne swallowed the sudden tightness in her throat. The blasted man was so overbearing and imposing that it was hard to think straight with him so near.

And he likely knew it. He seemed to take perverse pleasure in getting under her skin and threatening to undo her control. He wasn't afraid to cause a scene in front of the others at court. He made no qualms about scoffing at her beloved books. And every time he called her lass, he chipped away at her sanity.

He no doubt believed the epithet flustered her because it flew in the face of proper etiquette—it was rude and uncouth, just like him. *Oui*, that should have been the reason it ruffled her feathers so much, but the truth was far worse.

Every time he called her lass in that deep, rough brogue of his, a ripple of awareness rolled over her, puckering her skin and warming her insides.

It was shameful to be agitated so. It made her want to lean against that broad, hard chest of his and forget the world around her. But hadn't she learned her lesson seven years past when it came to such longings?

Apparently not, which she was reminded of whenever he was near.

Of course, she wasn't above seeking to rile him as he riled her. But that wasn't the only reason she kept calling him Monsieur despite his insistence that she use his given

name. It created distance and formality between them—
which she desperately needed, for he was already too close
to her, and the pull to be closer still was nigh overpowering.

As he continued to loom over her, waiting no doubt
for some sharp-tongued response, she realized that she'd
been gnawing on her nail again.

She ripped her hand away from her mouth, feeling
heat creep into her cheeks at the show of weakness. It
had been something she'd done as a child when she'd
been nervous. Her mother had helped her break the
unbecoming habit by rubbing raw cloves of garlic,
which Vivienne did not care for, on her fingertips.

But her mother was long dead. Vivienne was on her
own against the unnerving Scotsman.

She lifted her chin. "The day is too fine to spend it
arguing, *Monsieur* MacAdams. If we cannot speak pleasantly, let us not speak at all."

His only reply was a grunt, which she took as agreement. The day was indeed fine, probably one of the last
before autumn settled its cool touch on the land.

Vivienne turned away and glided toward the garden,
where the other ladies were already chatting and taking
up their gloves and shears to clip the last remaining
blooms.

She set down her wide-mouthed basket beside Marie
and Aveline, who were pulling on their gardening gloves.

"Your cheeks are quite pink, Vivienne," Marie
commented a little too slyly. "Mayhap you should have
worn a veil today to keep the sun off your skin. Or is
there another reason for your flush?"

Vivienne had forgone her veil in order to feel the

sun's rays on her hair, but now she wished she could
hide her cheeks and neck behind the fabric, if only to
put an end to Marie's prying.

"I am fine," she replied tightly.

"Are you sure? Because the way that giant bodyguard of yours is eyeing you may well set your gown
aflame." Marie and Aveline dipped their heads together
and giggled.

She shouldn't take their bait, but Vivienne couldn't
help it. Her gaze shot to Kieran, who was several paces
away. He stood awkwardly in the middle of one of the
gravel paths winding through the garden, looking about
as out of place as…well, as a fierce Highland warrior in
the middle of a sea of meticulously manicured flowers
and shrubs.

His commanding presence was undeniable. He
stood with his feet planted wide beneath his red-checked
plaid, his thickly muscled arms folded over his chest. He
didn't seem to bother shaving every day, for the brown
stubble on his face was a familiar sight.

As was the nigh-permanent scowl he wore.
Combined with the crook in his nose, which must have
come from a break long ago, he was a fearsome sight.
But most disconcerting of all was the way his blue eyes
remained sharp and watchful on her.

Though his features were rugged—his faintly
crooked nose, his prominent brow, and the hard line of
his jaw all set him apart from the refined nobles at court
—he was devilishly handsome nonetheless.

"He…he is only doing his job," Vivienne
murmured, unable to tear her eyes away from him.

"Don't worry," Marie said, nudging Vivienne softly with her shoulder. "We are only teasing you. *Mon Dieu*, I wish my husband looked at me like that."

"I wish *anyone* looked at me like that," Aveline said, ducking her head shyly.

"There is nothing wrong with enjoying it, either," Marie prodded. "Since he seems to be bound to your side for the foreseeable future, can you not…appreciate each other's company a bit?"

Vivienne yanked on her gloves and snatched up her shears before slinging her basket over her arm once more. Heaven help her, would she ever escape the man? He'd already become her shadow, inserting himself into the Queen's chamber and her evening fetes, and now his presence had invaded the light chatter of her friends?

"We are the Queen of France's ladies-in-waiting," she replied through gritted teeth. "We are meant to be models of propriety and elegance, especially those of us who are not yet married."

And Kieran threatened to ruin it all. Thierry hadn't approached her in nearly a sennight. Kieran's looming presence and blunt rebuffs seemed to have finally frightened him off for good. If Vivienne couldn't make a good match—a stable, safe match—then all might be lost, not only for herself, but for her father as well.

The *last* thing she needed was to dally with her Highland bodyguard, no matter that Marie and the others thought it amusing to concoct imaginary trysts for them. The scandal would smear her name once and for all. She had barely managed to survive *one* disgrace seven years past. *Two* would certainly be her end.

"Vivienne, don't be mad," Aveline called after her as she strode away with as much calm grace as she could muster.

She waved reassuringly at the two ladies, not trusting her voice to keep from wobbling with emotion if they pressed her further. She made a half-hearted attempt to cut a few flowers, placing them in her basket as she moved down the gravel path, but inside she was a tangle of confusion.

She needed to clear her head—and that wasn't possible in the presence of either her gossiping friends or Kieran's penetrating stare. So she made her way toward the large hedge maze in the middle of the garden.

The carefully-trimmed hedge stood well above her head. It would be pleasantly cool and lush inside. She'd ventured into the maze enough times to know that she couldn't truly become lost, but the winding pathways would allow her to amble for a while with her thoughts.

As she was about to enter the maze, one of the castle gardeners appeared from behind a nearby shrub, shears in hand. She didn't recognize him, but he smiled and gave her a little bow, resuming his pruning.

She dipped her head at him, but she was so distracted that she didn't even bother asking his name. It was rude of her not to greet a new member of the palace staff, yet that was the effect her brooding body-guard had on her—she was losing control of her well-ordered, tightly-managed life.

With a sigh, she stepped into the hedge maze, letting the earthy smell of sun-warmed leaves calm her. She wandered to the left, knowing it was the slower route to the center and would therefore give her more time to untangle her thoughts.

She couldn't deny it. She was attracted to Kieran. He was big and bold and ruggedly handsome—and entirely wrong for her. Her whole life seemed to hang by a thread. Her position with the Queen, her father's well-being, her own future—they all depended on her remaining in control.

And Kieran made her feel out of control. In a matter of a fortnight, he'd wheedled his way into her life, disrupting everything she'd so carefully arranged over the last seven years, and threatening to turn her into the foolish girl she'd been at sixteen.

He'd said she was in danger from de Soules, but she feared the real danger was in the blazing-hot spark that flared between them whenever they spoke or simply exchanged a look.

But she couldn't let this be her undoing. She'd worked too hard to get here. She had to—

A rustling in the leaves behind her made her pause. Had Kieran followed her into the maze? Heaven help her if he had, for if they were alone together now, she didn't trust herself not to touch him.

The rustling came again, closer this time. Her skin prickled with anticipation, but some instinct told her that something was wrong.

Before she could move or even draw a breath, the gardener she'd seen earlier stepped into the middle of the path. She nearly hissed a laugh at her own silly nerves when she saw what he held.

The large shears he'd been using to prune one of the

hedges a few moments ago were raised in his grasp like a dagger.

And pointed right at her.

Vivienne only had time to scream before he lunged toward her.

Chapter Eight

Kieran stared at Lady Vivienne as she stood talking quietly with two of the other ladies-in-waiting. They were speaking of him. He could tell by the way the older one—Marie, he thought her name was—kept glancing appreciatively at him.

He didn't give a damn if they gossiped, but he found himself frowning deeper as Lady Vivienne seemed to grow agitated.

It was hard to tell, of course, for she had an uncanny ability to keep her features smooth and her slim shoulders relaxed, but suddenly her gaze darted to him and her normally cool blue eyes sparked with dark intensity. She swept him over, her cheeks flushing and her petal-pink lips parting ever so slightly.

Bloody hell, if she looked at him like that again, he would not be held accountable for his actions. And damn if she didn't look especially stunning today as well.

When she'd emerged from her chamber that morning, he'd nearly choked on his tongue. She wore a blush-
pink silk gown that set off her strawberries and cream
skin—which was generously exposed thanks to the
gown's scooped neckline. Though she was on the slim
side, the expertly-designed garment put every delicate
curve on perfect display.

Her flaxen hair was coiled into plaits and pinned up
as usual, giving him the long expanse of her neck and
décolletage to stare at. She'd floated by him as she
always did, her violet scent curling around him and
tugging him after her like a leash.

In short, she was like a damn dessert ready to
be eaten.

As he stood before her now, leveling her with his best
glower, he could only pray that his cock didn't begin stirring beneath his kilt and give him away.

She tore her gaze from him at last, murmuring a few
more words to the two ladies through a tightened
mouth, then glided away to cut flowers. He remained
rooted in place, for she was directly in his line of sight.
Besides, she seemed agitated enough even without him
pestering her.

Aye, he enjoyed being a thorn in that sweet behind
of hers, for she seemed far too perfect for her own good,
but he didn't truly wish to torture her. She was wise to
suggest that they not speak today, for every time he did
he had to fight the urge to seal her tart lips with a kiss.

After snipping several flowers and placing them into
her basket, she ambled toward what appeared to be a

large hedge maze. He moved at last, stalking down the path slowly so that she remained a stone's throw away but still in his sights. She nodded to a gardener, then slipped inside the maze.

Kieran nearly went after her, but he hesitated. What would happen if he were alone with her in the leafy, shaded privacy of the maze? Would he be able to restrain himself, as he had in the alcove that first night, or would his control finally snap and have him doing something foolish like tasting her lips, dragging her against him, grinding his aching cock into—

He muttered a curse, stepping out of the path and behind a shrub. What was happening to him? It was only lust, he told himself firmly for the hundredth time since arriving at court. He was a man. He had needs—which he hadn't attended to for some time now. And Vivienne was a beautiful woman. It didn't mean aught.

But a nagging wee voice in the back of his head pointed out that there were plenty of other bonny women in the French court, some of whom had passed him suggestive and even openly inviting looks. Yet he didn't want them. He wanted sharp-tongued, strong-willed, ever-restrained Vivienne. He had to—

Unaware of Kieran's presence nearby, the gardener who'd greeted Vivienne abruptly stopped pruning and gazed at the hedge maze's entrance. With a surreptitious glance at the other ladies, who were all some distance away engaged in cutting flowers, the gardener slipped into the maze.

Kieran's instincts flared with warning. It was possible the man was simply seeing to his duty to trim the hedge, yet his furtive glance and slinking steps told a different story.

Kieran swiftly strode to the maze's entrance. The path immediately forked, each direction shrouded by the hedge's dense foliage. Neither Vivienne nor the gardener was anywhere in sight.

Hell and damnation.

Just as he was about to pick one direction at random, a high, frightened scream tore through the air.

Vivienne.

Without thinking, Kieran lowered his shoulder and plowed straight through the hedge toward where the scream had come from.

Leaves exploded around him and branches snapped in his wake, some snagging his shirt and plaid, but he did not slow. He barreled on like a charging bull, desperate to reach Vivienne.

She screamed again, and it was like a dagger to his chest, but he was closer. With a roar, he picked up speed, crashing through the hedge toward her.

Suddenly he broke into one of the paths, and there she was. She lay sprawled on the gravel path, her gown torn and stained. But she was conscious, thank God, and clutching the small pair of shears she'd carried earlier in trembling hands.

The gardener loomed over her, his shears raised as if he were about to plunge them into her. His head whipped around at Kieran's abrupt appearance, his face twisted in a snarl.

Without hesitating, Kieran lunged for him. The gardener turned his shears on Kieran at the last moment, attempting to stab him in the chest, but Kieran batted his arm aside. He plowed into him, driving them both to the ground.

With his greater size and strength, Kieran pinned him, but the gardener had managed to keep his grip on the shears. He stabbed again, this time aiming for Kieran's side. Kieran barely managed to twist out of the way, catching the man's wrist as the shears sliced through the air where he'd been a heartbeat before.

The man's hand trembled as he fought against Kieran's hold, but Kieran managed to torque the gardener's wrist so that the shears slowly tilted toward him.

With a bellow of rage, Kieran sent all of his strength into his arm and surged downward, plunging the shears into the gardener's chest.

The man went rigid, his eyes widening in shock, then sputtered a bloody breath before going still.

Panting, Kieran rolled off the lifeless man. His limbs trembled, but not from his battle with the gardener. Nay, he shook out of fear for Vivienne and what had almost just happened.

He looked up to find her still huddled on the ground, the shears in her hand wavering like a leaf in a stiff breeze. Her dark blue eyes brimmed with tears and her lips quavered.

Instantly, he was crouched at her side.

"Are ye hurt, lass?" Distantly, he knew she would not like him calling her that, but the gently spoken word slipped out like an endearment.

She blinked, struggling to focus her gaze on him. He

moved so that his body blocked the sight of the dead gardener, then took her chin carefully in his grasp.

"Vivienne, look at me. Are ye all right? I need to ken before I move ye."

When her eyes at last locked on his, the knot of anxiety in his gut loosened ever so slightly. She was alive, at least, and that was better than his worst fear.

"I…he didn't hurt me."

He swept his gaze over her, taking in the tear in her skirts and the dirt stains on the pink silk. But he saw no blood and her limbs all seemed to be working. If she truly was unharmed, his first priority was to get her to safety.

Carefully, he extracted the shears from her hand and tossed them onto the ground. Then he slid his arms under her and brought her against his chest. She inhaled in surprise, but as he rose to his feet, her arms looped around his neck and she pulled herself closer.

Rather than returning the way he'd come, which would have meant dragging Vivienne back through the hole he'd made in the hedge, he bore right at every fork in the maze until he reached the entrance.

They were greeted by the shocked faces of the ladies-in-waiting, who must have heard Vivienne's screams as well. Several gasped in dismay at the sight of Vivienne, disheveled and in Kieran's arms. One even sank to the ground in a half-swoon.

"Ye," he said, turning to Marie. "Fetch the guards and have them remove the man in the maze. Then go straight to the King and Queen and tell them to come to

Lady Vivienne's chamber. Dinnae take nay for an answer."

"*Oui, monsieur*," Marie, wide-eyed but clearly the most level-headed one in the bunch, replied quickly. She immediately scurried off to do his bidding.

The other ladies began swarming after Kieran as he strode toward the palace, wringing their hands and murmuring prayers.

"Off with the lot of ye," Kieran barked as he entered the palace and began winding his way toward Vivienne's chamber. "Go to yer chambers, or help Marie, but dinnae get in my way."

They scattered like startled butterflies, some flitting after Marie and others fleeing to their rooms.

When he reached Vivienne's chamber, he kicked the door open unceremoniously and strode toward her bed. He set her down on top of the coverlet as gently as he could, but her fingers sank into his shoulders as if she didn't want to let him go.

"I'm going to guard yer door until the King and Queen arrive," he said, gently prying her hands free. "Then we will have a talk about what happened—and what happens next. Understand?"

She stared up at him with wide, frightened eyes, nodding mutely.

"Do ye want me to send in one of the ladies to help ye change or wash?"

"*N-non*," she murmured. "I can do it myself."

"Verra well." He pinned her with his gaze. "I will be right outside. Ye can call for me if ye need aught."

She nodded again. Reluctantly, he straightened and

strode to the door. He forced himself not to look back at Vivienne, for if he did, he doubted he would be able to leave.

Closing the door behind him, he planted himself in the corridor and waited, thanking God with each passing heartbeat that he'd reached Vivienne in time.

Chapter Nine

Vivienne didn't know how long she sat on her bed, staring in a numb stupor at the door beyond which Kieran stood. After what felt like an hour but was probably only a quarter of that, she forced herself to stand on trembling legs.

With wooden fingers, she unlaced her ruined gown and carefully laid it over the chair in front of her dressing table. Though the gown was likely unsalvage-able, at least a few kerchiefs or mayhap a headdress could be saved from the undamaged silk.

Distantly, she realized she must be in shock, even as part of her mind tumbled on with disturbing normalcy, planning out practical uses for the gown that had been destroyed when she'd nearly been killed.

She donned a simple dress of gray wool, then splashed water over her hands and face. As the water in the basin turned muddy from the dirt on her hands, an overpowering exhaustion came over her. She stumbled to the bed and dragged back the coverlet, climbing in without bothering to remove the dress she'd just put on.

But when she closed her eyes, the gardener's face swam before her, his hazel eyes menacing as the shears came toward her.

Blessedly, Kieran's low, gruff voice suddenly drifted to her through the door. The King must have just arrived, for she heard his sharp, worried voice as well.

To her astonishment, Kieran didn't immediately admit the King to her chamber. He must have been waiting for the Queen to arrive as well. If Vivienne had been in her right state of mind, she would have been horrified at the idea of Kieran making the King himself stand outside and wait to see her, but as it was, she didn't have the energy to care.

Soon enough, the Queen's voice filtered through from the corridor, and then the door swung open and Kieran was there again. He stepped aside and allowed the King and Queen to enter, then closed the door, his hard features even grimmer than normal.

Vivienne struggled to throw back the coverlet and untangle herself from the bedding so that she could greet the King and Queen on her feet, but Kieran shot to her side, laying a hand over hers to still her.

"Be at ease," he said softly.

It felt ridiculous—if not downright treasonous—to lie abed instead of rising and curtsying to her monarchs. Yet neither the King nor the Queen seemed overly concerned with formalities at the moment.

The Queen moved toward the bed, her brow creased with worry. "Are you well, *ma chère*?"

Before Vivienne could answer, King Philip moved to his wife's side. Like the Queen, his brown eyes were tight with concern. "What happened?"

"I-I was walking in your hedge maze, *Majesté*," Vivienne began.

"Start before that. Ye nodded to the man—the gardener," Kieran interjected.

Vivienne abruptly realized that Kieran must have been watching her closely even as she'd tried to slip away from him into the maze. A sudden flood of gratitude hit her like a blow. If he hadn't been so attentive, she might be dead now.

"*Oui*," she said, her throat tight with emotion. "I didn't recognize him, but I assumed he was a new member of the staff. He nodded and smiled. Then I entered the maze and wandered until I heard something behind me. It was…it was him."

The Queen took her hand and gave it a reassuring squeeze, silently urging her to continue.

"He raised his shears as if to stab me, so I screamed. I ran as fast as I could, but I tripped on my skirts. He was about to strike when Kieran appeared."

Kieran jerked, his body going rigid where he stood beside the bed. Vivienne realized it was the first time she'd called him by his given name.

Just then, a knock came at the door. Kieran crossed the chamber and opened it, but instead of admitting whoever stood outside, he slipped out and spoke quietly with the man. When he stepped back inside, his face was set in stone.

"Yer captain of the guard has had a look at the

bastard's body. He confirmed that the man has never been seen before, and no one was hired recently."

King Philip muttered a curse, running a hand through his hair. "We will get to the bottom of this, Lady Vivienne," he said.

"Och, I *am* at the bottom of this." Kieran's voice bordered dangerously on insolence, yet he didn't seem to care. "He was one of de Soules's men. He had to have been."

"How can you be sure?" the King asked.

Kieran turned to Vivienne. "The man didnae try to steal from ye or—" his hands clenched so hard at his sides that his knuckles blanched, "—or touch ye, did he?"

"*Non.*"

"I watched him enter the maze. He did so with intent, checking to make sure no one saw him. And he only aimed to do one thing—kill Lady Vivienne."

The Queen returned her attention to Vivienne. "Did the man say anything, *ma chère*? Anything to give him away?"

Vivienne shook her head. He hadn't spoken a word. Nor had his appearance been in any way out of the ordinary.

As if reading her mind, Kieran spoke. "The bastard wore yer servants' livery, Majesty. The palace has been compromised. And I dinnae give a damn how, either." His gaze locked on Vivienne, his eyes as cold as ice. "All I ken is that I am getting Lady Vivienne the hell out of here come first light tomorrow."

Vivienne pulled in a breath, but to her shock,

neither the King nor the Queen reprimanded Kieran for his foul language or challenged his decision to remove her. Instead, the Queen nodded sadly and the King muttered another curse.

"I have failed your King Robert, *mon ami*," King Philip said quietly to Kieran. "I promised to stand with him in all things, yet someone he wanted protected nearly came to harm in my palace."

"*Non*, husband," the Queen cut in. "The failure is mine. It was I who refused to let Monsieur MacAdams take away my dear Vivienne. I exposed her to danger, and you to the displeasure of our Scottish allies."

"It doesnae matter," Kieran said.

From the storm brewing behind his eyes, Vivienne imagined that he struggling under the burden of his own share of guilt for what had nearly happened, despite the fact that she had been the one to wander away into the maze. Worse, she had questioned him at every turn, challenging the very idea that she was in danger, and making his job more difficult by refusing to leave court with him.

"All that matters is getting Vivienne to safety," he went on.

"Agreed," the King said. "And be assured, *mon ami*, I will not rest until the last of de Soules's allies are eradicated from my court—from all of France."

"I'll leave that to ye. And ye leave her protection to me," Kieran responded gruffly. "Och, and apologies for destroying yer hedge maze, Majesty," he added as an afterthought.

"That is nothing," the King replied quickly. "Lady

Vivienne's life is far more important."

The Queen bowed her head somberly as the King and Kieran clasped forearms. Then both the Queen and King quietly exited the chamber, murmuring wishes for Vivienne to rest well.

When the door closed softly behind them, Vivienne couldn't hold back the tears any longer. Everything was happening so fast. First the attack in the maze, and now the decision that she would leave court.

Not that she would argue with Kieran about staying any longer. The fact that someone had managed to get all the way inside the palace's walls and had nearly succeeded in killing her shook her to the bone. But the knowledge that her whole life would now be turned inside out had her stomach in knots and her throat closing on a sob.

What would happen to her position at court? And her father, who counted on that position?

Suddenly Kieran was beside the bed again, his large frame appearing to wobble through her tears.

"What is it?" His voice was soft yet insistent. "Did that bastard hurt ye after all?"

She shook her head, her throat too tight to speak, and tried to swipe away the tears.

"What can I do?" he asked, his tone now edging toward desperation.

"Just…" She couldn't find the words, so instead, she reached for him, circling her arms around his neck and pulling him toward her.

Though his strength was far greater than her own, he didn't resist. He allowed her to drag him down until he was perched on the edge of the bed. She buried her face into his chest and let one sob, then another, and another, escape.

He sat frozen for a moment, solid and warm yet rigid, before at last his arms came around her and he held her against him. His embrace was so hard that she had trouble breathing, yet she refused to ask him to loosen his grip. This was the only place she felt safe—enfolded in his powerful arms.

When the tears ebbed at last, he began to pull away, but she held him close.

"Please…don't go."

"Bloody hell, lass," he practically growled. "Ye dinnae ken what ye are doing to me."

Though his voice was rough and harsh, she knew he was not angry with her. *Non*, from the way his fingers sank into her waist and he inhaled deeply against her hair, he was fighting the same battle she was.

And losing.

She lifted her chin to meet his gaze. His pale blue eyes harbored a tempest of emotion as he stared down at her. When his gaze dropped to her lips, she knew they would both be bested by their unspoken desire.

He lowered his head until their lips brushed, a feather-soft contact. Vivienne's breath caught. It wasn't nearly enough to quench the longing within her.

When she deepened the kiss, he made a noise in the back of his throat that sounded feral and hungry. He claimed her mouth then, his tongue sweeping over hers. One of his hands sank into her hair, tangling in the arranged and pinned plaits. His fingers gripped her locks, sending pricks of sensation from her scalp across the rest of her skin.

She let her hands slide along his shoulders and down his arms. He was so hard and large beneath her palms. She imagined distantly that he'd been forged in an unforgiving wilderness and honed in battle just for this moment, for this kiss and her yearning caress.

At her touch, he growled again, his mouth and hands growing more possessive. With one hand still tangled in her hair, the other rose from her waist up her side to the slope of her breast. When his large, warm hand closed over her, she inhaled and arched. It had been so long since she'd known a man's kiss, his touch. She felt like a beggar starved for affection.

Her blood warmed and began to course faster through her veins. Heat pooled low in her belly as he further deepened the joining of their mouths.

When he circled the peak of her breast with his thumb, an aching pulse awoke between her legs.

Without realizing what she was doing, she leaned back against the bed, pulling him with her. One of her legs rose along the outside of his hip, and suddenly she could feel the hard length of his manhood wedged between them.

He hissed, a sound that was somewhere between ecstasy and agony, then abruptly released her, pulling himself away.

Without his heat and powerful form over her, Vivienne felt exposed. She sucked in a breath, realizing what they'd just done—and what they'd *almost* done.

He swore softly, raking a hand through his hair.

"That was a mistake."

Hot shame flooded her face. *Oui*, he was right—giving in to her desires so recklessly was the last thing Vivienne should have done. Still, it stung to know that he felt the same way.

"Forgive me," she murmured, her voice coming out strained. "I wasn't thinking clearly and—"

"Aye," he cut in brusquely. "We neednae discuss it further."

He rose from the bed, and Vivienne couldn't help but notice the evidence of his desire beneath the wool folds of his plaid. He had been just as swept away by the moment as she'd been.

Vivienne knew her own reasons for regretting her rash wantonness, but why had Kieran halted so abruptly? Despite spending so much time in close proximity to each other, Vivienne knew little of the man behind the gruff, hard shell.

And perhaps it was better that way—better to douse this mad spark between them before Vivienne did something she truly regretted, something that would ruin her carefully controlled life once and for all.

"Be ready to leave come first light tomorrow morn," he said, his voice brusque. He hesitated, glancing down at her. His gaze was unreadable, yet he gentled his tone. "I'll be right outside yer door if ye need aught."

With that, he strode out of her chamber, leaving her alone with a stomach full of knots and a head swirling with confusion. Thankfully, she was so exhausted that after only a few moments, the blessed oblivion of sleep claimed her.

Chapter Ten

Vivienne woke disoriented and hungry much later. She rose and pulled back the shutters on her small window. The sapphire-blue color of the sky told her that it was still an hour or two before sunrise.

Because it had been early evening when she'd fallen asleep, she'd missed the evening meal. But now that she was awake, nerves replaced the hunger in her belly at what lay ahead.

Today was the day she would leave court, her home for the last seven years. Her whole life seemed to hang in the balance—a stable marriage with a nobleman like Thierry, her position as one of the Queen's ladies, and her father's wellbeing all wavered with uncertainty. And of course her life was now literally in danger, with only Kieran MacAdams to protect her.

She donned one of her favorite midnight-blue silk gowns, then dragged a trunk from beneath her bed and slowly began to fill it with all her worldly belongings.

She had no idea where Kieran was taking her, so she tried to pack with numerous occasions in mind.

First she folded an assortment of silk and brocade gowns, along with chemises, stockings for cooler weather, and a variety of silk slippers, into the trunk. Then she wrapped her treasured books into a heavier fur-trimmed cloak and added them in. Last, she carefully folded her various vials and jars of oils and flower waters into a spare coverlet and tucked them in beside the rest.

The trunk was now far too heavy for her to move, and it only closed if she sat on it, but thankfully she'd just managed to secure the latch when she heard Kieran's distinct sharp rap on the door.

At her call, he entered, his features particularly stony this morning. He wore his usual plain shirt and belted plaid, but he also carried a set of leather saddlebags over one shoulder.

"The sun is nearly up," he said, closing the door behind him. "Ye'd best begin preparing to depart."

She blinked. "But I already have." She gestured toward the enormous trunk, which took up a good portion of the chamber's floor space.

He swept the trunk with his gaze, then leveled her with a look. "Ye must be jesting."

Vivienne bristled. Apparently the intense kiss they'd shared last eve was forgotten and they were back to taut verbal sparring.

It was just as well. If she were to set out with him for an indeterminate length of time to an unknown location, it would be better to have walls and boundaries between them once more. Kieran's fortification of choice seemed to be a mocking disdain for Vivienne and all she held dear. For her part, Vivienne would be the cool, mannered woman of court Kieran seemed to hate so much.

"What is the jest?" she asked, lifting her brows at him. "I rose early and packed what I need for our journey."

"More like ye packed half the damn palace," he grumbled.

"I wasn't sure what circumstances I would find myself in, so I selected an array of—"

He tossed the saddlebags from his shoulder. They landed with a dull smack on the stones before her feet. "Ye can take what will fit in there. Naught more."

She stared at the saddlebags. "That…that is all?"

"We arenae going on some lavish pleasure-tour as the King and Queen do when they travel," he replied. "We are on the run from those who wish to see ye dead."

Vivienne swallowed. "But even on the run, I will still be expected to wear clothes, will I not?"

As soon as the words were out, she regretted them. His eyes flashed with heat before they turned cold once more, and she knew he was thinking of being naked together, as she was now as well.

"A-and I will still have want of my books and my beauty tonics and tinctures," she went on hastily. "I cannot fit all of that in those small bags."

"Let me help ye then," he said, closing the distance between them in two swift steps. She jumped out of the way so as not to be bowled over as he halted before the trunk and threw back the lid.

He snatched up the coverlet filled with her vials and bottles and dropped it on her bed. Luckily, her mattress cushioned the glass well enough that none of them broke.

"First off, ye dinnae need any of this rubbish."

She began to object, but before she got far, he'd already returned to the trunk. He unceremoniously shook out her cloak, sending her carefully-packed books tumbling over the folded gowns below.

"This cloak could come in handy, but all these books will only take up space and weigh yer horse down."

"There is no need to—"

"And we arenae going to some grand feast every night," he interrupted, lifting a handful of her gowns and holding them up. "We will be riding, mayhap sleeping on the ground, and most importantly trying no' to draw attention."

A lump had risen to Vivienne's throat at his callous treatment, but luckily an equal portion of anger kept her fright and hurt at bay.

In truth, she should be thanking him. It made it much easier to remember what a detestable brute he was when he behaved like this. And thinking him a brute was far better than thinking him dangerously handsome and devastatingly enthralling.

She willed herself to hold her tongue as he dropped her gowns and crossed his arms over his chest, waiting. Brute though he may be, he had saved her life. She'd promised herself yesterday not to oppose him in his efforts to protect her anymore. If that meant swallowing her pride and somehow managing to cram her entire life into two small saddlebags, then so be it.

Holding her head high and keeping her features smooth, she glided to the bed and unfolded the coverlet containing all her cherished beauty potions. She sifted through them, rationally assessing which she actually used and which were simply nice to have.

"I told ye already, ye dinnae need all that nonsense," Kieran muttered, stepping toward her.

"*Oui*, but it is good to smell agreeable whenever one can—especially when one is traveling," she countered calmly.

To her shock, he moved closer still, until hardly a sliver of air separated them. He encircled her wrist with one of his big hands and lifted it to his nose. He inhaled deeply against the sensitive skin on the inside of her wrist, then released her.

But he wasn't done with her yet. He dipped his head, and for a heart-stopping moment, Vivienne thought he meant to kiss her again. But instead, he dropped his nose to her neck, inhaling once more against her skin.

He straightened, his eyes flashing with a challenge. "Ye smell fine to me. Leave them."

Thank goodness her skirts hid the wobbling of her knees. Yet if he meant to unnerve her with his overpowering presence and rude manners, she refused to be so easily cowed.

Mustering all her composure, she stared at him coolly for a moment before returning her attention to the pile of tinctures. After feigning a measured consideration, she selected the purple-tinted glass bottle of violet oil.

It was her favorite scent, and she treasured it all the more because it had been a gift from the Queen. But more than that, her thoughts flitted back to that first night when Kieran had sniffed it and commented about her wearing it often. He'd remembered from several months before that she preferred it.

Perhaps he found it as unnerving as she found his own scent, of soap and leather and warm male skin. Two could play at his little game of intimidation.

She moved to the tumbled pile of books heaped atop her disheveled clothes. It would be far harder to leave them than her flower waters and oils. She removed them one by one and replaced them into the drawers of her dressing table, all save one. Nothing—not even the foul-tempered Highland warrior glowering at her—would prevent her from taking the copy of *The Song of Roland* her father had given her.

That decision made, she crouched on the floor beside the trunk and slowly removed each rumpled garment. Everything from the gowns to the slippers to the silk chemises and stockings had been hand-made for her. They befitted her station as one of the Queen of France's closest companions, and showed the world her valued position.

To her surprise, a knot tightened her throat as she set each garment aside one by one. No doubt Kieran, who loomed over her, watching her closely, took her for a silly, vain chit. He likely thought her head so full of air that she would grow misty-eyed over a few scraps of silk and brocade when her very life was in danger.

But it wasn't the gowns and finery she cared about. It was what they represented. She'd nearly lost everything seven years past—her good name, her family's honor, and any hope for a future free of scandal and shame.

Yet when the Queen had taken her on as a lady-in-waiting, she'd been given a second chance. She'd remade herself as the perfect lady of court: well-mannered, demure, graceful, and restrained. And she'd proven it with her outward appearance. The gowns, the hair, the façade of cool control—they all covered her past mistakes.

So what was she without her fine clothes, her fancy fragrances, her position at court? She was a girl from a humble estate who had made a terrible error in judgment. She was nothing. It burned her pride to admit it, but far worse was the knowledge that in abandoning the palace, she didn't just hurt her own standing. Her father would pay as well.

Forcing herself to maintain her composure, she selected two practical gowns—the gray dress she'd worn yesterday evening and another of green-dyed wool that was warm and comfortable—and slipped them into the saddlebags.

When she held up two linen chemises, Kieran cleared his throat, but she ignored him. She tucked them, along with a pair of stockings and her book and violet oil, into the bags as well. Once she'd added a comb, a small pouch of coins, and a few other small personal items, there was no more room.

"Do ye have riding boots?" Kieran asked behind her.

She rose, kicking off her slippers and dragging out a pair of leather half-boots she normally wore in the winter.

Kieran eyed the blue silk gown she wore but decided —wisely—to refrain from commenting. Instead, he held out the fur-trimmed cloak she'd used to bundle her books together. When she took it and slung it around her shoulders, he hoisted up the saddlebags she'd just filled and strode out of the room.

Vivienne hesitated a moment, casting her eyes over her chamber. There was a chance she'd never see it again. There wasn't time to be sentimental, though. With a silent farewell to all that she had created for herself here at court over the last seven years, she stepped out of the chamber and hurried after Kieran.

He strode straight to the palace's stables, where a stable lad was already holding the reins to two horses. One was clearly Kieran's. It was a bay gelding large enough to hold his giant frame. The other was a smaller yet spritely looking white mare that must have been meant for her.

As Kieran went about fastening the saddlebags to her horse's saddle, a movement at the palace's double doors caught her eye. Hesitantly, the seven other ladies-in-waiting shuffled out and approached. Some eyed Kieran as if they expected him to snap at them to be gone again, yet he didn't seem to pay them any mind.

HER WILD HIGHLANDER

"Safe travels," Marie said, coming forward and pulling Vivienne into a tight hug.

"We'll miss you," Aveline murmured, moving in to embrace her as well.

One by one, the ladies hugged her and bid her well. Vivienne blinked back the tears as she reassured them that she would see them all again soon.

And then suddenly the Queen, who never rose at this hour, was gliding from the palace. The ladies all dropped into practiced curtsies, including Vivienne, but the Queen moved forward and took her hand, giving it a squeeze.

"Be brave, *ma chère*, and remember that you have our love."

Vivienne mumbled her thanks in a voice thick with emotion. When the Queen released her hand, Kieran suddenly grasped her around the waist and lifted her into the saddle. He mounted his own horse in one fluid movement and set the animal into motion.

As the others waved and called out their farewells, Vivienne trailed after him through the palace's thick walls and toward the bridge that led into the heart of Paris. She still didn't know where they were headed, and to give herself something to focus on other than her breaking heart, she nudged her mount alongside his.

"Where are you taking me?"

He gave her an assessing look for a moment. "Scotland."

A thought occurred to her that had hope surging past her sadness. "Will we sail via Calais?"

"Aye."

"Then I would make a request."

He lifted a brow at her. "A request, or a demand?"

She ignored the comment and said, "My family's estate in Picardy is on the way to Calais. I'd like to stop and see my father."

Kieran grunted, his rugged features darkening with a frown. "I told ye before, this isnae some grand tour for making social calls."

"Please," she said, unable to control the edge of desperation tinging her voice. "I...I may not have another chance to see him."

He hesitated another moment, but at last relented. "Verra well."

Vivienne breathed a sigh of relief. Her family's estate was only a two-day's ride from the palace, but it had been many long months since she'd had the opportunity to visit.

She could only pray that all would be well when they arrived.

Chapter Eleven

K ieran was being an arse and he knew it.
They'd ridden all day in stony silence, but it
was obvious Vivienne was struggling to keep up with the
grueling pace he set. She was so delicate and ethereal,
like some sort of angel. All airy refinement and graceful
composure, she was clearly not meant to ride long hours
with minimal breaks.

Yet the space between Kieran's shoulder blades
itched as they rode across the open, rolling French countryside. Without the cover of trees or a familiar landscape to use to his advantage, they were far too exposed
for his liking.

Still, insisting on a punishing speed until nearly dusk
might be for her own safety, but it didn't excuse being an
arse to her that morning. He'd mercilessly torn through
her trunk and had barely given her time to say her
farewells.

The blasted truth was, he was scared witless. His

worst fears had been confirmed—she was in danger, and William de Soules was likely behind it. Even from within Scone Palace's dungeon, the man still had influence as far away as France.

And if Kieran's instincts were right, which they almost always were, that meant the single attacker posing as a palace gardener was just the beginning. Kieran was the only thing standing between Vivienne and those who would see her dead.

But none of that was her fault, so he didn't bloody well need to take it out on her.

That was why, when blue dusk began to creep across the sky, he led them toward a nearby village's inn rather than insisting they sleep on the ground, as he'd told her they would.

Once they'd guided their horses to the inn's stables, handed over the reins to a stable lad, and Kieran had slung their saddlebags over his shoulder, they went inside.

The inn was quiet and mostly empty, yet the handful of men who sat nursing mugs of ale or wine at the counter all turned at their entrance.

And stared openly at Vivienne.

Hell and damnation. Even surrounded by other beauties at court, she had been a rare gem to behold. And they certainly weren't at court any longer.

He closed his hand possessively over hers, daring any man in the inn to continue ogling her. Most cleared their throats and returned their attention to their cups, but a few could not seem to help but gape at her.

Kieran strode to the counter, Vivienne in tow, toward a man whom he assumed was the proprietor.

"A room," Kieran said, placing a coin on the countertop. He glanced around at the narrow, rickety looking stairs that led from the sparsely furnished common room toward the chambers above. Vivienne huddled against his side, clearly exhausted.

With a muffled sigh, he set down another coin. "Yer best. And we'd like a meal—delivered to us." The last thing he needed was a room full of lonely, curious men gawking at Vivienne all night.

The innkeeper grinned at the coins, then hustled around the counter to show them to their room. He led them up the stairs and down a hallway to the last door. Inside, the room was simple but serviceable. Kieran was glad he'd paid for the "best," if the others were any worse than this.

A wooden table and two chairs were pushed against one wall. Opposite the table was a narrow cot. A small brazier with a fire laid and ready to be lit and a little stand with a pitcher and basin for washing rounded out the furnishings.

Once he'd closed the door on the innkeeper, who promised to bring up food and drink shortly, Kieran dropped their saddlebags in the middle of the floor and rolled his shoulders. Vivienne moved toward one of the chairs, gingerly lowering herself down.

It was only then, once they were alone in the small, plain room with naught to look at but each other, that Kieran realized just how much trouble he was in.

Bloody hell and damnation.

There was no way in hell he was going to let Vivienne out of his sight after the attack yesterday. Of course, even before the attack, they'd been forced into close proximity due to his role as her bodyguard. For the last fortnight at the palace, he'd been like her shadow, only leaving her side when she sought privacy or rest in her chamber.

But now even that extra sliver of space would not be afforded to them. He wouldn't risk getting his own room and leaving her alone in this unsecured inn just for propriety's sake. No doubt that would irk her refined sensibilities, but he didn't give a damn about that.

Nay, the darker, more insidious danger might be not in leaving her alone, but in remaining so close.

There was no denying it—he wanted her.

Their kiss, hot and needy, flooded back to him. Just as he'd suspected, a river of passion surged just below her prim and proper exterior. Despite being his opposite in nearly every way, she stirred him like no other. She was sophisticated and mannered where he was rude, polished where he was rough, and soft where he was so achingly hard.

Yet naught could come of the desire that sparked between them. They belonged to two different worlds, she the dazzling, complex realm of the French court and he the punishing, brutal conditions of the Scottish army. Hadn't he learned the hard way not to long for a life that wasn't meant for him?

The problem was, even after all that had happened ten years past, some part of him still hungered for more —more than a warrior's life. And more with Vivienne.

If he wasn't careful, things were liable to get intimate between them again in such close quarters. So to cool his blood and break the awkward silence hanging around them, he did the only thing he could think of—he brought up another man.

"What is de Pontier to ye?"

She lifted her drooping head, her eyes clouded with confusion. Leave it to Kieran to speak so bluntly as to be nonsensical. He drew in a breath and went on.

"He seems to pay a great deal of attention to ye." That was, when Kieran wasn't chasing the man off with a glower—or better yet, simply moving him bodily away from Vivienne.

"Thierry has made his interest clear, *oui*."

He eyed her. "Ye dinnae discourage him, yet neither do ye turn dunderheaded and moon-eyed in his presence."

She sniffed in offense. "*Ladies* do not become dunderheaded and moon-eyed."

Kieran liked to think he'd gotten more of a reaction from Vivienne than that de Pontier fop had, even if it tended toward anger and outrage rather than the more flowery emotions.

A sudden, gut-twisting thought hit him—had she kissed Thierry? Had the bastard elicited as passionate a response as Kieran had?

Mayhap this wasn't as safe a topic as Kieran had hoped. But he wouldn't stop now that his dander was up.

"Ye want him, though, dinnae ye?"

She seemed to pick her next words carefully. "He is a

nobleman with a large and important holding. He could provide me with a lifetime of security."

Of course—the bastard was everything Kieran was not. Wealthy. Refined. Powerful. Stable. Yet through the sudden surge of jealousy, a niggling voice told Kieran that she hadn't truly answered his question.

"Ye wish to marry him," he prodded, watching her closely.

"*Oui.*" She met his gaze then, and he saw the truth of the word in her eyes. But he also saw a flicker of pain and hesitation, too.

"Do ye care for him? Desire him?"

Bloody hell, these questions were mad. What could he possibly hope for her to say? She'd already more than confirmed what he already knew—that there could never be more besides lust between her and Kieran. Why did some perverse part of him wish to make her say so aloud?

Vivienne's throat bobbed as she swallowed, yet she held his gaze. "*Non.*"

Unexpected satisfaction surged through him, but before Kieran could parse what that implied, a knock sounded at the door. He rose and cautiously drew the door open a crack, but it was only the inn's proprietor with a tray of food, as promised.

Kieran snatched the tray and closed the door in the innkeeper's face with naught more than a grunt of thanks. He set the tray on the table and took up the chair opposite her. They ate the simple meal of lamb stew, bread, and wine in taut silence, but Kieran's mind wouldn't let the matter go.

"Why would ye marry that fop if ye dinnae care aught for him?" he demanded when she finished her last spoonful of stew.

She pulled up her chin, and despite her earlier fatigue, a new spark of angry energy lit her eyes. "Not all of us have the luxury of choosing a spouse based on affection or attraction."

"What the hell does that mean?" Of course, he knew that many nobles married purely for the purposes of alliance or advancement, yet there seemed to be something else lurking behind her words.

"It means that if I am to maintain my position at court, I must make a good match," she snapped, some of her composure slipping.

Kieran rolled his eyes. "What is so damn important about a position at court? I'll never understand yer obsession with all the extravagance and gossip and frippery."

She rose abruptly, stalking toward where he'd dumped her saddlebags. Her normally graceful gait was hindered by her obvious soreness, yet she still managed to look haughtily regal as she went.

"Others are counting on me," she said, bending to fetch her comb and violet oil. "You wouldn't understand, I'm sure."

His ire spiked at her barb—what the hell did she know about him, anyway—but he let it go, instead remaining focused on the topic of her marriage like a hound on a scent.

"But why de Pontier, then?" he persisted. "I've seen

the way men look at ye. Ye could have yer pick from any eligible nobleman at court."

As he spoke, a realization began to dawn. Aye, she could have any man she chose, including Thierry, whom she likely might have married by now if she truly wanted to—but mayhap she didn't want to marry at all.

"What are ye—three or four and twenty?" he asked, sweeping his gaze over her.

She straightened sharply from the pile of saddle-bags, her grip so hard on her comb and vial of flower oil that her knuckles blanched. "What does that have to do with anything?"

"If stability and security are so important to ye, as ye claim, why havenae ye married already?"

The question hung in the air for a long moment, the two of them staring each other down. Kieran had already pushed too far, but there was no going back now that he'd begun to find cracks in the carefully constructed wall she'd built around herself.

"Ye are the bonniest woman I've ever laid eyes on," he said, attempting to soften his bald question. "Ye could have any one of those idiots at court—or all of them, if ye chose. Why havenae ye picked one—like de Pontier—and married, Vivienne?"

She turned and strode slowly to the stand bearing the pitcher and basin. When she began pouring water over her hands and splashing it on her face, he feared she would never answer, but at last she stilled and spoke.

"I...I made a mistake many years ago," she said, keeping her back to him. "I trusted someone I shouldn't have. It has made me wary of making the same error again."

Kieran jerked in his chair at her softly spoken words. She began unwinding the plaits in her hair. It fell in luscious pale gold waves down her back.

"I know you think me silly and vain," she went on, taking up the comb and gently dragging it through her locks. "You think all I care about are feasts and dancing and silks and gossip."

"Nay," he said, his voice coming out gruff. Though he'd thrown just such an accusation at her feet a moment before, some part of him knew that wasn't all there was to her.

"*Non*? If not a fool, perhaps you think me cold and calculating, a shrew obsessed with remaining perfectly in control. And perhaps I am. Marrying Thierry would confirm that, wouldn't it?"

"Nay," he said again, rising and taking a step toward her. "In truth, I dinnae ken what to make of ye."

"It is not so complicated," she murmured. "I am a woman who nearly lost everything, and who learned the hard way just how powerful society's approval—or disapproval—can be."

"That is why ye have hesitated to marry, even though ye claim it's what ye want—because ye are afraid of making the wrong decision and falling out of society's good graces."

She turned then, her dark blue eyes flickering with pain. "As I said, I have erred in the past. If I do so again, I doubt I will get another chance. I…I am not one to trust easily."

He took another step forward, and in the small space, it was enough to bring them nearly chest to chest. Something in the air around them seemed to shift, to thicken with anticipation.

"And do ye trust *me*?"

"With my safety, *oui*," she answered without hesitation. Yet what she left unsaid struck him like a kick to the gut—she didn't trust herself to be alone with him.

The knowledge that she felt the same burning desire he did was like a swig of powerful Highland whisky. It warmed his blood and made his head spin wildly.

"Ye are safe with me," he said.

"Oh, I think we both know that is not true," she whispered.

"And what would be the harm if we were honest about what we want?"

Aye, there was the root of his frustration, and why he'd been behaving like such an arse, especially in questioning her about Thierry. He desired her, damn it. And he was no good at pretending he didn't.

Slowly, he slid his thumb and forefinger down one of her silky flaxen locks. "Society's eyes arenae here to approve or disapprove. Besides, ye should ken by now that I dinnae give a damn what others think."

A distant, sane part of his mind screamed at him that he was going down a path toward madness, but all traces of reason vanished when she brought a slim finger to her lips and began biting her nail. It was an unconscious gesture he was coming to recognize as a sign of nervousness, yet it told him she was considering his words.

Without thinking, he gently pulled her hand from her mouth and brought the abused nail to his own lips. Slowly, he kissed the pad of her finger, then drew it into the heated depths of his mouth.

She sucked in a breath, her eyes hazing with desire as he teased her with his tongue. He slid her finger free, then turned over her palm and sank his teeth into the flesh at the base of her thumb.

"Let me pleasure ye," he mumbled against her palm.

She stiffened, and he looked up to find her lips parted in surprise.

He'd assumed she was a virgin given her rigid adherence to propriety, yet something about the shadow that had crossed her eyes when she'd spoken of misplacing her trust years ago gave him pause. But even if she was innocent, she'd lived in the French court for some time, where trysts were an open secret and carnal indulgence was considered a natural part of life. Had no one ever offered to give her pleasure before without expecting aught in return?

"Why?" she asked.

"Because I want to see ye lose control," he rasped, holding her gaze. "I want to make ye come undone under my touch."

He moved his lips back to her finger, sucking it once more until she answered.

"*Oui*," she breathed, her eyelids sliding closed.

In less than a heartbeat, he was kissing her. She opened under him instantly, surrendering to his invading tongue. His hands fumbled with the ties running down the back of her dress, eager to free her skin from the garment.

When he'd gotten a few of the laces loose, he simply tugged on the material at her shoulders impatiently. To his pleasure, she helped him by wriggling until the silk was bunched at her waist.

He slid the gown over her gently flaring hips and let it pool at her feet, leaving her only in a silk chemise. The material was slippery-smooth and warm from her skin. Even with only her shoulders and arms bare now, it was nearly the most erotic thing Kieran had ever experienced.

Unable to hold back any longer, he nudged her against the wall, bracketing her body with an arm braced on either side of her. He tore his mouth away to trail hot kisses down her throat and across her exposed décolletage. Her chest rose and fell rapidly as he found inch after inch of sensitive, creamy skin with his lips and tongue.

One of his hands fisted in the silky length of the chemise, dragging it up until his fingers brushed her smooth, soft thigh. The other rose to cup one perfect, high breast. Her nipple was already pebbled with desire against the silk. He thumbed it, drawing a gasp and a moan from her.

His cock throbbed painfully beneath his kilt, but he willed himself not to lose control. Instead, he focused on her breast until he could feel her thigh trembling against his other hand. He moved up, brushing the curls between her legs. They were already damp. He shuddered with longing.

He slid a finger along the seam of her sex, making her moan again. Bloody hell, she would be his undoing even if she never touched him. She was so sensitive and alive under his hands, so responsive and nigh overflowing with passion beneath that thin veil of control.

When he parted her and brushed his finger against that bud of a woman's pleasure, she bucked against him.

So much for restraining himself.

He yanked down the front of her chemise, freeing her breasts to his gaze. They were round and soft and tipped with points of pink the same petal-soft color as her lips.

He closed a hand over one, letting his callused palm tease her, and his lips over the other, flicking his tongue over her nipple. Her fingers sank into his shoulders, clawing him wildly as her breaths came faster and faster.

When she was moaning and rolling her hips against his hand, he slid a finger inside her tight, wet core, dragging it in and out slowly while keeping the pressure on her bud with his thumb.

"Say my name," he rasped against her skin. "Let me hear it on yer lips."

"Kieran," she moaned. "Kieran."

She came hard against his hand, shuddering and crying out. He could feel her pulse around his finger until her breathing began to slow and she slumped against the wall.

Reluctantly, he withdrew from between her legs and lifted her chemise back in place over her breasts. He scooped up her suddenly boneless body and carried her to the cot, laying her down gently.

But when he began to move away, she gripped him around the neck. Her eyes lifted to his, dark and vulnerable.

He'd told her he wanted to see her come undone, to lose control. Now that he had, fear spiked hard in his gut. She was so damn beautiful, all disheveled and free, her defensive walls down.

He felt a stirring in his chest he'd thought himself no longer capable of—caring. But he already knew where this would end—in pain and loss. It always did. Opening one's heart only made it defenseless against being hurt.

Kieran drew away, unlooping her arms from his neck. "Rest," he said, his voice coming out rougher than he'd intended. "We have another half-day's ride ahead of us tomorrow before we reach Picardy."

She shuttered the emotion in her eyes, nodding.

Kieran settled himself on the ground in front of the cot, pulling his extra length of plaid around him. He'd made a grave error tonight in thinking giving rather than taking pleasure would keep him safe from the pull he felt toward Vivienne. Aye, there was no denying that lust crackled between them, but he had to ensure it didn't turn into aught more.

He'd lost everything once before, and he didn't plan on ever doing so again.

Chapter Twelve

"My family's estate is just beyond this rise." Those were the first words Vivienne had spoken to Kieran in hours. He grunted in response, not knowing what else to say.

That morning, they'd exchanged a few tense words in which they'd both agreed that it would be best to avoid the kinds of intimacies they'd succumbed to the night before.

For his part, Kieran should have been glad, for intimacy was exactly what he'd been trying to avoid for the last ten years. He needn't confuse lust with emotion. Yet it tweaked his ire to see Vivienne's cool, composed veneer in place come the light of day. Could she really return to that act now that he'd seen her true, passionate nature?

But of course he hadn't asked her that. Curiosity about what lay under her surface had been what had gotten him in trouble last night.

So they'd departed the inn without speaking further and had ridden north under a cloud-dappled sky for several hours.

Only now did she speak, pointing northwest beyond the hill they were mounting. As they topped the grassy rise, Kieran expected to see some grand keep surrounded by fertile, vast lands. Instead, a solitary tower house sat in the midst of an unkempt, overgrown plot.

They looked more like unclaimed, open lands than the holdings of a noble family. And it was a far cry from the pristine, wealthy estate he'd always assumed Vivienne had grown up on. In fact, it was downright humble.

He glanced at Vivienne to see if her face betrayed any embarrassment at bringing him here, but to his surprise, her eyes brimmed with yearning and her lips curved in a sweet smile. She tapped her heels against her horse's flanks to hurry the animal's descent down the hill and toward the tower house.

Kieran urged his horse after hers, quickly overtaking her. Though he doubted any danger lurked at her family's estate, he couldn't be too careful. She ignored him as she reined in her mount a dozen paces from the keep.

The round, conical-topped tower looked to have been built more than a hundred years ago. Mayhap it had once been a defensible holding, but it had long since passed its peak. An additional structure had been built at the base of the three-storey tower slightly more recently, creating what looked like a modest great hall with attached kitchens. Kieran saw no guards or other defensive measures as he swung down from the saddle.

The wooden door on the attached hall swung open just as Kieran was lifting Vivienne from her horse. Instinctively, he angled her behind him, but she slipped from his hold and darted around.

"Madame Claudette!" Vivienne cried, hurrying toward the woman standing in the doorway. The woman stepped into the sunlight with a wide grin on her face. She was perhaps twice Vivienne's age, and almost as strikingly beautiful, yet the two bore no resemblance to each other.

Madame Claudette wore a plain brown woolen dress with an apron tied over it. Her long black hair, which was liberally sliced with gray, hung in a simple braid down her back. Even from several paces away, Kieran could see the vibrancy of her green eyes.

Just before Vivienne reached Claudette, she pulled up, giving the woman a dignified tilt of the head rather than the hard embrace Kieran would have expected based on how excited she'd seemed a moment before. But ever the proper lady, Vivienne had apparently regained control.

Even with Vivienne's relatively staid greeting, Claudette smiled warmly, curtsied, and then squeezed Vivienne's arm.

"What an unexpected pleasure, *mademoiselle*. I'll fetch your father."

Claudette disappeared into the keep, then a moment later, a tall, lean man with blond hair turning to white filled the doorway. He carried a thin cane in one hand, extending his other toward Vivienne.

"Vivi?"

"*Papa*," Vivienne cried. Now she launched herself into his arms for an embrace. He chuckled as he hugged her back, his pale blue gaze drifting over her head to rest on Kieran.

"To what do we owe such a wonderful surprise?" the man asked, releasing Vivienne.

"And who have you brought with you, *mademoiselle*?" Claudette murmured from behind Vivienne's father.

Vivienne turned and beckoned Kieran forward. "Unfortunately," she said, her happiness dimming, "the circumstances aren't pleasant. I'll explain shortly. This is Monsieur Kieran MacAdams. Kieran, this is Seigneur Lambert de Valance, my father, and Madame Claudette Rougarde, the keep's chatelaine."

"Milord," Kieran said, sketching a faint bow. "Madame."

De Valance took a step forward out of the doorway, but instead of leaning on his cane, he tapped it on the ground before his feet. "A Scotsman?" he asked, cocking his head as if to listen to Kieran's voice again.

"Aye, milord," Kieran replied, a bit puzzled. The plaid around his hips should have given him away for a Scot before his voice had.

The man's white brows rose in surprise, yet to Kieran's confusion, he seemed to be staring with those pale, milky blue eyes at some point beyond Kieran's shoulder.

Then it hit him like a flash of lightning—Lambert de Valance was blind.

Vivienne was watching Kieran closely, her chin lifted defensively as if daring him to make a comment in his usual blunt, ill-mannered way. But all Kieran could think at the moment was how little he truly understood about Vivienne, even after all that had happened last night.

"We had best go inside and sit," Claudette said. "I'll make sure Pierre sees to your horses and refreshments are prepared. It seems as though the three of you have much to discuss."

De Valance moved inside, with Vivienne and Kieran falling in behind him. As Claudette set about making them welcome, Kieran took in the appearance of the small room.

Though far too modest to be considered a great hall, the purpose of the room was much the same. A large oak table and chairs for dining sat against the back wall, with a handful of ancient tapestries hanging over them.

A hearth sat unlit opposite the table. A few well-used, upholstered chairs were clustered in front of it. Off to the right, spiral stairs led up to the tower's higher floors, and to the left was a door that presumably opened into the kitchens.

That was all. No grand displays of wealth or power, and no indication of how a woman like Vivienne had come from a place like this.

De Valance moved to the table. The fact that he didn't use his cane told Kieran he was very familiar with the space. He lowered himself into one of the carved wooden chairs and waited for Vivienne and Kieran to do the same.

"Now, *ma fille*, what are these unpleasant circumstances that have brought you here?"

Vivienne glanced at Kieran, but he motioned for her to speak. She took a deep breath and began with Kieran and the Bruce's envoy arriving at court earlier that summer.

She explained how she'd recognized William de Soules from his visits to Edward Balliol's estate, which had not been far from here. And she told her father how she'd aided Jerome and Elaine in unraveling de Soules's nefarious scheme to dethrone Robert the Bruce and insert Balliol in his stead.

As she continued, her father's jaw slackened with shock. Apparently Kieran wasn't the only one who'd taken Vivienne for more of the demure type rather than a bold lady who'd managed to help thwart a traitor. When she described how she'd poisoned de Soules, leaving him incapacitated for nigh on a fortnight before Kieran had dragged him back to Scotland, de Valance cleared his throat.

"In short, milord," Kieran said when Vivienne was through, "yer daughter did something verra brave, but now she is in danger."

"Danger?" de Valance said, turning his head toward Kieran. His voice was sharp with worry. "What do you mean, Monsieur MacAdams?"

"Just Kieran," he said, his gaze flashing to Vivienne. A blush rose to her cheeks, and his own blood stirred at the memory of his name on her lips as she'd come apart last night. He swallowed hard, refocusing on de Valance.

"Though de Soules is being held indefinitely in

Scone's dungeon, he worked to build his rebellion on both Scottish and French soil. Apparently he was secretive about how many allies he had, never letting any one person ken everyone else involved in his scheme. Since de Soules's treachery and Vivienne's help in stopping him are now public knowledge, I feared that she would become a target if any of de Soules's allies sought to avenge him."

"*You* feared?" Vivienne cut in. "You told me Robert the Bruce was the one who worried for my safety and decided to send you."

Kieran barely managed to stifle a curse at his slip-up. The fact was, he hadn't wanted her to know that he'd been the one to urge the King to send him to France. Aye, he'd told the King and the others in the Bodyguard Corps that he merely saw it as his duty to protect one of Scotland's allies, but the truth was much more humiliating than that.

From the moment he'd laid eyes on her earlier that summer, he'd wanted to taste those petal lips and feel her soft, graceful body under his. But when she'd risked her life to incapacitate de Soules long enough for his scheme to be unraveled, Kieran had vowed that no harm would come to her. She was like delicate stained glass—too fine and valuable to come to ruin now that she'd been ensnared in Kieran's world of violence and destruction.

He shifted in his chair under her too-perceptive gaze. "Aye, well," he said, pausing to clear his throat. "I may have encouraged the King to consider yer protection. Ye did play a part in saving his life, after all. It seemed only right that I make sure ye were safe."

He turned back to de Valance, but he could still feel Vivienne's assessing eyes searching him.

"The long and the short of it is, milord," he went on. "Someone attacked yer daughter at court. I believe it was one of de Soules's lackeys seeking revenge against her. I'm taking her someplace safe until we can be sure the threat has been neutralized."

De Valance shook his white head slowly, clearly speechless. Vivienne took hold of his hand and squeezed.

"I-I didn't want to worry you," she said, her voice tight. "But I wasn't sure when I'd be able to visit again, and I had to make sure all was well."

De Valance reached for her and patted her face, his features softening with paternal love. "Don't fret over me, *ma fille*. Claudette takes good care of me now."

As if beckoned by the mention of her name, Madame Claudette appeared through the door leading to the kitchen. "A meal will be ready shortly. And I'll have a room made up for the two of you abovestairs, *mademoiselle, monsieur*."

Kieran rose from the table. "I'll be glad for a meal, but if ye dinnae mind, milord, I'd like to make a sweep of yer grounds to look for possible threats."

De Valance chuckled sadly. "I believe the only threat you'll encounter is being choked by weeds, Kieran. My lands are...not what they should be."

"I used to be a farmer, milord," Kieran said wryly. "Believe me, trying to grow barley in rocky Highland soil taught me an appreciation for nature's resistance to our control. I'm no' one to pass judgement when it comes to the struggles of working the land."

Vivienne made a little noise, and he turned to find her staring at him wide-eyed. Apparently he wasn't the only one who'd made assumptions during the time they'd spent together.

"I'll accompany you," she said abruptly, rising from her chair. "I can show you the borders of the estate so that you don't miss anything on your sweep."

He hesitated, but in truth, he didn't expect to encounter any real danger. He more wished to orient himself with his surroundings and, if he were honest, puzzle over his new insights into Vivienne.

"Verra well."

Chapter Thirteen

Vivienne clasped her hands before her as they strode from the keep to prevent from gnawing on her nails. Though she had been alone with Kieran many times before now, his casual comment about once being a farmer had thrown her off-kilter.

Despite all the intimacies they'd indulged in, she realized that she knew very little about her gruff, irreverent Highland bodyguard. She was embarrassed to admit that she'd never asked him about himself or his past.

"The estate is small enough to walk—unless you would prefer to ride," she said, hesitating.

"Walking is good."

She gestured toward the rise they'd crested on their way in. "I'll show you the bird's eye view from there, and then we can walk the edges."

They mounted the hill in silence while Vivienne fought to untangle her tongue.

"I never knew you were a farmer," she finally blurted, wincing at her lack of tact.

He rolled one muscular shoulder. "It was a long time ago. It doesnae seem relevant to my role as yer bodyguard."

"True," she said, "but nor is what we did last night."

"I thought we agreed no' to discuss that."

He had her there. "*Oui*, but if we are to remain in each other's company for the foreseeable future, don't you think we ought to get to know one another better? In a strictly proper context, of course," she added hastily, feeling her face warm.

He grunted, and she wasn't sure if it meant assent or disagreement, but at last he spoke. "What do ye wish to ken?"

He was like a vast, shrouded wilderness before her. Where to begin?

"How long were you a farmer?"

"I grew up in a family of farmers," he replied. "It was always in my blood. We had a small plot in the Highlands—a hard way to make a go of it, but we always managed to get by."

His voice dropped as he continued. "When my parents died, I took over the land."

"Then how did you become one of Robert the Bruce's warriors?"

They'd reached the top of the rise and he halted, his eyes carefully avoiding hers by scanning the landscape before them. "I realized I was wasting my time tucked away in my wee corner of the Highlands. Look at me."

She didn't need his encouragement. Her gaze swept

over the corded muscles in his shoulders and arms, the hard plane of his torso, and the powerful legs showing beneath his belted plaid.

"I've always been built like an ox," he went on. "Working the land made me strong, but there was naught to keep me tied to that place anymore. So I joined the Bruce's army and began fighting my way up the ranks. Ten years of hard work has brought me into his inner circle."

It was an impressive feat, one she should congratulate him on, but something he'd said a moment before kept nagging at her. "What do you mean there was nothing to tie you to your farm? Was it not a connection to your family even after they'd passed?"

He stiffened, a wary wall seeming to drop around him. "Why would I wish for a constant reminder that they are gone? I dinnae have a family anymore."

It was clearly not a topic he wished to discuss further, so she hastily changed the subject. She pointed to the west. "That is our estate boundary," she said, tracing a line with her finger. "That stream there is part of our lands. And the forested area is ours as well, though it has been overrun."

In fact, everything had been overrun. The fields spreading beneath them were weed-infested and wild looking. The woods bled into the croplands, and even from here she could see that the stables and other outbuildings behind the keep were sagging with disrepair.

"I meant what I said to yer father," Kieran murmured as they began their descent and cut westward. "Farming isnae an easy task. But how did the estate fall into such disrepair?"

"It didn't use to be like this," she said. "When I was a child, the fields were all tended and the land productive. It has always been a modest holding, but the soil was good and the tenants hard-working."

A tight lump rose to her throat, but Vivienne swallowed it. She'd wanted him to open up more to her. It seemed only fair that she do the same in return.

"When I was fifteen, my mother grew ill. My father and I both devoted a great deal of time tending to her—which meant he began neglecting the estate. Though I tried to take my mother's care on by myself, I simply couldn't do it all alone."

Vivienne's mind drifted back to those last painful, drawn-out days of her mother's life. She hadn't been the easiest or warmest of women, but she was protective of and loving toward Vivienne, wanting the best for her only child. She'd believed Vivienne was destined for more than a quiet life in this sleepy corner of France.

"That was when the trouble began. We had a cold spring that stunted the crops, then one of the tenant families died of a fever. When I was sixteen, my mother died. My father's eyesight was already failing by then, and there was simply too much to handle. The few tenants that remained moved to the nearby village when it became clear that my father couldn't maintain the estate by himself. I did my best to look after my father, but he simply couldn't manage it all any longer. And then—"

Her voice caught. It was hard enough to speak of

her mother's death and her father's deterioration. She could not bring herself to tell the worst of it, to reveal the depth of her shame and her near-complete ruin.

"And then when I was seventeen, I went to court," she said, hoping he didn't notice her heartbeat of hesitation.

He frowned, but his gaze continued to scan the over-grown fields they walked through. "So ye just left him?"

"*Non*," she replied, sharper than she'd intended. She drew a deep breath to calm her nerves. "I didn't want to leave him alone—he needed a great deal of help—but he insisted that I go. In fact, I learned years later that he organized the opportunity."

"Oh?"

"You see, the King and Queen were passing through Amiens on a grand tour of the countryside. Knowing that a position at court would open many doors for me, he arranged for us to be in Amiens to pay homage to the King and Queen during their visit. When it was my father's turn to be presented and pay homage, he brought me with him, insisting that I guide him due to his failing eyesight, and speak for him, though of course nothing was wrong with his voice."

"And let me guess," Kieran said, shooting her a knowing look out of the corner of his eye. "The Queen was so taken by yer beauty and grace that she wished to have ye as one of her ladies-in-waiting."

She felt her cheeks heat, but this time out of plea-sure rather than embarrassment. "It was a little more complicated than that, and involved several more meetings, but *oui*, the Queen took a liking to me and invited me to court."

"Yer father must have been pleased."

"*Oui*, for he hoped I would be able to find a husband and lead the grand, extravagant life my mother always wanted for me. I, however, didn't wish to leave him. But I knew such an opportunity would not present itself again. It was a chance to right my mistakes."

She felt his gaze on her and turned to find his eyes sharp and penetrating. Luckily, he did not ask her to elaborate.

Vivienne hastened her steps as they approached the stream, pretending to need a drink. "And being at court has allowed me to help my father in a different way," she said airily over her shoulder as she knelt and cupped water into her hands.

Kieran crouched beside her, taking a long drink as well. "I imagine the distance makes it harder than ye are making it seem," he commented evenly.

"The Queen gives her ladies an allowance," Vivienne replied. "I send *Papa* the coins, and anything else of value that I think might help him. And Madame Claudette is an immense help."

"Has she always been the chatelaine?"

"Oh, *non*," she answered quickly. "I hired at least a half a dozen before finding her. The others were…"

She felt her mouth tighten. Some had been cruel to her father, refusing to help him in the tasks he struggled with due to his loss of vision. Others had simply taken her coins and left.

"Madame Claudette came from the nearby village

three or four years ago and has been a Godsend ever since. Whenever the Queen is traveling with the King to the north, she brings me with her and allows me to check on things. But now that Claudette is here, I don't have to worry as much."

He rose slowly from the streambank, taking her hand to help her to her feet. All the while, he stared at her with those cool, assessing eyes.

At last, she couldn't take it anymore. "*Mon Dieu*, what? Do I have mud on my face, or has a bird dropped excrement on my head?"

To her shock, he actually laughed. The sound was low and rich just like his voice, and it instantly shot a warm, tingling awareness through her.

"Nay, lass," he said with another chuckle. "Ye dinnae have mud on yer face or bird shite in yer hair."

"Then what? I know you do not enjoy my company, so what can you find so amusing?"

He sobered, his features falling into their usual serious lines, yet his eyes clouded with some unreadable emotion. "Ye have that wrong. I dinnae mind ye or yer company. And at that moment I was struck by how mistaken I've been about ye."

Her heart suddenly leapt into her throat. He didn't mind her? Not exactly words that should set her pulse jumping, but there it was. "Oh?" she breathed. "What have you mistaken about me, then?"

"Here I was taking ye for a frosty, spoiled chit, only to learn that this whole time…" His words dried up and he waved vaguely as if to encompass all she'd just told him.

He suddenly shifted his gaze and cleared his throat, visibly uncomfortable at the way their conversation had veered toward sentimentality.

"I could fix that, ye ken," he said, pointing toward the long-dilapidated waterwheel that sat a stone's throw upstream. He strode toward it, Vivienne trailing behind him.

"Oh aye," he said, more to himself than to her as he eyed one of the broken wooden blades. "And this land could be brought back into productivity with a wee bit of sweat and effort." He muttered a curse. "But we dinnae have time for all that. We will leave on the morrow. I willnae put yer father at risk by staying longer."

Vivienne's stomach sank. She already got so little time with her father, and now she would be hiding out in Scotland for who knew how long. But she agreed with Kieran that they could not linger and risk bringing danger to his door.

She nodded, and they continued on in silence.

Chapter Fourteen

✦❦✦

K ieran leaned back in his chair, contentedly full and warm from the roaring fire in the hearth before him.

Upon returning from his tour of the de Valance estate, Kieran, Vivienne, and her father had eaten a simple but hearty meal of meat pies, fresh cheese, and roasted autumnal vegetables. Now they sat before the fire, sipping spiced wine while Vivienne read from her treasured copy of *The Song of Roland*.

Now that he knew how important the tale was to her, Kieran tried to listen more closely as she read. Yet instead of focusing on the words, all he could seem to pay attention to was the shape of her lips and the rise and fall of her voice as she recited the story.

Hell and damnation, things weren't going as he'd planned. But he couldn't seem to work up the energy to pretend indifference. Mayhap it was the wine, or his full belly, or the crackling heat from the fire lulling him into a relaxed torpor. Or mayhap it was because Kieran hadn't let himself indulge in a tranquil evening like this in ten long years. Whatever the case, he contented himself to simply sit and enjoy Vivienne's nearness.

What few servants Kieran had seen earlier during the meal had all been shooed away by Madame Claudette, yet the woman herself had remained at de Valance's bidding. She occasionally rose to refill their cups of wine, but she'd also taken up a chair beside de Valance and joined him in listening to Vivienne read.

When Vivienne reached the end of the tale, de Valance clapped a hand over his heart and sighed.

"Lovely, *ma fille*, simply lovely," he said, bending his head toward her. "Might you humor an old man and read another?"

Sadness flickered in Vivienne's dark eyes. "I only brought this one with me, *Papa*."

Even as guilt stabbed Kieran for so callously dismissing the idea of her bringing along all those books from court, de Valance spoke. "I still have a few volumes tucked away somewhere in my solar. Read to me from one of those. A tale of romance, perhaps. *Tristan and Iseult*?"

Vivienne's creamy skin flushed in the glow of the fire. "Why a romance?"

De Valance shrugged innocently, yet a knowing smile played on his lips. "Why not? It is a pleasant way to pass the evening. Besides, I thought those sentimental stories were your favorite, Vivi."

Reluctantly, Vivienne rose. "I'll go look in the solar."

"I'll accompany you," Claudette said, rising also. To

Kieran's surprise, her cheeks bore a rosy hue as well. "I reorganized the solar not long ago to make it easier for your father to navigate."

As the women disappeared up the stairs, Kieran settled into the silence, but to his surprise, de Valance set his cup of wine aside and tilted his head toward Kieran intently.

"I may be blind, but I am no fool," he said. "What goes on between you and my daughter?"

"I am her protector," Kieran replied, his shoulders tensing. "Naught more." Damn it all, he hadn't been expecting an inquisition from her father. And what the hell had the man noticed that made him so sure some spark kindled between them?

"I know my Vivi," de Valance said, narrowing his sightless eyes. "I can read her like one of those books she cherishes so much, despite the polished manners she learned at court. *You*, on the other hand, are a mystery."

"*I* am a mystery? Yer daughter keeps quite a few secrets herself," Kieran countered, suddenly eager to redirect de Valance's focus. The last thing he needed was an overprotective father calling him out for a connection he didn't understand himself.

De Valance hesitated, his lips working for a moment. "Vivienne has been through a great deal for one so young. And she hides it well, but she still carries the scars inside her heart."

"Aye," Kieran replied quietly. "She told me of the death of her mother, and the struggles with the estate."

"And did she tell you of Guy d'Aubert?"

Kieran stiffened. "Who?"

Just then, he heard Vivienne and Claudette's soft voices echoing in the stone stairwell.

"That is not my story to tell," de Valance said. "But listen well, Kieran MacAdams. My daughter may not show it easily, but she has a big heart. If you are truly just her protector, as you say, I would have your promise that no harm will come to her while she's under your care—either from another or from yourself."

The man's words sent a tangled knot of confusion into the pit of Kieran's stomach, but he didn't have time to unravel it. The women were about to re-enter the hall. "I promise," he said just as Vivienne appeared at the base of the stairwell.

"We found it," Vivienne said, holding up a dusty leather-bound book as she crossed to her chair before the hearth.

"Ah, wonderful," de Valance replied, his warm smile and relaxed air returning now that Vivienne and Claudette were back. "Might I hear the *Chevrefoil* section? I remember you always read that well."

"*Chevrefoil?*" Kieran said, glancing at Vivienne.

"It means honeysuckle." Her cheeks pinkened as she settled into her chair once more. "It is part of the story."

She cracked the book and began reading the verses, but it was an older dialect of French that Kieran couldn't follow. Still, her words seemed to have an effect on de Valance and Claudette, who'd taken up a chair at his side again.

As Vivienne continued to read, Claudette flushed once more, her gaze continually sliding to de Valance. For his part, de Valance's hand seemed to be drifting toward Claudette, first resting in his lap, then on his chair's arm, and at last dangling over the side mere inches from Claudette.

A soft smile came to Claudette's lips as she gazed down at de Valance's hand. But then she glanced up at Vivienne, who remained engrossed in her recitation, and the woman's green eyes clouded, her dark brows drawing together in worry.

Kieran released a surprised breath. Well, well. It seemed that Vivienne wasn't the only one keeping secrets. Some affection, or mayhap even love, clearly existed between de Valance and Claudette, but apparently they were hiding it from Vivienne.

Vivienne reached the conclusion of her reading and de Valance abruptly jerked his hand away from Claudette. He clapped lightly a few times to cover up the motion.

"You've outdone yourself, *ma fille*," he said, smiling.

Vivienne returned the smile, but her gaze flicked to Kieran, her eyes hesitant. "What did you think?"

Kieran rubbed a hand against the back of his neck. "Truth be told, I didnae catch most of that. I couldnae parse the dialect."

"It is a section in the great love story of Tristan, a noble knight, and Iseult, an Irish princess," Vivienne said, easing the book closed and hugging it against her chest. "Tristan has been banished from Cornwall by Iseult's cruel husband, who has learned of their love. They have been forced apart for a year. But Tristan hears that a feast is to take place and he has a chance to see her again. Tristan intercepts her caravan en route to the feast, placing a hazel bough across the path with his name carved into it."

"Why a hazel bough?" Kieran asked, intrigued despite his usual disinterest in such sentimental tales.

Vivienne's gaze warmed and grew distant. "It is a symbol of his love for Iseult. Just like the hazelnut tree and the honeysuckle, which grow so entwined that they cannot be separated, so too are he and Iseult bound together by love. They will both die if they are parted. *Ni moi sans vous, ni vous sans moi*," she said, reciting one of the lines from the tale. "Neither me without you, nor you without me."

She blinked, her eyes refocusing on him and that bonny blush returning to her cheeks. "That is why this section is called the *Chevrefoil*—the honeysuckle."

"You haven't told Kieran the ending yet, *ma fille*," de Valance prodded, leaning forward in his chair.

"Iseult sees the downed hazel branch and recognizes Tristan's signal. She slips off to the woods and meets him so that they can share a forbidden tryst. And when it comes time for Iseult to depart once more, they weep, vowing to find a way to be rejoined someday."

For a long moment, the only sound was the crackle of the fire. A blunt comment about silly, overly dramatic tales of courtly love rose on Kieran's tongue, but he locked his teeth to keep it from getting out. Why did some twisted part of him wish to ruin this moment when it clearly meant something to Vivienne?

The truth was, it was easier to hide behind his rough manners and hardened opinions about emotions like love. Yet a larger part of him was now consumed by the need to understand Vivienne better. For all her cold exterior, why was she so entranced by such tales? What hadn't she told him about her coming of age that made her this way?

And who the bloody hell was Guy d'Aubert?

"It is late," Vivienne murmured, breaking the laden silence. "I think I will retire for the night."

"Your old chamber is ready for you, Lady Vivienne," Claudette said, rising. "I'll return the book to the solar."

As Claudette shuffled off with the book, Vivienne moved to her father, who'd hoisted himself to his feet with his cane. They exchanged a kiss on each cheek before embracing warmly.

"All is truly well, *Papa*?" she murmured. "Madame Claudette is taking good care of you?"

Mayhap Kieran was wrong. Mayhap Vivienne *did* know—or at least sense—that something intimate existed between her father and the keep's chatelaine.

De Valance reached for her, cupping her cheek. "*Oui, ma fille.* I want for naught—except to touch your beautiful face, so like your mother's, more often."

Sadness filled Vivienne's eyes as she embraced her father once more, then moved off toward the stairs leading to the chambers above.

"I'll be outside yer door if ye have need of me," Kieran said as she mounted the stairs. He wanted not only Vivienne but de Valance to know that he wouldn't slacken in his duties to protect her—but he would also keep a solid wooden door between them.

She nodded in acknowledgement over her shoulder before gliding up the stairs.

But instead of following close on her heels, Kieran lingered in the great hall with de Valance.

"Ye are one to lecture me on mysteries and secrets," he said quietly when he was sure Vivienne couldn't hear. "I saw what passed between ye and Claudette when Vivienne was reading about forbidden love."

De Valance stiffened. "You are a warrior, Monsieur MacAdams. What do you know of love?"

"Och, enough to ken it when I see it," he replied, pushing back the dull ache that thrummed to life once more. "Ye and yer daughter clearly share a deep bond—which ye're liable to damage by keeping things from her."

De Valance leaned on his cane, his shoulders suddenly slumping. "Claudette and I…we do not wish to hurt Vivienne by disrespecting the memory of her mother."

Kieran inhaled, surprised by the man's candidness. But more than that, de Valance's words resonated like a struck tuning fork deep in Kieran's chest. Ten years past, he'd locked his heart away out of respect for Linette and their unborn child. Or had he abandoned his home and built an invisible wall around himself out of some self-preserving instinct that had naught to do with her or the bairn?

Hell and damnation, none of this—Vivienne's past, this d'Aubert man, de Valance and Claudette's secret connection—was any of his concern. So why was Kieran involving himself? His only mission was to protect Vivienne from de Soules's cronies.

Though many mistook Kieran for a brute and a

EMMA PRINCE

barbarian based on his size, strength, and blunt manner, he was no fool. He knew when others were lying to him —and when he was lying to himself.

The truth was, even before this damn mission got underway, he'd already been too involved, too entangled with Vivienne. Hell, the entire reason he'd petitioned the Bruce to be sent to France to protect her was because he'd already come to care for her in the short time he'd spent with her last summer.

But letting her into his heart meant making himself vulnerable to pain and loss once more—which he'd vowed never to do again. He'd made his own way in the world for the last ten years just fine without opening himself to anyone. He couldn't risk all that just for a wee slip of a Frenchwoman, no matter what his damn heart had to say about it.

"It isnae my business," Kieran replied, both to de Valance and himself. "I shouldnae have inserted myself in a family matter. Now if ye'll excuse me, I'd best get some rest. Vivienne and I will leave at dawn tomorrow."

De Valance nodded reluctantly. "You seem a good man, Kieran. Please, remember what I said about keeping my Vivi from harm."

"Aye, I will."

Kieran headed toward the stairs and began climbing. He'd already made a quick sweep of the keep upon returning from his walk with Vivienne around the estate, so he knew which chamber was hers.

He settled himself on the stone landing outside her door, pulling his plaid around him. But though he was weary, he knew sleep would elude him for a long time to come, for his mind swirled with thoughts of Vivienne.

He'd sworn to protect her, but the more time he spent with her, the more he feared that he was the one in danger of losing everything to the flaxen-haired beauty.

Chapter Fifteen

The next morning, Vivienne bid a tight-throated farewell to her father and Claudette. Though she tried her best to maintain her composure, she couldn't help the tear that slipped free as she embraced her father.

"I'll be back again soon, *Papa*," she murmured, her voice thick. "I promise."

Kieran stood like a granite mountain behind her as she gave her father one last hug. His silent presence was a reminder that she didn't know when—or, in reality, *if* —she truly would return to her family home.

She turned to Claudette and pressed the pouch of coins she'd brought from court into the woman's hand. "I'll send more if I can," she said. "I hope this will be enough to take care of—"

"Don't fret, Lady Vivienne," Claudette cut in, emotion filling her eyes. "I would never let anything happen to your father. I—" She bowed her black and silver head as if struggling with something to say. At last, she met Vivienne's gaze once more. "Rest easy," was all she said.

Pierre, a lad of no more than ten from the village whom Claudette had managed to bring on to the stables, rounded the keep with her and Kieran's horses in tow. After Kieran helped her into the saddle and mounted himself, he took the lead, urging his horse northward.

Vivienne remained twisted in her saddle for a long while, waving at the keep even though she knew her father couldn't see her. She hoped Claudette was describing it to him, remaining by his side until he returned into the keep.

She knew instinctively that she could trust her father's care to Claudette. The woman was kind and attentive, and she'd noticed more than once on her visits home that the two seemed to share a quiet affinity for each other.

Yet knowing her father was in good hands and banishing all her fears to be leaving him were two different things. Ever since her mother had died, Vivienne had taken on his care as her responsibility. But how could she help him now that she would be far away, without the means to send money?

The day-long ride to Calais was passed mainly in silence. Vivienne succumbed to her worries, realizing repeatedly that she was biting her fingernails. Each time, she returned her hand to her reins, only to catch herself doing it again not long after.

When the bustling port town of Calais came into view at dusk, she blinked as if waking from a fitful sleep.

Kieran guided them into the heart of the town, halting at a large system of stables. He helped her down and hoisted both their saddlebags over his shoulder, then approached the stable master to negotiate selling their horses. A short while later, Kieran accepted a pouch of coins and hefted it to measure its weight.

"This should be enough to buy us passage to Scone."

She perked up at that. "Is that where you are taking me? To Scone?"

Though she knew little of Scotland, having spent her entire life in France, she was aware that Scone was where King Robert the Bruce's palace lay. And though she would be a stranger in a new land, if there was one thing Vivienne understood, it was how to function in a palace court.

Kieran eyed her, clearly able to read her sudden hopefulness.

"Dinnae get yer expectations up," he replied. "We will pass through Scone, aye, but we willnae be staying. It is too public, too exposed, even with so many of the King's bodyguards there."

"Oh." Though her heart sank, she tried to keep her chin lifted.

She followed him as he wove his way through the cobbled streets on foot, heading for the docks. Even before they reached the water, Vivienne could smell the sharp brine of the sea, mingled with the scents of tar and fish.

The docks swarmed with activity. The air was filled with men calling orders and shouting to each other in a variety of languages, most of which she didn't recognize. Men lowered and raised crates onto ships of all shapes and sizes with rope pulleys. Others loaded cargo into wagons to be transported away from Calais. And a steady stream of ships seemed to be arriving and departing despite the fact that dusk was darkening into night.

Taking her hand in his to keep her close, Kieran began walking the length of the docks, making inquiries of the men as he went. When at last he got a nod of confirmation from one of the sailors about their destination, he pulled Vivienne toward one of the larger ships.

"Captain!" Kieran shouted up to the ship. A moment later, a blond head appeared above the gunwales.

"Who is asking?"

"Someone looking to line yer pockets with gold."

The man snatched up one of the many ropes dangling from the rigging, and to Vivienne's shock, he launched himself over the gunwales. But instead of landing with a bone-crushing crunch on the dock some fifteen feet below, he used the rope to swing down and plant his boots on the wooden planks with surprising grace.

Vivienne felt her eyes widen as she took in the sight of the man before them. He was a handful of years older than Kieran, yet he was a fair bit more weathered from the sun, wind, and salty air. His tanned face bore more than a few crinkled lines, yet his bright blue eyes shone with intensity even in the fading light.

He wore a simple tunic, breeches, and high boots on his lean, rangy frame. With his feet planted wide and his arms crossed, he rivaled Kieran for the most imposing figure on the docks. He looked like a fearsome Vikings from generations past.

"Oh?" the man replied, casually dropping the rope and eyeing Kieran and Vivienne. "And why would you do that, Scotsman?"

"Yer man there says ye are sailing for Scone. I'd like to buy passage."

"*Ja*," the captain replied in a Northern tongue, confirming Vivienne's impression that he was a Norseman. "But I am in the business of shipping spirits, Scotsman, not people."

"As I said, I'm prepared to pay ye handsomely." Kieran removed the pouch he'd gotten from the stable master and hefted it to demonstrate the loud clinking of the multitude of coins inside.

The captain grinned. "Ah, now you speak a language I understand well. What are you offering?"

Kieran considered. "Half for a spot for me and the lass. More if ye can provide her with a private cabin." He cocked a brow then. "Out of curiosity, what sort of spirits are ye transporting?"

The captain waved at the stream of barrels being loaded and unloaded from his ship. "From France to Scotland? Wine, of course. And from Scotland to France, whisky."

Kieran opened the top of the pouch and removed

one coin. "In that case, ye can have the entire pouch, assuming ye can provide the lady with a cabin."

The captain tilted his head in assent, but he waited, watching Kieran with open curiosity.

"And ye may have *this*," Kieran went on, lifting the single coin he'd removed. "If I can fill a waterskin with the whisky ye're offloading."

At that, the captain broke into a loud, barking laugh. "I like the cut of your jib, Scotsman."

"Kieran MacAdams," he said by way of introduction. "And Vivienne."

She noticed that he didn't introduce her as a lady, but given the way the captain's keen eyes assessed them, she doubted the man missed much.

The captain dipped his blond head in a quick bow. "Captain Ganger Larsson," he replied.

He turned from them and shouted to one of his men to fetch a waterskin and fill it from one of the kegs that was being rolled down the docks. As the sailor saw to his orders, Kieran approached the captain and handed him the pouch of coins.

"When will we depart?"

"As soon as the last of these barrels is loaded," Captain Larsson said. "The wind waits for no man, nor does she care if the sun or the moon lights her way. Come, I'll get you aboard."

Captain Larsson brought two fingers to his mouth and whistled. In a flash, a wooden gangplank was lowered, Vivienne assumed for her benefit, for the captain seemed more than capable of climbing back up the same rope he'd swung down on.

The captain strode nimbly up the gangplank, and Kieran started after him, but Vivienne hesitated. Kieran turned questioning eyes on her.

"I've never been on a ship before," she admitted, somewhat embarrassed. For as refined and sophisticated as she'd become at French court, in many ways she was still the girl from a small, humble estate in a landlocked corner of France.

"Dinnae fash, lass. Ye'll be fine," Kieran murmured reassuringly.

Reluctantly, she stepped onto the gangplank and let him guide her along, a steadying hand on her elbow.

Even though the waters of the harbor were sheltered and calm, she could feel even the slight sway of the ship beneath her. She could only pray that Kieran was right.

Chapter Sixteen

Vivienne was *not* fine. As she dry heaved into the bucket next to her cot, she began on the long list of curses she'd developed over the last two days onboard Captain Larsson's ship.

It started with Kieran, though of course the rough seas and her apparent complete incompatibility with sailing weren't his fault. But he'd told her she would be all right, and here she was, unable to keep even water and bread down, and barely able to do more than rise from the cot to use the chamber pot and crawl back to bed.

Then she moved on to Captain Larsson and the other sailors, who seemed no more affected by the rolling, tossing motion of the ship than if they were on solid ground. And then she cursed the sea itself, for the captain did admit that the waters were a bit rougher than normal, what with autumn upon them now.

She saved William de Soules for last, for she had an

especially dark corner of her mind devoted to him. If it weren't for the threat he and his cronies posed, Vivienne wouldn't be on this blasted ship to begin with. She would be safe and happy at court with the Queen and the other ladies-in-waiting.

But of course that would mean she wouldn't be with Kieran, either. He had been surprisingly attentive to her, bringing all sorts of foods to the captain's cabin where she huddled. He'd even emptied her sick bucket, to her horror and mortification.

As if conjured by her thoughts, a quick rap sounded on the cabin door before it swung open to reveal Kieran. With one look at where she lay curled on her side in the cot, his familiar frown deepened.

"Bloody hell, lass, yer skin is as white and damp as a thick Highland fog."

"You said I would find my sea legs in a day," she said, swallowing another wave of nausea. "It has been two and I might as well not have legs at all—or a stomach, for that matter—for how well I'm faring."

Closing the door, he muttered another curse. He moved to the bucket beside the cot, but finding it empty, he pushed it aside. "Captain Larsson says another storm is brewing ahead. It will get worse before it gets better."

Now it was her turn to murmur a few decidedly unladylike words. "I cannot take any more."

She hated that her voice bordered on a wail. It was already humiliating enough to be lain so low before Kieran, to be reduced to a huddling, heaving ball. But she didn't have the energy to care anymore. She'd been stripped of every scrap of pride and all that was left was the need for relief from the incessant, nauseating motion.

He crossed his muscular arms over his chest and leveled her with a stern scowl. She thought for a moment that he would chastise her for being so weak, yell at her to buck up, but instead, he just assessed her. "We need a new strategy," he said at last.

"I've already tried everything."

Captain Larsson, somewhat bemused at how utterly unsuited to the sea she was, had suggested she eat green apples. When that hadn't worked, they'd tried watered ale and bread. Even plain water only stayed down about half the time. And nothing had provided any true reprieve from the seasickness other than lying as still as possible on the cot.

"Nay, no' everything. I have a few ideas yet." Kieran began rolling up the sleeves of his linen shirt. "First, take a swig of this."

She recoiled when he lifted the skin of whisky from his belt, but he uncorked it and urged it into her hands.

"Have ye ever been drunk before, lass? I dinnae mean a wee bit tipsy, but good and soused?"

Vivienne swallowed hard against the thought. "*Non*."

"Well, it makes yer limbs loose. It's like being aboard a sea-tossed ship even when ye're on solid ground. A few of the sailors say when ye get drunk at sea, it negates the swaying. It's worth a try, anyway."

Tentatively, she took a sip from the skin. The whisky burned a fiery path down her raw throat, and she sputtered and coughed.

Kieran grunted. "I should have warned ye about that. Good Scottish whisky isnae for the faint of heart."

Vivienne forced herself to take another sip before passing the skin to him. He took a hearty swig himself, making a pleased noise as he swallowed and recorked the skin.

"Now," he said matter-of-factly. "Ye've been lying here two days without aught to do but think on how seasick ye are. Ye need a distraction." He strode to where he'd stored their saddlebags and began rummaging through hers. In the light of the lantern bolted to the cabin's low ceiling, she saw him pull out her copy of *The Song of Roland*.

He was right about one thing—she was so curious about what he intended to do that she propped herself on one elbow, forgetting her aim to remain motionless until the ship took a particularly stomach-dropping roll and she flattened herself on the cot once more.

"I cannot read like this," she said, squeezing her eyes shut. "It will only make it worse."

"Then how about ye just listen."

Hesitantly, she cracked one eye and peered at him. "You…you mean to read to me?"

"Why no'?" Kieran perched on the edge of the cot, angling the book into the lantern light. He opened the book and squinted at the writing inside.

"But I thought you hated this story," she went on when he frowned at the page before him. "You called it preposterous and foolish."

Kieran grunted again. "Aye, it is that, but ye like it."

His scowl deepened as if he'd just said something he hadn't meant to. "It is just silly enough to distract ye."

He returned his attention to the book, but as he continued to glare at it, a new realization hit her with the force of a blow.

"You…you *can* read…can't you?"

His head snapped up and he fixed her with a cool gaze. "Aye, I can bloody well read. I ken my numbers, too, if ye are interested."

"I didn't mean—" She drew in a breath. From his quick and frosty reaction, this wasn't the first time someone had underestimated his abilities. No doubt he'd been taken for little more than a muscle-bound brute more than once before.

"I meant no insult," she tried again, steadier this time. "I've seen myself that your wits match your brawn, Kieran."

His name on her lips made him stiffen for a moment before some of the tension drained from his features. "Aye, well," he said, rolling his shoulders. "I learned my letters when I was a lad, but the son of a farmer doesnae have a great need to read—or much opportunity to practice. Nor does a grown warrior in the Bruce's army. Besides, I dinnae have any use for fanciful tales of knights and damsels."

Vivienne nodded. "I understand." Though her own childhood had been relatively humble compared to many of the other nobles at court, it was a reminder that she'd still been born into a different world than Kieran. And even when things had been hard for her, she'd always been able to escape into one of her beloved stories. Kieran hadn't had any such escape.

He cracked the book once more. "Where should I start?"

"Oh, anywhere," she replied, her gaze settling on him.

He flipped a few pages and began where Charlemagne and his army launched an attack to avenge Roland's death.

His low, deep voice was halting as he read each word slowly, pausing over some of the longer ones. Occasionally, he would glance up at her, doubt in his eyes, but she knew the story so well that she could almost always supply the word he struggled to pronounce.

In fact, she likely could have recited the whole tale from memory as well as Kieran could read it with the book open before him, but she remained silent unless he prompted her. The story unfolded slowly under his careful reading, and to Vivienne's surprise, she savored it far more than when she recited it herself.

It was as if she were encountering it for the first time through Kieran. He wrinkled his crooked nose at the overly sentimental lines, and his dark brows rose at the particularly vivid descriptions of the battle.

When he reached a break in the verses, he paused, glancing at her with searching eyes. "How do ye feel?"

To her surprise, the sharpest edge of her nausea had been filed down ever so slightly. "A bit better."

He closed the book and set it aside, fetching her bread from the bolted-down table opposite the cot. "Try this, and another wee dram of whisky."

She acquiesced, taking a few bites of bread and a sip from the skin. But the act of rising on her elbows to eat and drink had her head spinning once more. She eased back down with a weak exhale, gripping the cot's edge.

"Och, dinnae turn green on me again, lass. I'm no' through with ye yet," he said, pinning her with a look that sent her stomach tightening with something that was decidedly not nausea.

"Oh?"

He crouched over her saddlebags once more, this time removing her bottle of violet oil. Her heart thudded hard against her ribs and he approached the cot, holding up the oil.

"There was an old healer woman in my clan who claimed that she could relieve many an ailment simply by pressing on various parts of the body," he said, sitting on the edge of the cot again. "The other lads and I used to call her a witch, but she was right more often than no'."

He removed the stopper from the bottle and took one of her hands in his, turning it so that her palm faced up. Gently, he dragged the stopper over her exposed wrist and into her palm, spreading a drop of the oil. Then he replaced the stopper and set the bottle aside.

"What are you—"

Before she finished the question, he took her hand in both of his and pressed his thumbs into her palm, massaging deeply. She gasped, then moaned, melting into the cot.

His chuckle rumbled through her. "Yer reaction is only more proof Old Maili was a witch after all. Either that, or she simply kenned how to distract from pain and discomfort."

Her only response was another moan as he worked on the pad of her thumb. The delicate scent of violets drifted to her nose, soothing her senses. Her body was beginning to feel warm and heavy from the whisky—either that, or Kieran's touch was intoxicating her.

"You mentioned other lads," she said, snatching up a topic of conversation to focus on rather than the heat beginning to kindle low in her belly at the feel of his hands on her. "Did you have siblings?"

His fingers slowed for a moment in their ministrations before resuming once more. "Nay," he replied. "My ma and da had many bairns after I came along, but none survived past the age of two. By the time I was twelve, they gave up, for my ma had grown weak. She died a few years later, and my da followed no' long after that. I was only eight and ten when the farm became mine."

Vivienne stilled. "I am sorry. That could not have been easy."

He lifted one shoulder, yet she didn't miss the hollow look in his light blue eyes. "Death is part of life."

"That doesn't mean it can't hurt," Vivienne countered, though she kept her voice gentle to take the sting out of the words. "Especially given how young you were."

Now his eyes turned hard like chips of ice. "Better to learn young that when it comes down to it, we are all alone in this world. Ye can only ever rely on yerself."

"*Non*, I don't believe that."

HER WILD HIGHLANDER

On her own, Vivienne had nearly destroyed her entire life—and her family's as well. It had only been with the help of her father, the Queen, the ladies-in-waiting, and countless others at court that she'd managed to return from the brink of ruin.

Truth be told, Vivienne was terrified of being left alone. Her whole life rested on a delicately woven web, where each thread held her aloft in society's eyes. Her clothes, her manners, her position with the Queen, her union with someone like Thierry—they'd all been stripped away. And Vivienne knew what would happen if one too many more of those threads snapped and she fell from society's good graces. It was only because of the generosity of others that she hadn't fallen completely.

"Everyone needs help from time to time," she went on quietly. "Even you."

Kieran moved to her other hand but kept her pinned with his sharp gaze. "Relying on people will only get ye hurt. Trust me, lass, I speak from experience. I ken more of the world than ye."

"I am not so naïve as you assume," she responded. "You admitted that yourself when we were walking my father's estate."

Kieran snorted. "Aye, ye've kenned yer piece of sorrow, I dinnae deny that. But explain something to me, for it doesnae make sense. Ye claim no' to be naïve, but ye are innocent enough to believe in tales meant to make wee lads and lasses dream." He waved toward the book he'd placed on top of her saddlebags. "Ye'd rather believe in noble fancies than the hard truths in this world."

Vivienne sensed some deeper wound beneath his words. He was directing his anger at her, but was it actually meant for himself? The problem was, her own frustration had risen now, and she could not let the barb go.

"You imagine you know me, but you don't. Just because I still have hope for the goodness in the world doesn't make me a fool. And besides, I am not innocent."

He froze, his hands still engulfing hers but his fingers halting in their ministrations. His eyes widened on her, and belatedly she realized what she'd just admitted.

She snapped her teeth closed, but the words had already gotten out. Curse the whisky for loosening her tongue!

"Ye arenae innocent," he repeated.

Though she lay on her back and he loomed over her from the edge of the cot, she lifted her chin. It was the truth, after all. There was no point in denying it now.

"*Oui.*"

His dark brows lowered as he considered something for a long moment. "This doesnae have to do with Guy d'Aubert, does it?"

He might as well have dumped a bucket of cold water over her. She sucked in a breath, her stomach dropping to the floor.

"How do you know that name?"

Chapter Seventeen

Kieran watched Vivienne closely for an indication that he was wrong in his guess about this Guy d'Aubert bastard, but all he saw in her midnight eyes was fear and pain.

"He hurt ye, didnae he?" Kieran demanded, his voice coming out low and hard.

He suddenly realized his hands were clenching into fists—with Vivienne's small, delicate hand still in his grasp. He released her instantly, rising from the edge of the cot.

"*Non*," she said quickly, but then she hesitated. "At least not in the way you are imagining. He did not...force me."

Kieran drew in a breath to loosen the knot of panic that had formed in his gut. Even though Vivienne hadn't been forced, d'Aubert had clearly played some nefarious role.

"What happened?"

Vivienne closed her eyes for a moment. She looked so damn frail and vulnerable lying there on the cot. She wore a plain green wool gown, too proud or modest to remove it and rest in just a chemise with Kieran coming in and out of the cabin to check on her, despite the fact that she was sick as a dog.

Her flaxen hair was secured in a single braid down her back, which made her look more like a simple country lass rather than a refined lady of court.

But she was more beautiful, even pale and depleted by seasickness, than any woman Kieran had ever seen. Though he would never wish misery upon her, a small, petty part of him was glad she had remained in the captain's cabin the last two days, for he was liable to kill every last one of Captain Larsson's crew if they so much as grinned or even simply stared at her.

"It was just after my mother died," she replied at last, her voice thin and small. "I was sixteen and though I still had my father, I felt terribly alone in the world."

Kieran forced his hands to unknot and lowered himself slowly onto the cot beside her again.

"What was more, a great deal of responsibility had been placed on my shoulders. I was now my father's caregiver and the only heir—a *female* heir, no less—to a crumbling estate. Then Guy found me."

"What do ye mean, he found ye?"

"I'd gone riding on my own—trying to outrun my problems, I suppose—when we crossed paths. He was on his way from his own lands in the south to Amiens on matters of business, so he said. He was…dazzling." Vivienne let a breath go. "He wore fine silks and a jeweled scabbard like some knight from the stories. And he made me feel special. He showered me with praise and flattery until my head was spinning."

Kieran had to resist the urge to spit on the cabin floor. A wild, irrational jealousy seized him. The bastard sounded like Kieran's exact opposite—slick, smooth-tongued, and everything polished and courtly that Kieran was not.

"He made me promise to meet him again the next day. So I did. And again the next day. He wooed me with every extravagant compliment and pledge that a girl as young and foolish as I longed to hear. So I gave myself to him." Vivienne stared at the ceiling, unblinking. "And thus was the start of a year-long affair."

"A *year*?" Kieran thought he knew how such a story ended. The bastard had gotten what he wanted from Vivienne—her innocence—and had then abandoned her. But apparently there was more to tell.

"*Oui*. He could not always get away from his estate to meet me, and sometimes weeks would go by between our trysts. During those times, I would lock myself away in my chamber, pining for him so desperately that I thought I might die." She chuckled sadly. "But whenever he could slip away and come to me, he would repeat the same promise he'd made when we first met—that he wanted to make me his wife."

Now Kieran was beginning to understand the bastard's game. "And he strung ye along like that for a whole year."

"I am ashamed now to admit how badly I wanted to believe him. Though it would have meant abandoning my father, I was too blind with love for Guy to see beyond my own desires. I wanted to live within the fantasy he painted with his promises."

"Ye were young and hurting," Kieran replied quietly. "Ye shouldnae blame yerself. He was the one who took advantage of ye."

"*Oui*, but I only thought of myself, even though my foolishness began to harm others as well. Whispers started in the nearby village about me. A few of the tenants who still remained at the estate had seen me slip away with Guy. And soon the rumors spread and grew louder."

Vivienne pressed her lips together for a moment before continuing. "I began hearing murmurs about myself and Guy when I would go to the village. They breathed the word *mistress*. Fool that I was, my first instinct was to fear that Guy had taken up with another woman, that he was wooing someone else behind my back. It wasn't until my father and I visited Amiens to see a healer about his eyesight that I learned the truth. I saw Guy with another woman—his wife."

"He was already married?" Kieran growled.

"Apparently *I* was the other woman, the mistress," Vivienne said through a tight throat. "Guy had only been looking for a dalliance, a liaison to distract him from his real life. He'd never intended to marry me, nor had he meant any of his extravagant promises of love and devotion. I was just a bit of fun on the side for him."

She shook her head as if to clear it of the memories, visibly fighting for her composure. "Of course, I was devastated, but soon it became clear that a broken heart was the least of my worries. My name was being bandied about as far away from my father's estate as Amiens. I had ruined any chance of securing a good marriage—which was my only hope as the daughter of a blind man whose estate was on the brink of ruin."

The last of the pieces fell into place as Kieran remembered what she'd said earlier about de Valance arranging for her to meet the Queen. "That was why yer father hoped to send ye to court—to help ye make a good match."

"It was more than that," she replied. "My…indiscretion was well known in Picardy, but going to Paris would grant me a fresh start. I was unknown at court, just another lesser noble hoping for a bit of luck and the favor of the King and Queen." She fixed him with an intent look. "I thank God every night in my prayers that the Queen took pity on me that day in Amiens. And every day since then, I have fought to make sure I never falter or put my name and family at risk again."

"What of Guy?" Kieran asked. "Ye seem to have borne the costs of his actions, but did the bastard pay for aught?"

Vivienne huffed. "As far as I know, he still holds an estate in the south." A faint smile touched her lips. "But he was never invited to court again. I believe the Queen may have known more of my circumstances than I realized when she first took me as one of her ladies. She only ever said that she enjoyed my company and our few conversations when she was visiting Amiens, and that she wished to fill the court with beauty and grace, for it reflected well on all of France. But my father may have had a private word with her."

Kieran considered all that she'd said for a long moment. So much made sense now—Vivienne's cool, controlled exterior, her hesitancy to marry for fear of misplacing her trust again, her reluctance to leave her position at court, both for her own sake and her family's. It was all the doing of that bastard Guy d'Aubert in so callously taking advantage of her.

But one thing still puzzled him.

"I dinnae understand," he said at last. "Ye fell under d'Aubert's charms because ye wanted to believe that all those tales of chivalry and love were true, aye?"

At her nod, he continued.

"But even after he betrayed yer trust, ye still read those stories."

In Kieran's view, it was pure madness to leave her heart vulnerable after what d'Aubert had done to her. How could she still believe in courtly love and honor after what she'd been through? Why hadn't she become like him after losing so much—withdrawn and alone, safe in his isolation from being hurt again?

She tilted her head so that she could fix him with her gaze. "I am no longer that naïve girl. I won't make the same mistake in believing a man like Guy's promises again. But what is the point in living without hope for a happy future?"

What indeed? Kieran swallowed hard. Here he was questioning Vivienne, when he hadn't had the bollocks to allow himself to hope or trust in ten long years since

Linette had died. He'd made his heart into a walled fortress, keeping everyone out.

But he'd gotten on well enough, hadn't he? He was in the Bruce's inner circle now, though other than Jerome, he didn't truly know or trust any of the others. He didn't need anyone besides himself.

She cleared her throat, interrupting his thoughts. "I cannot stop you from criticizing me for taking comfort in stories of honor and love—or for my error in trusting Guy, for that matter. But I would ask that you not share this information with anyone. I have worked hard to ensure that my place at court is not tainted by my past mistakes. My father's wellbeing and my future depend on it. You may think less of me for throwing away my innocence, but—"

"Hold there," he cut in. "Ye misunderstand me. I dinnae judge ye for no' being innocent."

She blinked in confusion. "But I saw the anger and disgust in your eyes."

"Bloody hell," Kieran breathed. "I wasnae mad at ye. Aye, I was out of my mind for a moment thinking that the d'Aubert bastard had hurt ye—and I still am, for the way he used ye. If he was before me now, I'd likely kill him. But I dinnae blame ye."

Vivienne eyed him warily. "But now that you know the truth, you…you do not care that I am not innocent?"

"Hell and damnation, lass, nay. I'm no saint either, that's for damn sure. I only care that he took advantage of ye."

Her gaze softened with surprise and vulnerability.

"Thank you." She let a shuddering breath go, and suddenly he feared she would start crying. "It is just…" she said, her voice choked. "I have held on to that secret for so long that I thought the whole world would come crashing down when it got out."

He couldn't help it. He dragged her into his arms and held her in a fierce embrace. She stiffened for a moment, but then she melted against him, surrendering to his hold and the rocking of the ship.

She took a few gasping breaths, clearly fighting against tears that she'd held back for so long. Though he'd often taken pleasure in wheedling his way under her perfect exterior, now he found himself admiring how valiantly she fought to maintain her composure instead of simply falling apart. She was a damn strong woman.

When she'd reined in the threat of tears and her breaths came evenly once more, he eased her back onto the cot. Yet his thumb lingered on her jawline, tracing the velvety skin there.

"I didnae mean to bring ye pain by dredging up yer past, lass," he murmured.

To his surprise, she laughed softly. "You promised to distract me, and that you have."

Something in his gut twisted as the sound of her chuckle, sweet and low. God, how he wanted to take away all her hurts and sufferings—and not just the seasickness, but the ache he knew still lingered inside at d'Aubert's cruel treatment.

"And ye've managed to keep the bread and whisky down as well. Will ye take more?"

"I cannot. I fear the whisky is already going to my head."

He grinned. "I told ye getting a wee bit pickled might help."

Instead of smiling back, a bonny blush rose up her neck and into her cheeks. "I'm not drunk yet, but I shouldn't have any more. I...I fear what will happen if I lose my wits around you."

Kieran froze, the pad of his thumb still resting on her warm cheek. Was she...was she saying what he thought? Was she admitting that she was dangerously close to losing control, as he was whenever they were near? "And what will happen, lass?"

"Please, don't call me lass," she murmured beseechingly.

His brows knit in confusion. They were back to that again? He'd thought they had dropped some of the pretenses between them, but if she was going to insist that he call her Lady Vivienne again—

"It has the same effect as the whisky," she went on, cutting off his thoughts. "It makes me warm all over and soft in the head. I don't trust myself when you call me that."

Bloody hell and damnation. She was about to be his undoing.

"I am no' Guy d'Aubert."

She blinked at his abrupt words, but he continued before she could form a question.

"I am no' one for flowery words or pledges. I'm a Highlander—when I make a promise, I keep it." His voice dropped. "And if I cannae keep a promise, I dinnae make it."

"What are you saying?" she murmured.

He swept her lovely features with his gaze, his pulse hammering in his ears. "I willnae make ye promises as d'Aubert did, nor deceive ye into thinking this can be something it cannae, Vivienne. I ken ye still dream of a life from one of yer romantic stories. I cannae give ye that."

He swallowed hard, the old, dull ache rising in his chest. Nay, never again would he let himself hope for a deeper happiness. But the spark between them was undeniable.

"All I ken is that I want ye. I *burn* for ye, lass. And what I can promise is to give ye pleasure enough to chase away the pain for a time."

Her breath caught in her throat and her eyes, dark and vast as a midnight sky, were unreadable. "You are suggesting that we…"

"…Surrender to what we both want, aye. It neednae be complicated." Aye, it was simply lust, Kieran repeated to himself. He couldn't let it be aught more.

A war waged on her delicate features. Beneath his thumb, he could feel her pulse pounding just under her jaw.

"If it is society's judgment ye are worried about—"

"*Non,*" she cut in, surprising him. "I fear the moment I left court alone with ye, any chance at remaining free from rumors was dashed. I can only hope that the Queen will take me back when this is all over, though I likely lost any chance with Thierry even before we departed."

She gave her head a little shake as if to clear it. "But I do not wish to think of Thierry or court or society or any of it."

"What do ye wish to think of then, lass?"

Her gaze locked with his, and suddenly he was drowning in the dark pools of her eyes, yet he'd lost the will to struggle free.

"I don't want to think at all," she breathed. "Only feel."

She lifted a hand to his face, grazing her soft palm against the bristled growth on his cheek. The intoxicating fragrance of violets enveloped him, scattering his thoughts and making his pulse spike in anticipation.

"I am so tired. Tired of worrying and fighting and resisting this."

He turned his head and pressed his lips into her palm. "I've wanted ye from the moment I saw ye all those months ago. And I've kept wanting ye with every day, every damn breath, that has passed since then."

"As have I."

Need surged hard in his veins at her admission. His heart thumping wildly in his chest, Kieran lowered his head and claimed her lips with his.

Chapter Eighteen

At the first touch of his lips against hers, the last of Vivienne's control shattered.

She'd been strong for so long. She'd sealed herself from emotion and desire, fearing she would turn into the sixteen-year-old girl who'd nearly ruined everything with her recklessness.

But as Kieran had said, he wasn't Guy d'Aubert. Giving herself to Guy had been based on the fanciful hope that all his pledges of love and devotion were true. Yet Kieran wasn't making any promises. In his blunt, brash way, he was being far more honest. They could share pleasure, and it needn't be more than that.

But could Vivienne keep it so simple?

She wasn't a naïve girl anymore. Though she still believed in the kind of love she read about in the stories of chivalry and courtly devotion, she knew now that the world was far more complicated than that. She was entering this moment with her eyes open.

Yet for all the rational explanations flying through her mind, some part of her knew they were just that—justifications for a need that defied all reason and logic.

From the moment she'd laid eyes on Kieran last summer, her heart had stuttered at his imposing, powerful form. He'd been all rough edges and untamed bluster amongst the refined, polished nobles at court. And every time he'd opened his mouth, she found herself ruffled by his plain, unapologetic speech.

He'd flat-out ordered her not to involve herself with William de Soules, but she hadn't listened. His overprotectiveness even before the threat to her life arose had stirred something deep within her, a long-buried part of her that yearned for someone else to be the strong one, to take care of her for once.

And if he made no other promise to her, that was what Kieran had vowed to do. To protect her. To never let her come to harm. And to give her pleasure enough to drive away her fears, at least for a little while.

His kiss stole her breath and ratcheted her pulse until all she could hear was her own blood pounding in her ears. His tongue teased her lips, demanding entrance to the depths of her mouth. When she yielded, she was rewarded with the hot, wet velvet of his tongue caressing hers.

She dragged him closer as their mouths mated, threading her fingers through his hair. Her nails sank into his scalp and he growled low in his throat, a sound that was half-pleasure, half-feral hunger for more.

Suddenly his hands were everywhere—sliding down her arms, in her hair, on her waist. He wriggled his fingers underneath her back, furtively tugging at the ties on her gown. She arched to give him more room to work, all the while letting her own hands explore the strong column of his neck and the rock-hard contours of his shoulders.

Though she could feel her gown's laces loosening, apparently the progress was too slow for Kieran's liking, for he muttered a curse and simply yanked down the top of her bodice. He worked the wool dress lower over her waist, revealing her linen chemise beneath.

Suddenly as impatient as he to feel his skin upon hers, she clutched his shirt and pulled it from his belt. She dragged it over his head, exposing the muscle-corded expanse of his torso. The cabin's lantern was behind him, casting him somewhat in shadows, but where the light touched, his taut, powerful form was outlined in gold.

He continued working her gown down the length of her body, easing it past her slim hips and over her legs. He tossed the green wool aside once it was free.

"Damn that chemise," he rasped, glaring at the innocent garment. She would have laughed if she hadn't been so consumed with desire, unable to concentrate on anything but the feel of his hands as he gripped the linen at her shoulders.

He began peeling away the chemise, and she hastily untied the ribbon at her chest to prevent it from ripping. She doubted he would care much if it did at the moment, for his eyes flickered with unguarded need where he traced her collarbone and her exposed décolletage.

The linen slid like a whisper down her body, making her nipples draw tight as it came away. The cool air of the cabin caressed her, but it was not enough to douse the burning of her skin under Kieran's fierce gaze.

"Ye are…" He swallowed hard, his Adam's apple bobbing as his eyes devoured her. "Ye are so beautiful, lass."

She'd been told that she was beautiful many times, and in far more extravagant terms as well, yet Kieran's plain-spoken declaration stirred her like none other. It felt as though he was looking not just *at* her, but *into* her, beyond her exterior and to her very heart and soul.

He reached out tentatively, barely brushing his fingertips against her shoulders as if she were made of glass and he feared shattering her.

"I am only flesh and blood," she murmured. "Touch me. Please."

His eyes darkened hungrily at her plea. His work-roughened hands closed over her breasts. She arched and moaned, sensation shooting through her as his callused palms rasped against her taut nipples.

He captured her mouth in a kiss once more, but soon he began kissing a path across her cheek to her ear. He nuzzled her ear, then nipped the lobe, his tongue darting out to tease and flick there.

"I need to touch ye, taste ye—everywhere," he growled.

Shivers of anticipation pricked across her skin. She nodded, unable to speak when his teeth claimed her earlobe again.

He slid down her body, the hard planes of his chest

scraping against her already-needy breasts. His lips and tongue left a hot trail of kisses down her throat before he licked one of her pearled nipples.

Vivienne gasped and jerked, the sensation sending liquid need pooling between her legs. He laved first one breast and then the other until she was writhing and moaning beneath him, her fingernails turning to claws on his broad shoulders.

He kissed his way over her flat stomach, pausing to nip her ribs with his teeth. Then he was settling between her legs, his lips grazing the delicate skin of her inner thigh.

Her heart lurched. She'd never experienced what she knew he would do next, but she'd heard tell of it before. Though the Queen's ladies-in-waiting were meant to be the court's paragons of propriety, some were married and others had simply discreetly dabbled in the indulgences to be had at court. Vivienne had overheard the knowing whispers about this act, but never had Guy given her such a selfless pleasure.

When his tongue slid along the damp seam of her sex, she nigh jumped out of her skin. His fingers sank into her hips, pinning her to the cot as he licked her deeper, spreading her sex and finding that point of pure, blinding sensation.

As he teased and tasted her, her hands twisted in the bed linens, desperately seeking purchase. She could no longer tell the difference between the rolling of the ship on the storm-tossed waves and the undulation of her own hips as the pleasure began to mount and swell.

"Kieran," she moaned, spiraling toward the heavens. "*Mon Dieu*, Kieran."

She came apart, crying out his name again as ecstasy crashed over her and swept her away.

As the last shudders of her release ebbed, he sat back on his haunches, his eyes blazing on her.

"I need to be inside ye—now," he hissed, unclasping his belt with shaking hands.

"*Oui*," she breathed, desire still humming in her veins. The pleasure he'd just given her was indescribable, yet she was already greedy for more, desperate to join fully with him.

As his belt came free, his plaid slid from his hips and pooled at the foot of the cot where he crouched. Desire making her bold, her gaze trailed down the stacked muscles on his stomach to the rigid, thick length of his cock.

She was no maiden, yet her breath still caught in her throat at the sight of him. His cock matched the rest of his large, hard frame. The crown was ruddy and faintly damp with his own desire.

Instinctively, she spread her knees, beckoning him in. He lowered himself onto one elbow, taking his cock in his hand and guiding it to her entrance. She arched to meet him, shivering at the first graze of his manhood against her sex.

He entered her slowly, pushing inside her inch by inch with torturous restraint. He was so large that Vivienne felt like an innocent again, stretched nigh to the point of pain as she took his length. Yet her body knew intuitively what to do. Her legs parted even wider to

EMMA PRINCE

accommodate his big form, her hips tilting to take all of him.

He panted next to her ear, and she realized his control was stretched far thinner than she'd first thought. He was being careful for her sake, she realized, moving with deliberate slowness to give her body time to adjust to his size.

Though she was grateful for his care, yearning kindled deep within her. She needed his untamed strength now.

She lifted her head and sank her teeth into his shoulder with a wordless moan, urging him on.

He growled in response, withdrawing slightly only to drive back into her with enough force to make her groan again. He began to move in earnest, delving in and out in a steady, hard rhythm. She clung to him, her breath catching with each thrust.

Yet just as pleasure began to coil tight within her, he snaked a hand under her back and flipped them both over. She found herself straddling him, her knees on either side of his hips and his cock still buried deep within her.

Another surprise. She had never experienced this before. She froze, uncertain what to do and feeling exposed propped atop Kieran, his hungry eyes feasting on her.

He gripped her hips, rolling them with his hands. The motion drew a moan from both of them.

"Move with the ship," he rasped, showing her again by lifting her up and dragging her down once more. "With the waves. Aye, like that."

She rocked against him, finding her rhythm. His hands skimmed over her, emboldening her motions. Her hair, which had come undone from its plait, cascaded over her shoulders and brushed against his chest.

He muttered something in Gaelic that sounded like a curse. One hand closed over her breast while the other slid to where they were joined. His thumb found that bud of pleasure above her opening, and suddenly she was shuddering and crying out as she shattered into a thousand pieces again.

Like lightning, he rolled her over so that he had her on her back once more. Even as she began to come down from her peak, Kieran grabbed her hips and thrust hard once, twice, thrice into her.

Oh, this was the wild Highlander who'd sent her heart pounding with just one look earlier that summer. Who'd stormed back into the palace a few sennights past and taken possession of her all over again. She yielded to this claiming, reveling in the unbridled power of his desire.

With a rough growl, he suddenly withdrew and spent his seed on the bed linens beside her. Panting, he collapsed over her, catching himself on one elbow so as not to crush her.

The ecstasy of their joining dimmed ever so slightly as Vivienne caught her breath. Guy, too, had always withdrawn just before his release to prevent getting her with child.

It made complete sense, of course. As an unwed woman with a father and an estate to look after, Vivienne was in no position to have a child. She was grateful that Guy had at least enough sense and regard for her not to leave her with both a ruined reputation *and* a babe.

Yet the reminder of Guy was unwelcome when she had just given herself to Kieran. Heaven help her, had she made the same mistake again?

Non, she told herself firmly, trying to shove the dark thoughts away. The connection she shared with Kieran was based on honesty, not lies. They desired each other equally, no more.

And there was no one here to pass judgment on her. Society's eyes couldn't reach her all the way in the middle of the North Sea.

Kieran eased himself down onto the cot beside her. He turned her on her side so that his chest pressed into her back, their legs tucking together and her bottom wedging against his lap. He rested a possessive hand on her hip, gently tracing an invisible pattern with one callused finger there.

"That was the last trick I kenned to combat seasickness," he murmured, his voice low and teasing in her ear. "Did it work?"

A surprised laugh leapt from her throat. Somehow, in the midst of losing herself to pleasure, the seasickness had abated. Perhaps the key had been mimicking the roll of the sea with her body, she thought, her cheeks heating at the memory. *"Oui,"* she replied, suddenly feeling shy. "A most effective method."

Now it was his turn to chuckle, sending vibrations through her back. When his mirth faded, the only sound for a long time was the muted slap of the storm-tossed waves against the ship's wooden sides.

"This changes naught," she said, unsure if she were speaking more to herself or to Kieran.

"Aye." Yet even as he said the single, blunt word, his hand tightened on her hip.

Vivienne wasn't a naïve child anymore. *Non*, she was acting knowingly. This time she would not succumb to the foolish fancies that had nearly been her ruin before. She could only pray that when this was all over, she could return to her old life without too much damage to her reputation—or her heart.

As she drifted off to sleep with the rocking of the ship, however, fear still crept into the darkest corners of her mind.

What if it was already too late?

Chapter Nineteen

"I trust ye can forget all of this."

Vivienne's head whipped around at the sound of Kieran's voice. He spoke quietly to Captain Larsson a few feet away on the ship's deck, giving the man a piercing scowl.

"A Highlander and a Frenchwoman traveling from Calais to Scone," Kieran went on. "No' something worth commenting on to anyone else, ye understand?"

The captain gave Kieran a blank stare. "I have no idea what you are talking about, friend," he said. "I am a simple trader and a man of the sea. Why would I know anything about any Scot or Frenchwoman?" He broke the façade then, flashing Kieran a grin.

"And I trust yer crew will follow yer lead," Kieran said, glancing at the men securing the sail and preparing the anchor to be lowered.

"Rest assured, friend, Ganger Larsson is not a man to be crossed," the captain replied. "My men know that—and anyone who thinks otherwise is in for a lesson."

Kieran nodded. "My thanks. I'm in yer debt."

"*Nei*, Highlander," Captain Larsson said, his blue eyes dancing. "You paid more than twice what you should have for passage, even including the use of my cabin and your…what do you Scotsmen call it? Your 'wee dram' of whisky?"

Kieran snorted and slapped the man on the shoulder. Despite the captain's strong, sinewy form, he was forced to take a staggering step forward or be knocked to the deck.

"Still, I appreciate ye being kind enough to take my coin and keep yer lips sealed."

"What happens at sea is best kept between oneself and the water," Captain Larsson said, glancing between Kieran and Vivienne with a look that was too knowing for her sense of modesty.

Feeling her face flush, she snapped her head back around and focused on what lay ahead.

After five long days at sea, Scotland had finally emerged against the misty horizon, blazing with the colors of autumn. Though the season's cool touch had only just begun creeping over France when they'd left, it seemed that fall's cold, damp grip had already latched onto Scotland. The air was heavy with the threat of rain, and the grass-covered hills were turning from green to amber beneath the steely sky.

In the last two days, Vivienne had finally begun to find her sea legs, though even now she still had to grip the railing to avoid stumbling with the incessant roll of the ship beneath her. At least she'd been able to hold down food and water and didn't feel quite as weak as she had at first.

Despite Captain Larsson's ribbing praise that perhaps she could be turned into a sailor yet, Vivienne had said more than a few prayers of thanks when one of the men had spotted land that morning.

But more than simply feeling solid ground beneath her feet once more, she was grateful to be headed to Scone, if only for a little while, as Kieran had warned her.

Ever since leaving the French court, Vivienne had felt off-balance. After seven long years of living entirely inside the world of carefully orchestrated manners and highly regulated performances of everything from dancing to sipping wine, it was disorienting to live without rules and rituals.

Though she had never set foot on Scottish soil, let alone visited the King's palace in Scone, Vivienne understood how to be a lady at court—far better than she knew how to be a woman alone with Kieran.

They hadn't spoken further of the intimacies they'd shared three nights past. Kieran had remained close, as he always did, despite the fact that the captain and his small crew clearly posed no danger to her. Yet he hadn't suggested that they partake of his "cure" for seasickness again.

Vivienne assumed that with the proverbial itch scratched between them, Kieran's lust was slaked and his interest on the wane. For her part, their wild, passionate joining had the opposite effect. Even more than she'd been before, she was acutely aware of his every move, his every glance and breath.

It was maddening. She cursed her traitorous body for its wantonness, but there was no denying it. She wanted more of him. So much more than he could give.

"We should be on land in a quarter of an hour at most."

She jumped at Kieran's voice right behind her. He stepped to the rail beside her, his gaze scanning the mist-shrouded hills on either side. To her surprise, they hadn't merely anchored along the shoreline, but had sailed right into the mouth of a wide, slow-moving river that drew them deeper inland.

Ahead, she spotted other masts and sails through the fog.

"There," Kieran said, pointing to the cluster of ships. "We'll anchor with the others, then disembark even before the captain's cargo."

She nodded, not trusting her voice with him standing so near.

Kieran headed below deck to fetch their saddlebags while the crew began their final preparations to anchor. Men dashed about as the captain shouted orders, while Vivienne tried to stay out of the way.

Two small dinghies, which were lashed to the side of the ship with rope, were lowered into the water. At the captain's command, a rope ladder was also dropped over the side.

"This is farewell, milady," Captain Larsson said, giving her a little bow. "Until the seas bring us together again."

"Hopefully that will not be anytime soon," she replied, making him bark a laugh.

She carefully picked her way down the ladder and into the waiting dinghy, where one of the crewmen had already settled himself behind the oars. Kieran descended after her, their bags over one shoulder.

As their own boat drew away, Vivienne watched the other dinghy being loaded with the barrels of wine, each one lowered on a rope from the cargo ship's hold. In a matter of moments, they bumped into the wooden docks built along the river's edge, and with Kieran's help, she climbed out of the dinghy.

To her horror, though the docks were clearly rooted and unmoving, it felt as though they swayed beneath her. She staggered toward the riverbank, but even with her feet planted on solid ground, the soil seemed to have turned to water.

"Good luck finding your land legs, milady!" Captain Larsson shouted from the ship. The chuckles of his crew were nearly swallowed by the fog.

"It willnae be so bad as before," Kieran assured her as he took her arm, steadying her as he guided her away from the docks.

By the time they had walked up a damp, grassy rise on the north bank of the river, Vivienne was already beginning to feel better. On the other side of the hill sat a sleepy little village that didn't look so different from the quiet hamlets in Picardy. Thatch-roofed buildings sat clustered together, many with tendrils of smoke rising from their chimneys, and the streets, though mud rather than cobblestones, bustled with villagers going about their day.

Kieran led her into the village, moving through the buildings until the familiar scent of animals and hay reached them. He halted before a large, tidy stable and called for the stable master.

To her surprise, Kieran pulled several coins from the pouch on his belt and traded them with the stable master for two serviceable if rather weathered-looking horses.

"We'll only need these for the ride to the palace," he said quietly as he helped her mount. "It is an hour away."

Keeping their horses close, Kieran took the lead, guiding them westward.

They rode along the river, past small villages like the one they'd bought the horses in and through clumps of wild, tangled forests. Vivienne drank in her surroundings in quiet wonder.

Even only a short distance from the King of Scotland's palace, she felt as though she were in a remote half-wilderness. She realized now that France was tamer and far more cultivated that Scotland. Here, they seemed never more than a stone's throw from some thicket of trees or overgrown patch of forest where humans rarely set foot.

As in Picardy, the landscape rolled gently, though many of the trees and grasses already flared orange and red and yellow now that Michaelmas had come and gone and October was upon them. She was grateful she had on her fur-trimmed cloak, for the air held a damp bite to it.

Soon Kieran guided them away from the river and cut northwest into the more wooded hillsides. A soft rain began to fall, and Vivienne pulled her hood up against it. For his part, Kieran hardly seemed to notice that his head and shirt were growing wet. It seemed he was as immune to the effects of the cold and rain as the tall, solid pines surrounding them.

Ahead, the trees began to thin, and Vivienne glimpsed two stone edifices rising from behind a wooden palisade. One of the towers was clearly a church spire, pointed and inlaid with a few valuable panes of stained glass. The other was square and squat, and beneath it she could make out a sprawling series of connected buildings before the palisades cut off her view.

"Welcome to Scone Palace," Kieran said, glancing at her over his shoulder.

Vivienne felt her eyes widening. This looked more like a rudimentary, cobbled-together keep than a palace. The tower and rambling attached buildings seemed to have latched themselves onto the church a hundred years belatedly. And the palisade was clearly an afterthought. Though they stood nearly twenty feet tall, the sharpened wooden poles wouldn't offer much protection for the likes of a King.

Where was all the finery fit for a monarch? Perhaps it would be different inside, yet Vivienne suspected she'd been quite wrong to imagine Scone Palace would be anything like the French court. And even more mistaken in assuming her experience at court would make her feel at home here.

As they approached the gate at the front of the palisades, several guards halted them. But when Kieran reined in his mount, one of the guards blinked in surprise.

"MacAdams. Ye've returned."

"Aye," Kieran replied acerbically. "As ordered by the King."

The guards leapt into motion then, several opening the wide, heavy gate and another darting inside to announce their arrival.

As they rode into the small courtyard in front of the palace, worry formed a knot in Vivienne's stomach. Would she be granted time to rest and refresh herself after their long journey, or would she be presented to the King of Scotland straightaway?

And how was she to behave when she met him? Because she was part of the Queen's inner circle, she was granted certain liberties in formality with both the King and Queen. Even still, they were royalty and she a lesser noble from a small and relatively humble family line. Decorum and propriety meant everything in all her interactions at court. Would King Robert expect the same?

Kieran helped her dismount and handed the reins to a stable lad who came running from behind the palace. He gave the lad instructions on having their saddlebags delivered to them, then guided Vivienne toward the palace's double doors.

Vivienne hesitated as the doors were thrown open by two guards. "Don't you think we should—"

But before she could finish her entreaty, she was standing in the entrance to the King's great hall. Though it boasted vaulted ceilings and a long row of trestle tables and benches, the space could have fit five times over into King Philip's preferred great hall—and he had three of them.

The walls were lined with delicately woven tapestries depicting Scotland's great victories in battle. Candlelight softened the otherwise plain and rather austere space, as did the clean rushes on the floor. Several servants, who had been shuffling about preparing the hall for the evening meal, stopped and stared curiously at Vivienne.

"Dinnae fash," Kieran said softly as they strode across the hall under the eyes of the servants. "Things are a wee bit different here than in France. But ye neednae worry."

She didn't have time to ponder what he meant, for at the other end of the hall, a tall man in his middle years stepped from one of the many doors at the back. He wore a well-made yet modest tunic and breeches, with a length of red and green plaid looped over one shoulder. His russet hair and beard were liberally slashed with gray, yet his brown eyes were keen and lively even from this distance.

It wasn't until Kieran halted and dipped his head in his usual marginal show of respect that Vivienne belatedly realized she was openly staring at the King of Scotland himself.

Mon Dieu. She was in the thick of it now.

Chapter Twenty

B eside him, Vivienne gasped and abruptly dropped into a deep curtsy.

Even in a damp cloak, travel-worn wool dress, and muddy boots, she managed to make the gesture look both humble and preposterously graceful at the same time.

"Vivienne, ye dinnae need to—"

From her lowered position, she shot him a look that could have frosted over a midsummer sun.

Well, she would understand soon enough that they weren't in her high and mighty French court anymore. God, it was good to be back in Scotland.

The Bruce hurried toward them. "Nay, nay," he said with a frown. "Dinnae do that, Lady Vivienne."

Vivienne kept her gaze lowered, but her delicate brows drew together, clearly uncertain of what she'd done to offend the King, and what she should do instead.

"Rise, milady," the King said, a grin playing behind his beard as he offered a hand to help her up. "And let me do the genuflecting. I owe ye much."

Hesitantly, Vivienne took the King's proffered hand and let him assist her in straightening.

"Och, that's better," the Bruce said, smiling warmly at Vivienne. "Allow me to extend my deepest thanks, milady. If it hadnae been for yer aid, I might be six feet beneath the ground rather than beholding yer lovely face." The Bruce turned to Kieran. "Ye didnae tell me what a great beauty Lady Vivienne is, man. No wonder ye were so eager to fetch her."

Kieran made a choking sound that turned into a cough. At least Vivienne managed to only delicately clear her throat.

They were both saved from having to form a response, for at that moment, Elaine burst from one of the corridors behind the King.

"Vivienne!" She launched herself at Vivienne, colliding into her with a hard embrace. "Welcome to Scotland. I'm so glad you're well. *Are* you well?" Elaine drew back, her blue eyes filled with sudden worry as she scanned Vivienne.

"*Oui,*" Vivienne breathed, but before she could say more, Jerome strode into the hall behind Elaine.

"Forgive my betrothed. When she got word ye'd arrived, there was no stopping her."

From the way her head snapped between the King, Elaine, and Jerome, Vivienne was clearly overwhelmed. It was time Kieran put a stop to this. He stepped to Vivienne's side, leveling Elaine with a scowl fierce enough that she released Vivienne of her own accord. That earned him a glare from Jerome, but he didn't care.

"Vivienne needs rest. She didnae fair well on the sea crossing."

"Forgive me, of course," the Bruce said. "I'll want a report on matters in France, but that can wait until this evening when the others are gathered."

Kieran nodded grimly "There is much to tell, unfortunately."

The Bruce's eyes clouded with worry, yet when he turned back to Vivienne, he smoothed his features. "I'll have ye both shown to yer rooms so that ye can refresh yerselves after yer—"

"One room," Kieran cut in. When the King blinked at him in confusion, he added, "Ye said 'rooms' but we only need one."

A slow, knowing smile began to spread over Elaine's features. Jerome coughed, clearly trying to hide a grin. The King's eyes widened a fraction, his gaze flicking to Vivienne.

Belatedly, Kieran realized what they all must be thinking. *Hell and damnation.*

"I'll be sleeping outside," he snapped. "To ensure Lady Vivienne's safety. Bloody hell, Jerome, do ye need me to pound that tickle out of yer throat?"

Jerome swallowed his next cough, but his dark eyes pinned Kieran with a wry look. "Nay, that willnae be necessary."

"I'll see you settled," Elaine said brightly, looping her arm through Vivienne's and pulling her away toward one of the many corridors that branched from the hall.

Vivienne attempted to curtsy again to the Bruce as Elaine tugged her away. The King only waved a hand. "No' necessary, milady."

Kieran gave the Bruce a nod before falling in with Jerome behind the ladies.

"Don't worry," Elaine was saying to Vivienne. "When I first met the King, I was travel-weary and bedraggled as well—not that you are bedraggled. Gracious, even after what sounds like a trying journey, you look fit for a grand court feast!"

Damn if Jerome's wee English fiancée wasn't right. How Vivienne managed to look elegant and bonny even after nigh a sennight of being seasick Kieran would never understand.

Vivienne relaxed in the presence of Elaine's warm, easy air. She dipped her flaxen head to Elaine's copper one and breathed a chuckle. "You are far too generous, *mon amie*. All the same, I cannot wait for a hot bath and a change of clothes."

Jerome gripped Kieran's arm, slowing him so that the women began to pull away slightly.

"Ye ken we were teasing ye earlier," Jerome said, keeping his voice low. "And I expect to hear the whole story later, but do ye truly believe ye must remain posted outside Lady Vivienne's door even within Scone's walls?"

Kieran jerked his head in a nod. "She's a target. There isnae any doubt now. And I willnae take any chances with her safety."

Jerome's dark brows rose. He opened his mouth to

say more, but just then they caught up with the ladies, who'd halted before a chamber door.

"He prefers when I let him do this part," Vivienne commented to Elaine.

"It isnae a bloody preference," Kieran muttered as he moved to the door. "It is for yer safety."

Mayhap it was all the knowing looks passing between Jerome and Elaine, or mayhap it was being back in a palace, even one more modest than France's, with curious stares and questions to answer. Whatever the case, a sour temper was building within him. The sooner they could leave Scone the better—not only for Vivienne's protection, but for his own sanity.

He pushed into the chamber, giving it a quick sweep with his gaze, then moved slowly around the space. It was simply appointed but functional and comfortable, with a four-poster bed, a table and chair with a pitcher and basin for washing, and a fire laid in a brazier.

"I'll call for a bath," Elaine said, squeezing Vivienne's arm before slipping down the corridor. With a curt nod, Jerome followed, leaving them alone.

With naught to do but stand awkwardly in the middle of her chamber, Kieran's heart leapt against his ribs. Elaine was right—Vivienne was so damn lovely, even travel-worn and rumpled.

But she was so much more than bonny. He watched as she ran her fingers longingly over the bed linens, clearly eager for a night of sleep in a real bed, but then straightened and clasped her hands before her. The steely composure he'd once found so grating had somehow become a source of his admiration for her.

Here she was meeting the King of Scotland—who'd unnerved more than one iron-willed Scot with his uncouth ways, Kieran included—and being thrown headlong into the unknown every step of the way. Yet she met each new challenge with poise, determination, and grace.

She lifted her dark blue gaze to him then, and his heart lurched again. Luckily, Kieran was saved from having to explain why he'd been staring at her, for at that moment, a servant arrived with their bags. At Kieran's instruction, the lad deposited the saddlebags near the table.

Close on the lad's heels were the other servants with Vivienne's bath. They rolled a large wooden tub on its side into the chamber, then began filling it with a stream of buckets. Kieran oversaw the process, arms crossed over his chest and eyes sharp on all those who came and went.

Elaine slipped in, promising to have Vivienne's favorite night-blue silk gown cleaned for her. Then there was naught left to do but for Vivienne to bathe. With a mumbled word about being right outside the door if she needed him, Kieran made a hasty retreat.

Once he'd closed her inside, safe and sound, he leaned against the door and tried to think of anything other than Vivienne stripping bare and easing each creamy inch of skin into the hot water.

Chapter Twenty-One

"There was an attack in Paris."

Vivienne winced at Kieran's blunt words, spoken before the King and the others gathered around the table, but they were true.

After indulging in a divinely long bath and dressing in her gray wool gown—shamefully plain for holding court with a King, but there was no getting around that —she'd found Kieran waiting for her outside her door, as promised.

He'd led her through a series of corridors, but instead of returning to the palace's great hall, they'd arrived at a chamber that was clearly meant for the King's private meetings.

A simple meal of buttered bread, stew, and ale was laid out on the long, rectangular table that took up most of the room. The King had already been seated at the table's head at the far end. A handful of other people stood inside as well.

Vivienne was introduced to the others, a most unusual group of men and women who were all apparently part of the King's inner circle. Elaine and Jerome were there, blessedly familiar faces amongst the curious gathering. Colin and Sabine MacKay greeted her warmly, as did Elaine's brother Niall. Will Sinclair assessed her coolly with his one eye. Most strange of all was Mairin, a young woman with quiet, watchful gray eyes who sipped whisky with several of the Scottish men as they ate their meal.

Once the introductions were complete and everyone was seated at the table, Kieran had launched directly into news of the attack.

At Kieran's curt announcement about the incident at the palace, the King sat forward abruptly.

"What sort of attack?" he demanded with a frown.

"The sort that confirmed my suspicions about de Soules," Kieran replied gruffly.

"Retreat a wee bit," the King said, holding up a hand. "How did King Philip receive ye? Was there any indication of danger in his court before ye arrived?"

Kieran lowered himself into a chair beside Vivienne. "Philip was most accommodating. He was distressed to learn that we suspected de Soules's lackeys might still be on the loose in France, and eager to help in any way he could."

The Bruce nodded, his weathered features relaxing somewhat. "Good."

Vivienne blinked in surprise. It had never occurred to her that the Bruce might not fully trust King Philip, yet the assassination attempt against him had been fomented in part on French soil. Luckily, her French King seemed to have passed whatever assessment the Bruce had sought to make of him.

"And as to any danger before I arrived…" Kieran turned to her.

She swallowed, collecting her composure before the motley gathering. "*Non, Majesté,*" she replied. "The palace was quiet before Kieran's arrival. Though my actions against de Soules were known, there was no indication of danger."

"Lady Vivienne, I allow a certain informality when I am alone with my closest advisors and the members of the Bodyguard Corps. Since ye played no small part in saving my life, ye may call me Robert in private."

Vivienne straightened in her chair, pressing her lips together for a moment as she determined how best to refuse a King. "*Non, Majesté,*" she simply said at last.

His russet brows rose and a soft ripple of chuckles traveled around the table.

"Nay?" the Bruce said, clearly baffled.

"*Non.* You are the King. It would not be right."

Now Colin was outright laughing into his hand. Sabine elbowed him, but she couldn't reach Kieran, who snorted and shot her a look that made heat rise to her cheeks.

"Well," the Bruce said. "Suit yerself, I suppose."

"Never thought I'd see King Robert the Bruce take orders from a wee French lass, and one who was arguing for propriety at that," Colin murmured, drawing another wave of chuckles from the others before Sabine could swat his shoulder.

The Bruce leveled Colin with a look that likely would have sent another man's knees quaking with fear, but the camaraderie between the King and his inner circle was plain to see.

"Back to the matter at hand," the Bruce said briskly. He and the others sobered as they refocused on Kieran. "What of this attack?"

Kieran described first noticing the suspicious gardener, then following him into the hedge maze after Vivienne. When he told of tearing through the maze to find the man looming over Vivienne, about to strike, an involuntary shudder swept over her.

Elaine reached across the table and squeezed her hand reassuringly. Kieran went on, giving a terse explanation of killing the man.

"I should have left him alive long enough to question him," Kieran said, his voice edged with anger. "But I wasnae thinking clearly in the moment. Still, I am certain he was one of de Soules's men. He didnae go for coin or…" He gritted his teeth. "…Or aught else of Vivienne's. His only purpose was to kill her."

The room fell silent for a long moment.

"We have to assume the threat came from de Soules, Robert," Colin said quietly.

The King muttered a curse, tugging on his beard. "Simply killing the man willnae solve this problem, ye ken. He'll be made a martyr by those still loyal to him. And in any case, his cronies are clearly acting independently of him, for he is rotting in the bowels of the palace as we speak."

Though she knew she was safe with Kieran at her side and several members of the King's elite Bodyguard Corps surrounding her, Vivienne couldn't repress another shiver of foreboding. And unfortunately, thinking of William de Soules, the seemingly unassuming man she'd met at court earlier that summer, sitting far below her in a dungeon cell, gave her surprisingly little comfort.

He was a man capable of plotting the assassination of his own King, and whose followers wanted her dead. How could she ever hope to be truly safe from that sort of fanaticism?

As if reading her troubled thoughts, Kieran planted his elbows on the table and fixed the Bruce with a steady stare.

"We will be departing Scone as soon as possible— tomorrow morn, if ye'll give us two strong steeds, Robert."

Across from them, Will frowned, and Vivienne had to resist the urge to draw back from his fierce visage. "Surely ye cannae think the lass is in danger here at the palace."

"Ye're damn right I do," Kieran replied bluntly. "It was within the bloody palace's walls that de Soules and the other nobles plotted their rebellion. And if de Soules has men seeking to avenge him in France, he sure as hell could have others here in Scotland—in Scone itself, for that matter."

Kieran turned his gaze back to the Bruce. "Ye requested that I bring Vivienne here so that ye could thank her for her aid. Well, I've done that, but ye kenned I didnae intend for her to stay here in the public eye."

The Bruce bristled slightly at Kieran's tone, his mouth tightening with annoyance behind his beard, but after a moment, he dipped his head in acknowledgement.

"Aye, that was the deal. And will ye still insist on keeping yer destination from us?"

Kieran shifted in his chair. "All I'll say is that we are bound for the Highlands."

A few of the others, including Will and Colin, frowned, but Kieran's features were set in stone, his cool gaze daring anyone to challenge him.

"The clear danger presented to Lady Vivienne justifies yer secrecy," the Bruce said, steepling his hands in front of his mouth. "It also justifies adding more members of the Corps to her guard. Mayhap ye should take Niall with ye. Or Mairin."

"The lad is too green," Kieran replied without hesitation. "Besides, I wouldnae leave it to an Englishman to watch my back, Corps member or nay."

Niall jerked in his chair, his bright blue eyes flashing with anger. "I've pledged my loyalty just like you, MacAdams. And I've been training in the Highlands these past four years—"

"And the wee Mackenzie isnae ready for an assignment, either," Kieran went on, ignoring Niall and eyeing Mairin. The young woman remained silent, her wide gray eyes guarded.

The Bruce cleared his throat, and the room instantly fell quiet.

"Ye proved right that de Soules still has lackeys willing to harm our allies, MacAdams," the King said, his voice grudging. "And ye saved Lady Vivienne's life." He gave Vivienne a little nod. "Because of those things, ye've earned my respect. But it seems to me ye still need to learn a thing or two about being a member of a team."

Kieran rolled his shoulders. "Ye entrusted me with Vivienne's protection, and that's what I'm doing. I wouldnae have been a verra good choice for the mission if I needed to rely on others to see it done."

The Bruce considered Kieran's words, his dark, keen gaze settling on Vivienne. She remained still, but inside she was a tangled knot of worry.

It was disconcerting enough to be sitting at a table with the King of Scotland and his most trusted confidantes, all of whom were focused on her safety at the moment. Yet far more disturbing was how serious Kieran and the others were taking the threat against her.

Ever since the gardener's attack, she'd been forced to accept the fact that she was indeed a target. But with no danger greater than seasickness since then, some part of her had hoped that the entire matter could be resolved sooner rather than later and she could return to her old life at the French court.

What was more, her protection had apparently become some sort of unspoken battleground between Kieran and the others. Of course she knew Kieran could be an overprotective, domineering brute when he chose to be, but he seemed intent on proving that he could see to her safety all on his own.

At last, the King reluctantly nodded. Kieran had won this battle, if not the larger fight.

Which meant she and Kieran would be thrown together—alone—yet again. Vivienne would be whisked away somewhere into the heart of the Highlands, even farther away from everything she knew in this world. And with only Kieran to protect her.

Now if she could only manage to protect *herself* from the traitorous stirrings in her heart.

Chapter Twenty-Two

William de Soules squinted against the approaching flicker of a torch.

He'd grown accustomed to the guards' rotating schedule a few months ago. They usually snuffed the torches at midnight, climbing the stone stairs that led aboveground to the palace and sealing the door to the dungeon with a creaking thud. Then two guards would return sometime around dawn to light the torches again and take up their positions at the base of the stairs.

Though it was nigh impossible to tell the exact time in the inky darkness of his cell, he was certain dawn hadn't come so soon. To confirm his suspicions, only one slash of orange light illuminated the dark, dripping dungeon, not two.

William pushed himself up from his cot, slinking toward the iron bars to get a better look. In the gloom, he could make out the coarse features of his man Bevin approaching his cell.

EMMA PRINCE

He drew in a sharp breath, his pulse jumping. It had been nearly two months since he'd received any news, and if Bevin bore the information he hoped, William was in for a treat that he could savor for years to come.

Bevin strode closer, peering warily into the shadows stretching beyond the light of his torch.

"Psst."

Bevin nearly leapt from his skin at William's soft hiss. He swung around, lifting the torch high. William held up a hand to shield his eyes from the glare.

"Lower that, ye fool," he breathed.

As Bevin did his bidding, William stilled, listening for any sounds of movement from the cell next to him. Countess Agnes of Strathearn—*former* countess, that was —usually slept soundly through the nights, but William couldn't risk her overhearing aught. The bitch had already sold him out once before. She would do it again if it meant that whoreson Bruce King would take pity on her further.

"What took ye so bloody long?" he demanded in a low whisper when he was satisfied that Agnes didn't stir.

Bevin, slow-witted beast of burden that he was, ducked his head at William's sharp tone.

"Forgive me, sire, but I didnae think I should risk visiting ye until the flurry surrounding the executions had died down."

"It isnae yer job to *think*, Bevin," William replied. "Only to follow my orders."

"Aye, sire." He dipped his brown head once more, waiting on William.

That was better. "It has been more than a month

since the executions. I was expecting good news by now. What has happened?"

"A great deal, sire," Bevin said, his thick brows dropping. "It…it isnae all good."

William's grip on the iron bars separating them tightened. "Speak, fool."

"St. Giles failed in France."

"*What?*" William swallowed, fighting to lower his voice. "I thought you said everything was arranged."

"It was, sire, but there was an… unexpected obstacle at court. A Scottish warrior."

"Who?"

"Kieran MacAdams, sire."

William froze, but inside a storm unleashed, lashing his rage to life. *Kieran MacAdams*. The Highland brute had been the one to drag William from the clutches of the French whore who'd poisoned him, only to deliver him to the Bruce, bound, on his knees, and named a traitor.

"What the hell was Kieran MacAdams doing in France?"

Bevin shifted from one foot to the other. "Apparently no' long after the executions, the King sent him to protect the woman."

In an instant, William's blood ran from hot to cold with trepidation. Then the Bruce had taken Richard Broun's final words to heart.

Though it had been a joy to watch the King and the others squirm at Broun's pronouncement, William cursed the man for revealing the fact that he still had a few allies tucked away in hiding, waiting for his word to revive the rebellion against the pretender King.

"Why didnae ye tell me this sooner?" he hissed through his teeth.

"As I said, sire, I didnae think I could risk a visit so soon after the executions. It was already nigh impossible to get the sleeping draught into the guards' ale, and—"

"Then why didnae ye alert St. Giles to beware of that Highland beast?"

Bevin dropped his gaze. "I...I didnae realize until MacAdams had already departed for France what he was about. By then it was too late to get word to St. Giles through the normal channels."

William scrubbed a hand over his face, breathing a curse. "What good is having ye placed in the palace stables if ye cannae even keep track of who comes and goes?" He fixed Bevin with a cold stare. "Mayhap David de Brechin was wrong about ye. Mayhap ye arenae any use to me after all."

He let Bevin squirm for a moment before going on. "In which case, I'll tell the guards all about the wee mishap with that young cousin of yers. Yer clan willnae want ye back once the truth comes out—assuming ye arenae simply killed on the spot when the guards learn that ye raped and strangled that sweet girl, then sank her body in the loch to make it all disappear."

"Nay, sire, please, I beg ye, dinnae tell—"

"Shut yer trap, ye blithering idiot," William snapped. The wheels in his mind ground slowly as he contemplated what to do. In only a few months, his brain had grown rusty and dull as a nail left out in the rain with naught to do but stare at the stone walls of his cell. He needed to think, needed to regain control of the situation.

St. Giles had been one of his few remaining contacts in France. Through Bevin, William had managed to get word to the man shortly after being sentenced to rot in Scone's dungeon. Even then, with his wits sharp and his rage against the Bruce to fuel him, William had known he'd have to play things carefully at first. He couldn't strike directly at the whoreson King yet.

The galling truth was, William no longer had the resources to plot a direct attack against the Bruce. In hanging the nobles who'd conspired with William in the Bruce's overthrow, the King had sent a message that had frightened off many of William's few remaining allies. He still had Bevin, of course, and a small handful of others who knew that crossing William would be far worse than anything the King would do to them.

Weakened and imprisoned, William had to bide his time, wait until the dust settled, and slowly gather his allies once again to strike against the King who had taken so much from him. Besides, the palace was crawling with the King's Bodyguard Corps. The Bruce was never without at least a few of his elite warriors, according to Bevin. It was too early yet to attempt another assassination.

But that didn't mean he couldn't strike at someone else. Someone who had humiliated and belittled him. Someone he burned to hurt as she'd hurt him. Oh, there were others he yearned to eliminate—that English bitch Elaine Beaumore, for starters, who'd killed his closest ally, David de Brechin, and Jerome Munro, who'd helped Elaine unravel his plan. And of course he would take pleasure in orchestrating Kieran MacAdams's death from within Scone's dungeon.

But Vivienne de Valance was meant to come first. She was supposed to be well outside the Bruce's notice, tucked away in the French court imagining that since she'd rid herself of the scheming William de Soules, all was quiet and well. If aught, William had regretted sending St. Giles to kill her, because it would mean that he wouldn't be able to make her suffer at his own hands.

But for once, Bevin was right. Their backchannels for communication were slow and delicate. It had taken a month just to arrange for the French bitch's murder. There wouldn't have been time to change course even if William had learned right away of MacAdams's presence.

And now thanks to that brutish Highlander, William had neither his ally in France nor the knowledge of Vivienne's death, which he'd meant to savor while he bided his time against the Bruce.

Damn it all, he was thinking in circles again. He needed to focus. Who knew when Bevin would be able to slip down to the dungeon to give him a report again?

"You said a great deal has happened since last we spoke," William said, leveling Bevin with his gaze. "Is there aught else?"

Bevin nodded eagerly, his eyes widening. "Ye'll never believe it, sire. They are here!"

Confusion tumbled through him. "Who is here?"

"The woman and MacAdams," Bevin said, his

breaths coming faster now. "He killed St. Giles, but then he brought the woman to Scone—right into the palace."

Why would the idiot Highlander do such a thing? It didn't matter, William told himself firmly, his own breath coming short with his excitement. He thought of the French whore just above him, gliding about in all her fine clothes and jewels, her bonny head held at that damn haughty angle. He thought of touching that creamy skin of hers, then breaking her neck with his bare hands.

Nay, nay, he would do it slower than that if he could. But beggars couldn't be choosers.

"They are likely departing in a matter of hours," Bevin said, interrupting William's thoughts. "The Bruce sent someone to the stables to select two fine horses for them. What should I do, sire?"

William frantically searched his mind for a plan. She was so close, but if he wasn't careful, she would slip through his grasp again.

"Gather whatever men ye can find. Use the stash of coins I told ye about to hire mercenaries if ye have to—whatever it takes. Follow Vivienne and MacAdams out of Scone. Dinnae strike right away, else the Bruce's men will be close enough to give aid. But dinnae let them slip away."

"And once we have them, sire?"

William's lips drew back from his teeth. "Kill them."

Chapter Twenty-Three

Somewhere behind the thick, steel-gray clouds overhead, the sun peeked above the horizon. Kieran turned to the Bruce, who stood beside him in the courtyard before the palace, and gripped his forearm in a firm shake.

"Luck be with ye, MacAdams," the King murmured. "I still dinnae like sending ye out who kens where without anyone to watch yer back, but…" His keen eyes flicked to Vivienne, who was saying her farewells to the others. "…I suspect ye would give yer life to protect the lass—and mayhap even rise from the dead to ensure her safety."

It seemed there was no point in trying to deny what everyone already thought—that some special connection bound Kieran and Vivienne together—so instead of fighting it, Kieran simply replied, "Ye can count on it, Robert."

The King flashed him a wry smile before his features settled into serious lines once more.

"I think I shall move de Soules away from Scone," he said, lowering his voice.

Kieran frowned in surprise. "Oh?"

"If he is to spend the rest of his life in a dungeon, he neednae be right under my nose here at the palace."

"Do ye think that will lessen the threat he poses to Vivienne?"

The King stroked his beard, considering. "I dinnae ken, but tucking him away somewhere more remote would at least remove attention from him. And it may dissuade his allies from seeking to keep his cause alive. Out of sight, out of mind, ye ken."

Kieran wouldn't count on a simple change in de Soules's location to keep Vivienne safe, but it was better than doing naught, he supposed. He nodded to the King. "A sound thought."

"I'll try to get to the bottom of this blasted rebellion from here," the Bruce added. "So dinnae turn into a complete hermit. Get word to us every now and again, man. And hopefully verra soon I'll be able to bring ye and Lady Vivienne back in—when the last of de Soules's allies are weeded out and she'll be truly safe."

"Thank ye," Kieran replied soberly.

Vivienne, who'd been tilting her head respectfully to the members of the Corps who had gathered to see them off, now turned to Elaine. The two clasped each other in a long hug that ended with Elaine wiping tears from her cheeks.

"Farewell," Elaine said, her voice tight with emotion. "We will see you at Scone again soon, I am sure of it."

Vivienne smiled warmly at her friend. "And just think, when I return, you will be a married woman. I hope you'll plait your hair the way I showed you. You'll be the most beautiful bride, *mon amie*."

Elaine nodded, trying to blink away more tears.

Vivienne turned to the King, and despite his insistence that she needn't be so formal with him, she dipped into a graceful curtsy. The Bruce took her hand and helped her rise, then bowed over it.

"Ye have the King of Scotland in yer debt, Lady Vivienne," the Bruce said, straightening. "Dinnae forget that."

Their horses were already saddled and ready, held by a young lad a few paces away. Kieran helped Vivienne mount the fleet-footed chestnut mare the King had provided, then swung onto the back of his own dappled silver stallion.

With a final nod to the Bruce and the other members of the Corps standing in the courtyard, Kieran urged his horse through the open gate in the palisades, Vivienne following.

He had assumed that as they rode away from Scone, the knots in his shoulders would ease and his jaw would loosen. He was on Scottish soil, after all, and what was more, he was headed into the Highlands, the land that had forged him into the man he'd become. He was made for wilderness, not Kings' palaces, and never was he happier than when he was alone.

But he wasn't alone. His skin pricked and his pulse

leapt traitorously at Vivienne's nearness. Though he preferred the sprawling, empty forests and moors of the Highlands to the crowded courts in Paris and Scone, there was a certain safety in being surrounded by others —safety from himself and his desire for her.

When they were alone together, he couldn't seem to think of aught else but kissing her, touching her, being inside her. His mind drifted back to Captain Larsson's cabin, the creamy glow of her skin, her gasps and moans of pleasure filling his ears, and the erotic roll of her hips as she'd ridden him.

Hell and damnation.

She'd said that their surrender to desire didn't change aught, and he'd agreed, but that had been a lie. Even before they'd succumbed to pleasure, things had already begun to change in the darkest, most secret corners of Kieran's heart.

Damn it all, with each passing moment, he was breaking his vow to himself never to get involved with someone again, never to let himself care as he once had with Linette.

His only hope as they left Scone behind was to keep her at a distance, even while staying close to her side at all times. Without being able to put any physical space between them, his only other alternative was to stretch the silence that hung around them as they rode north. Aye, this silence would be his salvation.

THIS SILENCE WOULD BE the death of her.

EMMA PRINCE

Besides a few grunts and monosyllabic commands, Kieran had been taciturn since they'd departed Scone several hours ago. It was particularly maddening because there was so much left unsaid between them.

Vivienne shifted in her saddle, still unused to riding for so many hours straight without a break. At least her physical discomfort gave her something to focus on besides the laden silence between them.

There were far too many unknowns ahead for her peace of mind. How long would she be in hiding? When would it ever be safe to return to her old life? She hadn't truly let herself consider it before, but now that they had set out into the Highland wilds, she realized that she had no idea when—or if—there would ever come a time when she would be safe again.

The thought was terrifying, not only because it meant she might never be able to go home again, but also because she would be alone with Kieran—indefinitely.

And that fear led to a series of questions about what lay between them—mere lust? Something more?—that she didn't want to contemplate at the moment.

So to keep from driving herself mad with the worries and unknowns spiraling through her mind, she blurted the safest question she could think of.

"Now will you tell me where you are taking me?"

He glanced at her, his brow furrowed and his eyes distracted. Perhaps Vivienne wasn't the only one lost in troubling thoughts.

"Ye wouldnae ken the place even if I told ye," he replied gruffly.

Of course he was right.

They'd ridden over gently rolling hills dotted with farmlands and clumps of trees all morning, but by afternoon, they'd entered a denser pine forest. He might as well have been leading her in circles for all that she could distinguish where they were, except for the fact that the weak October sun had broken through the gray clouds behind them not long ago and proven that they were indeed riding north.

Vivienne gingerly adjusted her cloak on her shoulders and lifted her chin. "*Oui*, that is true, but you could at least tell me how much longer we will ride."

Kieran grunted, but luckily he deigned to add a few words as well. "Four days. Mayhap three if the weather doesnae turn."

He glanced up at the sky with a frown. Judging from the darker clouds to the west, the dry conditions wouldn't hold.

They fell into another silence, broken only by the occasional snort from the horses. Vivienne tried a different tack, determined to get at least a few answers to the questions making a muddle of her thoughts.

"I was surprised the King offered to send another member of the Corps with us," she began carefully. "Or rather, I was surprised at how quickly you refused him." Of course, she knew Kieran to be a proud, stubborn man, but was there more to it than that? Did he hope to have her all to himself in whatever remote corner of the Highlands he was taking her?

He snorted. "Ye already ken how I feel about relying on others. It is a fool's errand."

She worked her lower lip with her teeth for a moment in thought. "*Oui*, I remember. But I don't understand *why* you are so set against letting anyone help you."

"Something *I've* never understood," he commented, "is why ye agreed to drug de Soules back in Paris."

She blinked, caught off-guard by his blatant redirection of the conversation.

"Ye kenned de Soules was up to trouble when ye recognized him from his little plotting liaisons with Edward Balliol," he went on, "and it was right of ye to say something to Elaine. But that could have been the end of it. Ye could have passed on yer bit of information and left the rest to Jerome, Elaine, and me."

He leveled her with a piercing blue stare. "But ye didnae. Ye practically jumped at the opportunity to slip that draught into his wine. Nor did ye hesitate to offer to keep him incapacitated at court while Jerome and Elaine unraveled his plan, and I delivered the King's declaration of freedom to the Pope. Why?"

Vivienne frowned. "Because it was the right thing to do."

"Nay, it was the *dangerous* thing to do," he shot back.

She narrowed her gaze on him. He'd been like this —overprotective and domineering—when he'd first learned of the part she would play in thwarting de Soules last summer.

"Ye risked yer life and made yerself a target by drugging him," he said. To her surprise, he took the edge from his voice. "I still dinnae understand why."

Vivienne swallowed. "I suppose it was because of Guy."

Kieran stiffened at the mention of the name, a muscle in his jaw twitching behind his dark stubble.

"De Soules reminded me of him, in a way," she continued. "I…I couldn't stand the thought of a man like that—a cruel, callous man who was only looking out for himself—ruling the world. Or at least ruling a country."

She lifted her shoulders in a little shrug. "Putting a target on my back was a small price to pay to prevent a man like that from overthrowing his own country. And of course there was France's alliance with the Bruce and Scotland to think of."

She glanced at him to find his gaze pinning her, his blue eyes simmering with respect. Despite the crisp edge to the air, heat climbed up her neck and into her face.

Mon Dieu, he was most effective at befuddling her thoughts and redirecting her attention.

"Here we are again, discussing my story, which you already know anyway," she said, straightening in her saddle. "But what of you? Why are you so set against accepting help from others?"

He cleared his throat, the leather of his saddle creaking as he adjusted his position. "I dinnae see what all these questions have to do with my role as yer bodyguard."

"What about your role as my lover?"

Kieran's eyes rounded and he sputtered for a moment. "Yer what?"

Vivienne knew she would have to shock him in order

to keep him talking. She savored his stunned reaction for a moment before continuing. "What would you call what we did on the ship? Or against the wall at that inn?"

"I wouldnae exactly go so far as to call me yer—"

"We are to remain in close quarters for an indefinite stretch of time, are we not?" she went on.

He swallowed hard, his eyes flaring with a blue fire hot enough to still her tongue for a moment. His thoughts, which he so often guarded with a stony countenance, were plain as day. Indeed, they would be in close quarters—and they both knew exactly what that would lead to.

Fantasies about his lips and hands exploring her, his cock driving into her, pushing her to the heights of ecstasy, threatened to scatter every last rational thought she possessed. She forced herself to shove aside the sudden flood of desire and focus on her interrogation.

"Should I simply pretend you are nothing more than a warrior?" she murmured. "A guard no more capable of emotion or intelligence or interest than a rock? *Non*, of course not. If we are to remain in each other's company, to be thrust into such…*intimate* circumstances, you ought to be able to share something of yourself, as I have with you."

Oui, she'd definitely managed to shock him. His jaw worked for a long moment, but he couldn't seem to form a response.

At last he let a long breath go. "I dinnae like speaking about my past," he began haltingly.

She waited while he searched for more words.

"I wasnae always so guarded," he continued at last, shooting her a wary glance. "But when ye've lost everything ye hold dear—"

He cut off abruptly, but this time, it wasn't because he was at a loss for words. He'd gone rigid in his saddle, his head snapping around and his gaze scanning the surrounding woods.

Trepidation clawed up Vivienne's throat. "What is—"

His hand flew up, silencing her. He reached for the hilt of his longsword, which stuck out from one of his saddlebags. As the metal rasped against its leather sheath, he whispered, "Stay close, and do as I—"

But before he could finish, all hell broke loose.

Chapter Twenty-Four

The thwack of a bowstring was all the warning Kieran had.

An arrow flew past Vivienne's head, narrowly missing her. The mare she rode spooked, whinnying in distress and rearing on its hind legs. Vivienne screamed, desperately fighting to keep her seat in the saddle.

Blessedly, Kieran's enormous stallion proved steadier than the mare, even as he dug his heels into the animal's flanks and yanked on the reins to bring him closer to Vivienne's rearing horse.

Another arrow flew by, this time just wide of him.

"Kieran!" Vivienne cried, her voice high and frightened.

Bloody cowards! His sword was no use against an enemy that lurked behind the cover of the trees, firing on an unarmed woman. He could curse them later, though. Vivienne was mere seconds from being thrown to the ground—if she wasn't struck by an arrow first.

He rammed his sword back into its sheath, urging his horse still closer to hers. Just as she began to slip from the saddle, his arm snaked around her waist and snatched her up. He dragged her before him onto his own saddle, then wheeled his horse around so that his back was to the arrow fire, shielding Vivienne.

Suddenly, pain exploded in his right shoulder. An arrow hit him with such force that he jerked forward hard enough to knock Vivienne over his horse's neck, nearly unseating her. Thankfully, she somehow managed to hold on, even as he bellowed in pain.

His roar was apparently the last straw for her skittish mare, who flattened her ears and prepared to bolt into the trees. Kieran had the presence of mind to lean over and snatch the horse's reins, though, preventing her from dashing away.

Pain radiated down his injured sword arm. Thank God he wasn't still holding his blade, for he likely would have dropped it when he'd been shot. As it was, he might as well be weaponless, for there was no way he could wield a sword with an arrow protruding from his shoulder.

He dared a glance behind him, where the arrow fire had come from. The underbrush rustled and four men slowly emerged, swords drawn.

Every fiber in Kieran's body screamed at him to protect Vivienne at all costs. But with his injured arm growing heavy and stiff, he didn't stand a chance against the men.

Just then, the archer stepped from the trees, taking aim with a slow smile right at Kieran. Kieran's big frame protected Vivienne, but if the archer managed to fell him, she would be completely unguarded.

Calling up all his strength, he gripped the mare's reins in his good hand and slung his injured arm around Vivienne. He dug his heels into his stallion's flanks, sending the powerful animal surging into the trees.

Their attackers shouted in surprise as they tore off through the woods. Kieran hunched around Vivienne's small form in front of him, using his body as a shield. Though it might be easier to shift her back into her own saddle and let her control the mare, there was no way in hell he would expose her to more arrow fire.

Just as he'd expected, an arrow sailed past them, but thankfully it missed both him and their horses.

With a groan of agony, he dragged his injured arm from around Vivienne's waist and fumbled for the stallion's reins. In the heat of the attack, it had been enough to simply spur the animal into a gallop and let him run unguided, but now Kieran needed to see them to safety.

Once he had the stallion under control, he wrapped the mare's reins around his saddle's pommel. Then he switched the stallion's reins into his good hand, letting his injured arm hang at his side.

There was no telling how long it would take their attackers to mount and set after them, or how quickly they would pick up their trail. Their only hope was to lose them in the thick forest and then outrun them.

Gritting his teeth against the burning pain in his shoulder, Kieran spurred his horse faster.

TIME BLURRED and bent nightmarishly as they plunged through the darkening woods. Vivienne only knew that it must have been several hours since they'd been set upon, for the muted gray light of midday had slid into blue twilight.

Kieran had driven his powerful stallion to the brink of exhaustion before slowing him to a walk. Even without a rider, her spritely mare had barely been able to keep up. Now both horses breathed hard, no doubt grateful for some rest.

Kieran gave himself no such respite, though. He searched the surrounding trees relentlessly with his gaze, his body pulled taut behind her.

For her part, now that the initial terror had begun to wear off, cold shock was setting in. She'd long ago lost feeling in her legs from being wedged before Kieran astride his enormous horse. Her head felt filled with stones, heavy and dull.

When she began tipping forward over the animal's neck, her limbs like pudding from fatigue and numbness, Kieran muttered a curse and reined the horses to a halt.

With a grunt, he swung himself to the ground. It wasn't until he stood before her, reaching for her with only one hand to help her down, that she saw the shaft of the arrow protruding from his shoulder.

"*Mon Dieu*," she breathed. "I did not realize. You are injured."

"Aye," he said tightly. He tried to give her a weak smile, but because his features were drawn with pain, it was more of a grimace.

She slid from the horse's back, her knees nearly

buckling under her weight. Her legs wobbled precariously, but she managed to stay upright. Heart in her
throat, she stared wide-eyed at the arrow shaft.

"W-what should I do? I could...I could remove the
arrow, and try to——"

"Nay," he cut in. "There isnae time. I'll no' have us
dawdling here like lambs waiting for the slaughter while
those men hunt us down."

"But you cannot leave it in," she said. She hated the
way her voice was rising toward panic, but she couldn't
stop it. They were alone in the middle of a night-dark
wood, being chased by men who meant to kill them.
Kieran was injured, and she had no idea how to
help him.

"We'll have to," he replied grimly. "If we ride like
hell and manage to lose those men, we can be someplace safe in two days' time. It will have to wait
until then."

She began shaking her head, her chest squeezing
with fear, but Kieran caught her chin in his good hand
and forced her to meet his gaze.

"Look at me, Vivienne," he ordered, scowling down
at her. "If ye can face the Queen of France and earn a
place as one of her ladies, if ye can meet the King of
Scotland without losing yer composure, and hell, if ye
can square off with me even when I'm growling and
huffing like an enraged bear, ye can damn well do
this, too."

She swallowed hard, blinking away her frightened
tears. He was right. It was time to put all her years of

practice being strong into action. She gave him a curt nod, lifting her chin. "*Oui.*"

"There's my steel-spined lass," he said, his voice warm. "Now, I do need ye to do something."

He bent and reached for the dagger he carried in his boot, hissing a curse of pain as he straightened. "I need ye to cut off the arrow shaft," he said, handing her the dagger.

She took the knife with trembling fingers, but she willed herself to maintain a white-knuckled grasp on her composure.

"Get as close to my skin as possible. Aye, that's it," he said as she positioned the blade. "Now hold the arrow steady with one hand and saw through it with the dagger."

He spouted a colorful stream of curses when she closed her hand around the arrow and began working the blade along it. By the time the shaft snapped free, Kieran was sagged over, his brow beaded with sweat.

"Good lass," he mumbled, his hand shaking with pain as he took back his dagger and re-sheathed it in his boot. "Now, do something else for me. Untie yer mare's reins from my pommel."

She blinked in confusion. "But should I not ride her? Surely we could go faster if—"

"Nay," he growled, straightening. "I'll no' have ye exposed and vulnerable atop yer own horse. I nearly lost ye earlier, and I cannae—" He dragged a hand over his face, muttering a curse into his palm. "Ye are safer riding with me," he said after a moment. "Besides, the mare willnae be able to keep up this pace for another two days, even without ye riding her."

He was right. Though finely formed, the animal clearly wasn't meant for such hard trekking. "Then… then what will you do with her?"

He moved to the animal's side, unfastening Vivienne's saddlebags and hoisting them over his own behind the stallion's saddle.

"We'll send her on her way. Her tracks will confuse our attackers, forcing them to split, double back, or choose only one path to follow. And dinnae fear for her. She's far too bonny a beast to go more than a day without being noticed. Whoever finds her will think he's the luckiest man alive to gain such an animal."

Vivienne reluctantly did as Kieran bid, unlooping the mare's reins from the pommel. She patted the mare's neck, then stepped back as Kieran lightly swatted her haunch to send her off into the dark trees.

He turned to her, fixing her with a searching gaze. "Can ye continue riding through the night?"

"*Oui*," she replied, fighting to keep her voice steady even as a fresh wave of fear hit her.

Even if she truly could stay upright in the saddle through the long, dark night, what if Kieran couldn't? In the diffuse light of the moon behind the clouds, his skin was pale and his face pulled taut with pain.

With a boost from his good arm, she swung into the saddle. He dragged himself up behind her, growling in discomfort as he did. He took up the reins, settling his injured arm onto his thigh, then urged the horse into motion.

As they rode, the hours stretched. With each passing jolt of the horse's stride, Kieran's body grew more and more rigid with pain behind her. At last, she took the reins and looped his good arm around her waist to keep him from toppling out of the saddle.

And when he leaned against her, agony having wrung the strength from his body, she willed herself to bear his weight, all the while praying that they would reach safety in time.

Chapter Twenty-Five

Through fever-bleary eyes, Kieran squinted at the pine trees around them.

Focus, damn it! His thoughts tried to amble away for the thousandth time in the last two days, but he needed to concentrate if they had any hope of finding the cottage.

With his shoulder blazing in agony and his mind clouded with fever, he cursed himself for taking Vivienne to this place. Yet he knew of nowhere else to go.

He'd always planned on bringing her to this remote spot, tucked away from even the most curious clansmen and wide-roaming hunters, but now that he could barely keep his seat in the saddle, he realized it had been a mistake to take her someplace so isolated. Even if he told her now what he sought, there was no way she would be able to guide them through the dense forest to the wee hidden clearing.

The last two days had been a blur of pain and fear

as they'd ridden like the very Devil was on their heels. And in a way, he was; at least for the first day, Kieran was sure their attackers had been tracking them.

Even after turning Vivienne's mare loose, he'd taken extra steps to shake them off their trail. At times they'd cut across streams and made circles with their tracks. But mostly they'd simply ridden for interminably long stretches, pushing both the horse and themselves to the edge of collapse.

Blessedly, the dappled stallion was stronger than any other he had seen—and stronger than Kieran, as well. Even when the horse was able to continue, they were forced to stop several times as Kieran teetered on the brink of unconsciousness, threatening to fall from the saddle and drag Vivienne with him.

Through the pain, through the dread, and through the heavy fog of fever that had settled over him the day after the attack, Kieran fought to hold off the darkness until he could get Vivienne safely to the cottage. But first he had to find the damned thing.

He swept his unfocused gaze over the forest once more. Thank God there had been no indication that they were being followed this past day. The terrain had grown rougher and the woods thicker, making their enemies' pursuit far more difficult. But even wounded and fever-addled, this was his home territory. This land had made him. He wouldn't be bested by it.

Aye, he recognized their surroundings now. Up ahead, the trees thinned, though the underbrush was wild and overgrown. He caught a glimpse of a sagging thatch roof. He blinked to be sure he wasn't hallucinating, but the cottage held steady before his eyes.

"There," he ground out, lifting his good arm to point at the clearing in front of them.

Vivienne sucked in a breath. "We are safe, then?"

If only he could simply say aye. "I doubt anyone will find us here." Whether Kieran would be able to protect her if someone did was another matter.

He urged the stallion across the weed-clogged clearing to the cottage. Through the fog of pain, he silently cursed. The wee hut looked about as bad as he felt.

It was untouched, just as he'd left it ten years past—except for the destruction nature had wrought. The thatch roof drooped inward and would likely leak when the rains they'd ridden through earlier that morning reached them here.

One of the shutters on the sole window hung askew from its hinges, meaning that for however long it had been like that, the cottage had been open to wee beasties as well as the elements. The door looked solid enough, but worn by a decade of neglect, just like the rest of the small structure.

Vivienne slid from the stallion's back, her movements stiff. Kieran swung down after her, but when his feet hit the ground, the whole world seemed to sway and tilt. Suddenly he was toppling into Vivienne, his weight nearly knocking her to the ground.

"Easy," she said, struggling to keep him upright. He fumbled for the saddle's pommel, anchoring himself even as the world continued to spin.

Her bonny face, drawn with worry, swam before him.

"We need to get that arrow out of you."

He barely suppressed a wince at the mere thought. Aye, it had to be done, else there was no hope of remaining in the land of the living to ensure Vivienne's safety.

At his grunt, she wedged herself under his good shoulder and guided him toward the door. She had to throw her weight against it before it opened with a groan of distended wood and a squeal of rusty hinges.

From the look of things inside, not a soul had set foot in the cottage since Kieran had abandoned it. The wooden table and chairs still sat off to the left near the empty hearth. A few of the cupboard doors hung open along the back wall, but naught seemed to have been touched. The straw-filled mattress pushed into the far right corner was in bad shape, but the wooden bedstead beneath it looked sturdy enough.

Dried leaves and twigs had collected in several corners, and there was a puddle in the middle of the floor where the thatch roof had leaked. A few moths fluttered through the open shutter at their entrance, but at least there were no signs that rats—or worse—had taken up residence in the cottage.

With Vivienne's help, he stumbled to one of the chairs and lowered himself with a muffled groan.

"I should see to the horse," he muttered, trying to rise almost immediately.

"*Non*," she said firmly. "I'll do that later."

He must have been even weaker than he'd

thought, for he didn't argue. "There is a barn on the north side of the clearing. And a stream running behind it."

She nodded, then hesitated. "I...I don't know how to remove the arrow," she said, her brows creased with concern as she eyed his shoulder. Her hand drifted to her mouth and she took her fingernail between her teeth before pulling it away abruptly.

"Dinnae fash. I'll talk ye through it." That was, if he could maintain his threadbare grip on consciousness. "Can ye carry our saddlebags inside, lass?"

"*Oui.*"

She hurried out of the cottage, returning a few moments later with one of the heavy leather bags held awkwardly in her arms, the other in tow behind her. She struggled inside, managing to avoid the puddle in the middle of the cottage before her strength gave out and she dropped them both.

"Pull out that skin of whisky I packed." He'd had the wisdom to refill his waterskin at the palace in Scone, yet he'd meant to savor it over the sennights they were to remain here. But desperate times called for desperate measures.

As Vivienne approached with the skin, he removed the dagger from his boot and extended it toward her.

"Ye'll have to cut away my shirt."

As she began gingerly slicing at the linen, which was stained and stiffened with his dried blood, he took a long pull of whisky. The burn down his throat and into his stomach was a welcome distraction from the throbbing pain in his shoulder.

When the last scraps of his shirt lay at his feet, he took one more swig and reluctantly handed it to her.

"Pour some of that over the wound."

His shoulder exploded in fire when the whisky hit it. He hissed every curse he knew through gritted teeth, squeezing his eyes closed for a long moment.

"I'm sorry to hurt you," Vivienne breathed, handing back the skin.

"Nay, lass, ye didnae," he lied. "It's just a bloody shame to waste such fine whisky."

She exhaled a weak chuckle, but then sobered as she fixed him with a tense gaze. "What now?"

"Ye willnae be able to pull it out without the arrowhead doing far more damage. Ye'll have to push it through."

Confusion and disbelief widened her dark eyes. "But—"

Taking her wrist, he guided the point of the dagger to the front of his shoulder. Holding her there for a moment, he splashed more whisky over his unbroken skin and the tip of the blade, muttering about the proper uses for good Highland whisky.

He could feel her hand shaking beneath his. "It's all right, lass," he rasped, giving her a reassuring squeeze. Then without preamble, he plunged the dagger into his shoulder, giving it a twist for good measure.

Her horrified gasp reached him distantly through the ringing in his ears. He withdrew the dagger and released her trembling hand. She stared at her fingertips, which were tinged red with his blood, before lifting wide, midnight eyes to him.

"Now," he said through gritted teeth, "push it out."

Shifting the bloodied dagger to her other hand, she reached out tentatively and touched the wound on his back. He locked his jaw to prevent from growling.

She drew a deep breath, and suddenly he was engulfed in pain again as she pushed against the sawed-off end of the arrow shaft.

The damn thing was buried so deep that in a single heartbeat the arrowhead was already emerging, slick and bloody, from the cut he'd made in the front. When the tip thrust out of his skin, he snatched it and yanked it free in one swift motion.

He gulped lungfuls of air as his head swam, darkness encroaching on his vision. "Now the whisky again," he ground out, handing her the skin.

When she poured more of the spirit into the open wound, both front and back, he roared in agony. He slumped forward in his chair for a long moment afterwards.

"Now I need to stitch you up, *oui*?" Vivienne asked.

"Aye."

He didn't have the wherewithal to say more, but luckily she seemed to know what to do now. She rummaged through her saddlebags until she came across a mending kit with needle and thread. After quickly dipping the needle into the whisky, she threaded it and held it poised over his shoulder.

"Do the front first," he managed. His last shreds of control were slipping, and he feared if she started with the raw, angry wound on his back, unconsciousness would claim him before he could get to the bed.

Vivienne drew in another steeling breath, moving around to eye the cut on the front of his shoulder. "It is no different than the needlework I've done all my life," she murmured to herself.

Kieran grunted. "Aye, but remember that I am no' some scrap of silk for ye to embroider."

He earned a smile for his gruff comment, which distracted him from most of the pain as she carefully stitched closed the exit wound. Still, as she tied off the last stitch, he was so woozy that he felt like he'd drunk the entire skin of whisky. If only.

"Ye'd best help me to the bed before ye finish," he said. "Unless ye want to drag me there."

He pushed himself up with a hand on the table, then leaned against her as he stumbled toward the bed. He eyed the ragged, damp straw mattress dubiously, then decided even fevered and injured, it would be better to sleep on the bare wooden slats beneath.

He grabbed the mattress with one hand and tugged it free of the bedstead, dropping it on the floor. Vivienne hurried to their bags once more, removing several extra lengths of plaid. She laid one over the bedstead's slats and piled the others at the bottom to be used as blankets.

There was no more putting it off now. She took up the needle once more and he turned to give her the back of his shoulder. As she carefully closed the raw, burning wound, his vision began to blur.

He fought against the darkness, unwilling to leave Vivienne alone in this isolated wilderness to fend for herself, but it was a losing battle. As she tied the last stitch and pinched off the remaining thread, he collapsed onto the bed.

His last thought before unconsciousness swallowed him was that he was supposed to be looking after her, but he was damn lucky she was looking after him, too.

Chapter Twenty-Six

W hen Kieran's big, powerful body folded like a rag doll onto the bed, Vivienne feared the worst.

She pressed a hand to his damp brow. His fever raged, but his pulse still beat strongly at the base of his throat. She rolled him onto his good shoulder and pulled one of his plaids over his bare chest, tucking another one under his head.

Fear began to squeeze her throat and compress her chest as she stared down at him, but she couldn't succumb to it. There were so many things to do, and Kieran would be awake and on the mend in no time. She couldn't let him down by wallowing in doubt and distress.

The dilapidated hut needed a great deal of work, but the steadfast, unwavering horse that had carried them here deserved her attention first.

She went outside to find him munching on the overgrown weeds that filled the cleared section of forest. Taking his bridle with a soothing word, she guided him across the clearing toward a small wooden barn tucked against the tree line. Just as Kieran had said, a stream ran behind the barn. She let the animal drink while she washed the blood from her hands, trying to ignore their shaking as she did.

Then she led him back toward the barn, letting him chew on the tall grasses again while she struggled to remove his heavy leather saddle. She dragged the saddle to the barn and pulled back the door, peering inside.

The faint, familiar scents of hay and manure still lingered in the barn, but the small handful of stalls had been swept clean as if someone had cleared out long ago, never to return. She retrieved the stallion and guided him into one of the stalls, leaving him to rest after their trying journey.

Now it was time to tackle the hut itself. She started with the outside, propping the skewed shutter into place by wedging a rock between it and the windowsill. There was nothing she'd be able do about the leaking roof, so she went inside to face what she could.

She rummaged through the cupboards, finding them mostly empty except for a hodgepodge assortment of clay bowls, a few cups, and two iron pots. She positioned one of the pots over the puddle, hoping the water that had already dripped inside would dry and the pot would catch any new leaks.

She also found a bucket, which she carried back to the stream and filled. Once she'd tottered back to the hut and set the water aside, it was time to tackle their bags.

Unpacking gave her a chance to inventory all they possessed. Besides, she had to believe that they would be staying here indefinitely—that they were safe here. And that Kieran would wake soon and be pleased to find that she'd gotten them settled.

Luckily, the cook at Scone Palace had sent them off with more than enough food. Vivienne stashed the satchel full of oatcakes, dried meat, apples, a wrapped wheel of hard cheese, and a few autumn root vegetables in one of the cupboards. Then she folded their few items of clothing and tucked them, along with all the other items in the bags, into a lower cabinet.

From the crack in the shutters, she could tell that it was growing dark outside. She could gather a bundle of dry twigs or mayhap stalks of tall grasses to make a broom to clear out the leaves and debris in the corners, but that would have to wait until daylight.

As would seeing about a fire. It had been years since she'd lain and lit her own fire, but she knew enough to be wary of the clearly neglected hearth. If there was a bird's nest or squirrel's den blocking the chimney, she just might manage to kill them both from the smoke alone if she attempted to light a fire there.

Which meant she'd done all that she could for now. Her gaze landed on Kieran, and the fear she'd been so valiantly holding at bay suddenly seized her by the throat.

Never had she been so profoundly on her own. Even when society had turned its back on her for her indiscretion with Guy, she'd still had her father to help her find her way back. But now she was completely alone in the middle of the Highland wilds, with no one to watch over her.

Non, that wasn't true, for even with him lying unconscious before her, she could still hear Kieran's gruff command that she keep hold of her composure, could imagine those steely blue eyes leveling her with a piercing stare. Perhaps she was capable of far more, even on her own, than she'd ever imagined.

Still, she had been strong for so long. She was tired, and so very scared for Kieran. She lowered herself onto the edge of the bed, watching him draw the slow breaths of deep slumber. When the first tears pricked her eyes, she gave over to them, sinking down beside him.

Please let him heal, she prayed as she dragged another plaid over them both and muffled her sobs with her hand. *Please*.

THE MOMENT the light from the torch flickered behind his eyelids, William de Soules jerked up from his cot and bolted to the bars to wait for Bevin's arrival.

With his transfer to Dumbarton Castle's dungeon coming in a matter of hours, he'd feared Bevin wouldn't return in time. But now that the hulking brute lumbered toward him, William's heart leapt in giddy anticipation.

"What news?" he whispered the moment Bevin reached his cell. "Is the bitch dead?"

Foreboding stole up William's spine when Bevin hesitated, his eyes fixed on the damp stone floor.

"Nay, sire."

It took all his control not to howl in rage and frustration. Only the knowledge that Agnes of Strathearn would be roused in the next cell kept him from screaming.

"*What. Happened.*"

Bevin's coarse brow lifted pleadingly. "I did as ye said, sire. I hired mercenaries—the best to be had on such short notice. We tracked them outside of Scone and attacked. But the Highlander prevented us from getting to the woman. He took an arrow, but they rode off before we could finish them."

"How could ye let them escape?" William hissed. "Did ye track them?"

"Aye, sire, but their horses separated, and we lost them as they entered the Highlands. We havenae given up," Bevin added hurriedly. "Two of the men are still searching. The other two returned with me."

William sagged against the bars, the air whooshing from his lungs. What could he possibly hope would happen even if the mercenaries did manage to find MacAdams and Vivienne now? The Highlander had already bested them once—and that had been against five men, not two.

He'd been so close to victory against the French whore. St. Giles should have been able to kill her, but even after his failure, William had been given a second chance. She'd been only a few paces above him in the palace, Devil take it!

And now she'd slipped through his grasp yet again. She was somewhere in the Highlands with that barbarian MacAdams, and William would be sent to Dumbarton come morning, left to rot far away from Scone…

A mad idea began to form in the dark corners of his mind. He straightened, clutching the bars to keep himself upright as his thoughts swirled wildly.

"…would ye have us do, sire?" Bevin was asking. "If the others find her—"

"Shut yer mouth, ye fool," he breathed, "and let me think."

Aye, aye, the pieces were beginning to come together. If he wanted something done right, he could no longer entrust it to others. He had to do it himself.

"The guards informed me no' long ago that I would be transferred to Dumbarton Castle's dungeon for the rest of my days come morning," William said. "Which means ye only have a few hours to gather all the men ye can."

"I dinnae underst—"

William reached through the bars and closed his hand over Bevin's throat, squeezing until the big brute wheezed. "This isnae complicated," he said through clenched teeth. "Find all those who remain loyal to me and follow my escort when we leave Scone."

Bevin held up a hand in surrender. William released him, and the thick-skulled oaf rubbed his throat for a long moment before speaking.

"I-I have made inquiries, sire. Even before ye had me go after the woman, I have been searching, but…"

Bevin swallowed hard. "But no one is willing to stand with ye."

The words hit him like a kick to the gut. William exhaled sharply. Here he was, thinking himself a symbol of the uprising to unseat Robert the Bruce from the throne and restore order to Scotland under England's control once more, when the truth was, even his lowest allies had abandoned him.

"They all saw what happened to the others," Bevin went on. "If the Bruce was willing to hang nobles, imagine what he'd do to untitled men like me." He licked his lips, his gaze imploring. "Please, sire, dinnae dwell on it. Ye still have me. Tell me what to do and I'll do it."

Aye, he had thick-headed, bumbling Bevin's loyalty, but only because William held the man's life in his hands with the secret he knew. If the brute hadn't been a murdering rapist, he would desert William just like the others.

He gripped the bars until his knuckles blanched in the flickering torchlight. Nay, he would not give up now. He could not die in the pit of Dumbarton, abandoned and alone, and let the French bitch win.

His plan could still work, even without the support of his former allies.

"Use the rest of the coin," he said quietly. "All of it. Hire as many mercenaries as ye can."

Bevin nodded vigorously. "What shall I have them do, sire?"

"They are going to help me escape."

Bevin's eyes widened, but William went on, his

tongue barely keeping up with the rush of his thoughts. "Aye, ye'll attack the convoy taking me to Dumbarton. Then we'll head north to find the two men tracking Vivienne."

His heart hammered wildly against his ribs at the thought. Oh aye, he would get to hunt her down himself after all. He would be the one to take her life. But first, he would make her suffer as he had at her hand.

"If aught should happen to separate us when ye attack the convoy, we will meet on Ailsa Craig," William went on. "Ye ken the island?"

Bevin nodded again.

"Good."

With all that had gone wrong for him thus far, William would be a fool not to have a secondary plan, but he prayed he wouldn't need it. Of course, his escape from the Bruce's clutches would be a great coup, yet what he burned for more than anything was to have the French whore in his grasp.

"Good," he murmured again to himself, anticipation squeezing his chest.

Vivienne would be his at last.

Chapter Twenty-Seven

Kieran was hot. But not the hazy, aching burn of a fever. It was more the toasty heat of several layers of wool.

And a warm body pressed against him.

He cracked an eye to find midday light streaming through a gap in the shutters. He lay on his side, with Vivienne's golden head tucked beneath his chin. She curled into him, her legs intertwined with his and her hand tucked against his bare chest.

For a long moment, he didn't remember where he was or how he'd gotten there. All he knew was that Vivienne was in his arms, her delicate scent of violets and woman's skin enveloping him, her touch warm and soft.

Well, she was in *one* of his arms. He had a hand snaked underneath her and around her back, holding her close, but his top arm lay stiff and still against his side.

Recollection crashed over him like a breaking wave.

The attack. Their flight into the Highlands. Her careful ministrations and his collapse into unconsciousness.

She must have crawled alongside him on the bedstead, exhaustion dragging her into a deep slumber. They'd been awake for two days, unable to do more than nod off briefly atop his stallion. And she'd been left with the burden of looking after him for the last... He had no idea how long he'd been out, but it must have been at least a full day judging by the light filtering into the cottage.

He shifted slightly, careful not to disturb her. He needed to get a better look at her, to reassure himself that she was well even though he'd failed to look after her in his injured, fever-addled state.

Her delicate features were smooth with the peace of sleep, yet he noticed dried tear tracks cutting through the smudges of dirt on her cheeks. He silently cursed himself for allowing her to come to any distress under his watch. Hell, they'd both been damn close to losing their lives to their attackers—they had to be de Soules's lackeys, for who else would target her so single-mindedly? He could never let danger get so near again.

He must have tensed, for she stirred, her brows furrowing for a moment before she slowly blinked. The breath caught in his lungs as eyes darker and more dazzling than the finest sapphires met his.

"You are awake." Her voice was thick with sleep and confusion. Then her eyes widened. She snatched her hand from between them and placed her palm against his forehead. "And the fever has broken."

"A wonder what sleep—and whisky—will do," he

murmured, giving her a lopsided smile. "I feel much better."

He rolled his shoulder experimentally, and though the skin felt tender where the arrow had pierced him and pinched from the stitches, it no longer throbbed with his pulse.

Vivienne lifted her head and peered at the shuttered window. "It is past midday!" she exclaimed, tossing back the plaids covering them.

He caught her waist with his good hand, stilling her. "Be easy. These last few days have been hell." He lifted his fingers to the dried tear tracks on her cheeks and gently brushed them. "And ye have borne a great deal."

Her eyes flashed with embarrassment and she scrubbed her palms over her face, wiping away the dirt and the remnants of her tears. "I…I was worried about you."

Hell and damnation, he would be ruined if she kept looking shyly at him like that under her lashes. Her flaxen hair was tousled from sleep, her cheeks and lips rosy.

She'd worried over him. And from the deepening color in her face, it wasn't simply because she'd nearly lost her bodyguard yesterday.

Though he knew it was wrong, his heart swelled at the thought of gaining her trust, her affection. Aye, desire flared between them, as bright and undeniable as the sun. But a traitorous voice in the back of his mind whispered that he wanted so much more.

"Careful, lass," he murmured, his lips quirking. "Else ye'll make me think ye dinnae loathe me quite as much as ye'd have me believe." When she opened her mouth for a retort, he quickly added, "Och, dinnae fash. Remember, I dinnae mind ye overmuch, either."

Damn him, he was a bloody fool for teasing her. The bonny blush that stole over her face made her look all the more delectable. What was worse, in echoing the words he'd spoken to her at her father's estate, he was coming dangerously close to confessing something he shouldn't.

If he were honest with himself, he'd have to admit that the sweet ache in his heart had become stronger than the heat in his veins. He couldn't deny it—he already cared deeply for her. But caring was complicated. And dangerous.

Lust, on the other hand, was simple. Straightforward. They'd already acknowledged their desire for one another—and acted on it. Surrendering to it again would be easy given the fire of need that was burning him from the inside out at the moment. Far better than admitting the truth in his heart.

Shoving aside all rational thought, he leaned forward and kissed her soft, petal-pink lips. She pulled in a surprised breath, giving him access to the warm recesses of her mouth.

When their tongues met, she melted back onto the plaid beneath them, one hand sliding around his neck to tangle in his hair.

Sensation shot through him at her touch—straight to his cock, which already stood painfully erect beneath his kilt. He growled, sinking his teeth into her bottom lip to show her how he hungered for her.

Damn all the layers of wool separating them. At least he was shirtless. Her dress rasped against his bare skin as she arched into him. Beneath, he could feel the soft swells of her breasts, needy for his touch, his kiss.

She sighed as he delved deeper into her mouth, their tongues tangling in an erotic preview of what he longed to do with the rest of their bodies.

He rolled on top of her, but when he took some of his weight onto his elbow, his injured shoulder barked in protest. He winced and sucked in a breath.

Vivienne froze beneath him, her eyes flying open.

"We cannot."

"Och, aye, we can," he countered, sending her a smoldering look. "There is naught wrong with my cock, I assure ye."

"You are injured. You need to rest and heal." To prove her point, she placed a single finger on his wounded shoulder and pressed lightly.

The dull ache there turned into a quick flash of pain. He rolled onto his side with a curse, bested by her delicate touch. She took the opportunity to scramble up, straightening her gown modestly.

In truth, she was right that he needed to let his shoulder mend and get his strength up, but the fact was, too much needed doing around the crumbling cottage for him to lie back at his leisure.

Kieran exhaled. "Rest may have to wait. I need to tend to the horse and see what can be done about the leaking roof. This is October in the Highlands, after all —rain isnae a question of if but when and how much."

"But I've already done that."

Confused, he propped himself up with his good arm and frowned at her.

"I saw to the horse last eve after you passed out," she went on. "He is in the barn, though he will likely wish to be let out to graze in the clearing." She tapped a finger to her lips in consideration, then moved to where her boots sat at the foot of the bed.

"But ye couldnae have fixed the roof," he said, eyeing her incredulously.

She waved with one hand as she pulled on a boot. "*Non*, of course not, but I think my solution will have to do for now."

The clever lass had put out a pot to collect the drip, allowing the puddle beneath it to dry.

"The food is just there," she continued, pointing toward one of the cupboards. "And the rest of our things are below. I can help you get into a new shirt if you like, but first I think you had better drink and eat something."

He noticed the full bucket of water in the corner and couldn't help but gawk. "Ye...ye did all this while I was sleeping?" he murmured. "On yer own?"

"*Oui.*"

By God, this woman never ceased to surprise—and impress—him. She was a lady-in-waiting for the bloody Queen of France, for heaven's sake. When was the last time she'd had to tend a horse, or carry water, or come up with a solution for a leaking thatch roof?

Yet she'd done all that—after removing an arrow from his shoulder and stitching up the wound.

"Ye...ye are..." He shook his head. "I've never kenned a woman like ye, Vivienne."

A slow, radiant smile broke over her face before she regained her matter-of-fact air. "Let me fetch us something to eat, then I'll see to the horse."

She set about her task, moving gracefully through the small, dilapidated cottage as if it were the King of France's palace. Kieran sat in silent wonderment, his chest swelling nigh painfully.

He'd forgotten just how damn good it felt to let someone look after him, to give him attention and care.

And how good it felt to wake up with a woman in his arms. But not just any woman.

Vivienne.

Hell and damnation. Aye, he was indeed in danger. But worse, he no longer wanted to keep himself safe.

Chapter Twenty-Eight

"Let me do that, lass."

Vivienne scurried out of Kieran's reach, which was hard given how small the cottage was in relation to the long span of his arms.

"*Non*. You already have your hands full with your task, *Monsieur* MacAdams," she retorted teasingly.

He growled in response to her faux primness, leveling her with a cool blue glower. Still, he settled back onto the bedstead and lifted her book before his face once more, leaving her to finish chopping the vegetables that would go into their stew.

A smile tugged at her lips as she chopped to the sound of his deep, gruff brogue reciting the chivalric tale. He was accompanied by the soft ping of the drip from the roof into the pot on the floor. A gentle rain had been falling all day, yet the inside of the cottage was cozy, somehow made even more so by the soothing rhythm of the drip.

How things had changed since their frantic arrival at the isolated hut. These last five days had been some of the most idyllic Vivienne had ever experienced.

For the first two days, Vivienne had insisted that Kieran remain in bed. The straw mattress hadn't been salvageable, so she'd dragged it behind the cottage to be dealt with later, but the bare wooden slats of the bedstead had been made into a cozy nest of woolen plaids.

Soon, though, he'd declared that there was naught wrong with his legs, and had risen to survey the cottage, the clearing, and the barn. Still, without the use of his right arm, he was limited in what he could do. Vivienne didn't mind, however, for she was becoming quite adept at running the little cottage on her own.

They'd subsisted thus far on the food stores they'd brought from Scone, but with Kieran's instructions on what to look for, Vivienne had gathered the last late-season berries and root vegetables from the surrounding woods.

Today she was determined to give them more than hard oatcakes and dried meat to eat. She dropped a handful sliced turnips and carrots into the iron pot—more of a caldron, for it was round-bellied and had a handle for hanging over the fire—that rested on the table beside her.

Blessedly, they were able to light a fire in the hearth. With the weather growing colder and a plenti-tude of cracks and gaps letting frosty air into the cottage, Vivienne had tentatively sparked a few dried bark shavings using Kieran's flint stones and held her breath as she waited to see if the smoke filled the cottage.

To her relief, it had drawn straight up the chimney without spewing any back into the room, indicating that the chimney was clear. With Kieran unable to chop wood—and without an axe to do so anyway—Vivienne had gathered fallen twigs and branches behind the cottage, and every evening they'd had a small but cheery fire.

And when the fire had gone out each night, they stayed toasty by curling up together underneath the plaids. It was for warmth only, she'd told herself firmly, for Kieran was still on the mend. The truth was, she felt drawn to him like a moth to fire. But just like the moth that got too close, she feared she had already been singed beyond repair.

Oui, their lust for each other burned hot—perhaps even hotter in these last few days because they'd denied themselves pleasure while Kieran healed. But the raging passion between them did not explain the way Vivienne's stomach fluttered at the mere sound of his voice, or the warmth in her chest at his simple nearness.

She'd fancied herself in love with Guy once, but now she realized she'd only felt a childish infatuation for him. She'd liked his extravagant words of praise and the elegant way he rode his horse, but that wasn't love. She hadn't even truly known him—his thin façade concealed no greater depths or deeper emotions.

Perhaps it hadn't even been an infatuation with Guy, but with the picture of *herself* he'd painted and held before her. She'd wanted to believe Guy loved her too, but none of it had been real, for he hadn't known her either.

Kieran, on the other hand, had seen sides of her that no one—not even her father or the Queen—had witnessed. He'd seen her be strong, and vulnerable, and frightened. He'd seen her stripped bare of her finery, her frosty composure, and her control, yet he accepted it all with grace and ease. Well, more like with a grunt, a scowl, and a blunt word or two, but she'd learned that was as close to grace and ease as Kieran got.

Vivienne realized belatedly that her hands had stilled in their chopping and Kieran's voice had stopped. She looked up to find him eyeing her keenly over the top of the book.

"Where did ye just wander off to?"

"Oh, nowhere." She hurriedly dropped the rest of the vegetables into the caldron and began cutting up the dried, salted meat they'd brought from Scone.

"Dinnae fash, lass. I cannae take offense if ye find my reading horrendous. Besides, how many times have ye heard this tale? More than a hundred, I'd wager."

It was true, she'd heard it countless times, and Kieran did still read with halting slowness, but he was utterly wrong about the reason her attention had drifted.

"I *like* hearing you read it," she blurted, feeling heat climb into her face. "It makes the story different some-how, more…compelling." Oh, she was making a fool of herself now. She swallowed, pretending to be engrossed in chopping the meat. "Besides, it is a pleasure to be read to, don't you think?"

Out of the corner of her eye, she saw the sides of his

mouth lift. "Yer and my idea of *pleasure* is a wee bit different, lass."

Now her face would surely go up in flames for how hot it was. Luckily, he took pity on her and went on in a safer direction.

"That juniper, for example," he said, pointing at the little bundle of sprigs she'd gathered and put into a tall cup on the table. "Ye say it is for enjoyment, but it doesnae serve any purpose."

She resisted the unladylike urge to roll her eyes. "Oh, it serves a purpose," she countered tartly. "The juniper smells lovely, and a bit of greenery indoors is pleasing to the eye."

He set the book aside and crossed his arms—as best he could given the fact that his shoulder was still healing. "Hmph." He eyed her grudgingly, but then relented. "I suppose I can admit that having a woman's touch around this place is agreeable enough. It hasnae had it since—"

He cut off abruptly, his frown deepening.

"Since your mother passed away?" she offered hesitantly. Once the terror of their flight from their attackers had waned and she'd had time to consider how they'd reached this place, she'd realized that the cottage wasn't just a lucky find. "This is your family's home, is it not?"

His eyes flickered with surprise, then tightened with pain. "Aye."

"And you thought to bring me here to keep me safe."

He exhaled wryly. "Ye've seen for yerself how isolated we are here. I dinnae even ken if my own clan knows this plot of land exists."

He waved a hand over the sparse interior of the cottage. "When I decided to join the Bruce's cause, I sold off our animals—we had a few goats and pigs as well as a draft horse—along with all the tools and almost everything else. From the way the tradesmen were staring at me in the nearest village, I imagine they thought me a wild barbarian come down from the mountains, no' a fellow MacAdams who'd been working the land all his life."

Vivienne smiled softly. "And you've never returned in all the time you've been gone?"

"No' since I walked away when I was but twenty years old," he replied, his gaze drifting to the fire that crackled in the hearth. "I wasnae sure what to do with the place, in truth. What with it being my family's land, it seemed wrong to sell it. Yet I couldnae stay anymore, so I simply sealed everything up and left. That was ten long years past."

A memory of his earlier words pricked the back of her mind. She pursed her lips, confusion tugging at her.

"You mentioned before that you came into this land when you were eighteen," she said.

"Aye."

"But you also said that you left to join the Bruce's cause immediately after you inherited this stead," she went on, cocking her head. "That leaves two years unaccounted for."

He tensed, and his features went hard as if they were a stone wall—sealing her out.

"Aye, well, mayhap it took a bit longer to clear out of this place than I said before."

He fell quiet, apparently ending that line of conversation, but Vivienne couldn't help but feel unsettled. The tickle of apprehension in the back of her mind and the gnaw of unease in her stomach told her that he was keeping something from her. But Kieran wasn't a man to be forced into opening up, so she didn't press.

After a moment of laden silence, Kieran picked up the book again and resumed reading. As Vivienne dropped the meat into the caldron and brought over the bucket to add water, the comfortable, relaxed air she'd felt earlier began returning.

Kieran stopped reading abruptly with a sigh, drawing her out of her contented lull.

"I'm glad ye like my reading, lass, but this isnae my strong suit." He was frowning at her over the top of the book. "I'm simply no' made to sit abed all day like a wee old biddy."

A surprised laugh bubbled up in her throat. It was true, her delicate, finely made book looked preposterously out of place in his big, gnarled hands. And though she very much enjoyed the sight of him partially reclined in the bed, his large, powerful frame was simply not meant to lie in repose all day.

"Dinnae ye have something else for me to do?" he asked, setting aside her book once more. "Something to lift or move or…or smash?"

Now she was laughing hard enough to put a stitch in her side. "*Non*, I'm afraid not," she breathed through her mirth.

She took up the caldron's handle to move the stew to the fire. But the caldron, which had already been heavy enough to give her a little trouble when it had been empty, was now even heavier with the added water. The caldron tipped precariously on the edge of the table, threatening to spill the entire uncooked stew.

Like a bolt of lightning, Kieran shot from the bed to her side, grabbing the caldron's handle and righting the liquid inside.

"Och, this is something I can help with," he said, lifting the iron caldron with his good arm as if it weighed naught more than an empty basket.

He strode to the fire, easily placing the caldron on the hook over the flames.

Vivienne couldn't help it. Her cheeks warmed at his show of strength and the easy power in his body as he turned and walked back to her.

"Ye shouldnae have to be doing any of this, lass." He halted before her with a frown. "I should."

Unexpectedly, she bristled at that. "Why? Because you do not think me capable?"

"Nay, it isnae that," he replied with a definitive shake of his head. "Ye've more than proven ye are capable of aught these past five days. But I dinnae like seeing ye struggle under these lowly burdens."

He stilled, his pale eyes intent and penetrating as he fixed her with a stare. "Ye are the sort of woman who should be pampered, Vivienne. If I had my way, ye wouldnae ever have to lift a finger for such menial tasks."

"Oh?" she breathed, her pulse quickening as he swept her slowly with his gaze. "Then what would I do all day?"

"Och, lass," he rasped, his voice low and drawn. "All ye should ever have to do is lie back and be pleasured."

He slowly dipped his head until his lips were only a hair's breadth from hers, but then he halted, teasing her with his nearness as if to challenge her resolve.

But Vivienne had already admitted defeat against her desire for him. She rocked forward, their lips connecting in a searing kiss.

Chapter Twenty-Nine

Kieran's pulse spiked hard when Vivienne's lips met his. Aye, she wanted this as badly as he did.

That knowledge nearly made him push her against the nearest wall, yank up her skirts, and thrust into her possessively. She was his, damn it.

But nay, he'd offered her far more pleasure that a swift swiving against the wall. He would take his time and make sure she knew he'd meant every word.

He deepened their kiss, mating his tongue with hers in a slow promise of what was to come. She sighed into his mouth, making the skin on the back of his neck prickle in anticipation and his cock stiffen beneath his kilt.

He began backing her toward the table, wicked plans taking shape in his mind. Oh, there was so much he wanted to do to her, but he was already weakened by his own raging need. He could only hope to show her just how serious he was about pleasuring her before he came undone himself.

She gasped when her legs bumped into the table. Without breaking their kiss, he hoisted her onto its edge, but when her hands came down on his shoulders to steady herself, he winced and muttered a curse.

Vivienne pulled back reluctantly. "We shouldn't," she breathed, eyeing his injured shoulder with worry. "You aren't well enough yet."

Like hell he wasn't. The slight discomfort from her touch had already faded—and it was naught compared to the aching need beneath his kilt.

"Let me show ye just how well I am recovering," he rasped, capturing her mouth with his once more. He took her wrist and guided her hand to his cock, which strained against the scratchy wool of his plaid.

She pulled in a breath as her hand encountered the hard, thick length of him. "Aye," he growled. "It isnae my shoulder that needs relief."

Her lips curled into a coy grin before he reclaimed them with his own. He kissed her until she was sighing and reaching for him once more. This time she threaded her arms around his neck, lacing her fingers in his hair.

He groaned his approval, his own hand tangling in the tresses at the nape of her neck. He tilted her head back and kissed a path down her throat to the top of her dress.

"Blasted clothes," he muttered at the offending garment.

He reached behind her and began fumbling with the laces running down her back. When they loosened, he tugged on the material at her shoulders, working the gown away from her chemise.

She shimmied to allow him to pull the wool over her hips and down her legs, all the while remaining perched on the table's edge. As he reached for her chemise, she pulled his shirt free of his belt, sliding her hands up his sides slowly.

He had to pause in his efforts to disrobe her when it came time to pull his injured shoulder free of his shirt, but the faint twinge of pain was quickly subsumed by the need coursing through him.

When at last he'd glided her linen chemise down and tossed it aside, he let himself feast on the sight of her. She hadn't bothered to plait her hair that morn, so it hung in long, flaxen waves around her. Her lips were already rosy and damp from his kiss, and they parted on a breath as she gazed up at him. Her depthless blue eyes were dark and hooded with desire.

Taking her shoulders, he eased her back onto the table so that she lay sprawled before him. Hell and damnation, she looked more delectable than the finest meal he'd ever seen splayed out on the table like that. Her skin was all berries and cream, her lithe, slim limbs and delicious curves mouth-wateringly tempting.

Unable to hold back any longer, he leaned over the table and flicked his tongue over one pearled, petal-pink nipple. Her back arched off the table in invitation, her breath catching in her throat as he teased the peak. He shifted his ministrations to her other breast, the sound of his own blood hammering in his ears mingling with her moans and gasps of pleasure.

When she was writhing beneath him, her legs falling open of their own accord, he trailed a path of kisses down her flat stomach. He ached with the craving to pleasure her with his mouth, but he wanted to draw out her anticipation.

His lips found first one of her soft, creamy thighs and then the other, dropping kisses on each. He dragged his teeth over the sensitive skin there, moving ever closer to her womanhood.

But soon he could take no more of torturing her, or himself. He found her center, kissing her deeply.

When his mouth closed on her, she bowed off the table with a strangled moan. God, he loved the taste of her, all earth and woman and something that was uniquely Vivienne. He licked and teased her, bringing forth passionate gasps from her and then backing off, letting her catch her breath.

Soon her legs were trembling with need, his name on her lips in a plea for release. Just as her breath began to hitch toward ecstasy, he pulled back.

"Nay, no' yet, lass," he growled. "I want to be inside ye when ye come."

He rose up from his knees, making quick work of his belt buckle. When it snapped free, his kilt slid down his legs and pooled at his feet.

She lifted her head from the table, her eyes sparking with passion as her gaze devoured him. Her breath came short with expectancy as he stepped between her open legs and positioned himself at her entrance, holding her eyes with his.

He took her slowly, savoring the sounds of her

panting moans despite the raging need to thrust deep and hard. Once he was buried to the hilt inside her, he halted, still holding their stare.

Joined as one, she bared herself to him, revealing the contours of her soul—her strength, her vulnerability, the secret heart that she so often kept guarded. And he bared himself as well, unshuttering his eyes and lowering the wall around himself.

Something expanded in his chest, a stuttering and seizing that had naught to do with lust or bodily desire. He'd thought he knew what affection felt like, but this went far beyond the comfortable warmth and contentedness he'd experienced before. He might as well have been shot with an arrow again, but this time straight through the heart.

Vivienne moved beneath him, rolling her hips in a wordless entreaty. Lust hammered him, yet he could not lose himself solely in physical sensation anymore. Nay, his desire was entwined with the aching need in his chest, which he saw mirrored in Vivienne's dark, defenseless eyes.

He began to rock in and out of her, feeling her shuddering pleasure as his own as they moved as one.

"Kieran," she moaned, a half-plea, half-prayer.

The last shreds of his control slipped through his fingers at that. He thrust hard now, unable to hold off any longer. She lifted her hips, taking him fully. Her breasts bounced with his rhythm, taunting him with their lush sway and the pink tips he'd tasted earlier.

Suddenly she cried out, shattering in ecstasy. It was the most beautiful thing he'd ever seen—her face flushed with passion, her breasts arched into the air, her lithe legs trembling around his hips.

He felt his own release surging over him and began to pull away, but Vivienne hooked her feet behind his back, halting him.

"*Non*, don't," she breathed, her eyes locking with his. "Stay inside me."

His breath hitched in his lungs. He didn't have time to contemplate all that it would mean between them, all that could come, for some primal instinct in him wanted this just as she did.

With a swift nod, he buried himself inside her once more. With two more thrusts, he came undone, the force of his release wringing her name from his lips.

As the last shudders receded, he folded possessively over her, catching himself on his good elbow.

Sometime later, he scooped her up and carried her to their nest of plaids on the bedstead, then fetched them each a bowl of the now-hot stew. He couldn't help but swell with pride to feel her eyes following his naked form as he moved about the cottage, or to catch her staring and blushing when he turned to hand her a bowl.

The rain must have stopped, for water no longer dripped through the roof, making the cottage quiet except for the soft crackle of the fire. They ate in silence, for which Kieran was grateful. His mind churned with tangled thoughts, but more than that, his heart twisted strangely.

He couldn't deny it anymore. Something had passed

between them, *grown* between them, changing him down to his very soul.

The longer he sat with it, the more it worried him. Hadn't he been in this position before? And didn't he know what came next? Nay, he told himself, it had never been like this, but if his feelings were only more intense than they had once been, did that mean the inevitable pain and loss would be that much worse as well?

"What is wrong?"

Vivienne was looking at him with drawn brows. He realized he was frowning and clutching his bowl hard enough to make his knuckles white. He shook his head to clear it, but the thrumming in his heart—some mixture of longing and fear—continued. "Naught," he replied, then muttered, "naught that a wee dram of whisky wouldnae chase away."

"I'll fetch the skin," she said, setting her bowl aside and rising from the bed. He watched her move gracefully away, all soft curves and creamy skin, but she was more modest than he. She bent and retrieved her chemise, slipping it over her head before continuing on to the cupboards next to the table.

She opened one of the cupboard doors but apparently didn't find the skin, so she opened another, peering inside. "Where did I put it?" she muttered as she continued to search. She pulled open the last door and rose up on her toes to see the top shelf. "Ah, there—"

She reached up, but when she removed her hand, she held not only the waterskin, but also some small wooden object.

"What is this?" She held up the carved piece of

wood, turning it into the light of the fire for a closer look.

Kieran's stomach dropped even as his heart leapt into his throat. Over the roar of blood in his ears, he heard himself say, "It is a carved horse. A bairn's toy."

Vivienne blinked, then realization dawned across her face. "It...it must have been yours, *oui*? From when you were a child?"

Mayhap it was a sign that the time had finally come to tell her the truth. Aye, why else would she have found that forgotten hunk of wood he'd carved as a man of twenty, full of hope for the future? It was a perfectly timed reminder from fate of all he'd lost, and all he stood to lose again if he let anyone into his heart.

How could he have been such a fool? Hadn't he learned ten years past that loving was only an invitation for pain and suffering? How could he let himself hope, even in the most secret corner of his heart, that things could be different this time, that he could find ever-lasting happiness with Vivienne?

"Kieran?" Vivienne's soft, worried voice pulled him from his thoughts, but the darkness had already descended around him.

He should never have let himself care for her. He should never have lowered the wall around his heart.

It was too late, of course. Love throbbed like a pulse deep inside him. Yet the memory of emptiness, of utter isolation after Linette's death, clawed at him, making him wild to escape the same fate again. So he sealed his heart away behind cold stone, meeting Vivienne's eyes with a hardened stare.

"Nay," he ground out. "It wasnae mine, though I made it."

Vivienne's brow furrowed. She set aside the skin of whisky and looked at the carved horse, then back at Kieran.

"For whom?"

"For my bairn."

Chapter Thirty

Vivienne's breath stilled in her lungs. At Kieran's suddenly flat, hard stare, trepidation slithered up her spine.

"You have a child?"

"*Had.*"

The word was sharp and cold as a shard of ice. Before Vivienne could comprehend the depth of such a loss, Kieran went on.

"And a wife, too."

"You…" Vivienne swallowed hard, forcing down the panic rising in her throat. Kieran wasn't Guy, she reminded herself. He wouldn't hurt her like that. And she was not the other woman again. "You were married?"

"Aye. But she died, along with our unborn bairn."

"I-I don't understand," she began. "Why have you never mentioned either of them?"

He lifted one shoulder coolly. "What is there to tell? It is in the past now."

For all his sudden frostiness, it was obvious that something had abruptly shifted within him when she'd found the carved horse. When they'd made love, they'd been raw and vulnerable with each other. She'd seen the emotion burning in his eyes and had let herself believe that something far greater than lust lived in his heart for her. She could not give up so easily.

"What was your wife's name?" she tried again.

"Linette."

"And how did you come to be married?"

"I met her at a clan gathering when I was seventeen. I thought her bonny, so when my da died and I was left with this stead at eighteen, I asked her to wed with me and join me here."

Blindly, Vivienne reached for one of the nearby chairs and pulled it out. Legs trembling, she sank down onto it.

"So you lived here with Linette for two years before she passed." She could barely think over the loud thud of her heart in her ears. Part of her tried to push down her mounting fear and listen to Kieran with under-standing and tenderness. If his current detachment was any indication, he'd been through hell and didn't want to revisit the dark memories.

But another part of her was stunned to only be learning all this now, after revealing so much of her own painful past to him. She had shared his bed—his and Linette's bed—without knowing any of this.

"Aye," he replied. "After the first year, she discovered

she was carrying our bairn. Six months later, they were both gone. So I left."

"Slow there," she said, holding up a hand. She swallowed. "How did they die?"

He blew out a breath and suddenly sprang from the bedstead, still naked. "Must ye poke and prod, Vivienne? Why does it matter?"

His sharp words stung. She watched in silence as he bent and snatched up his shirt, shoving it over his head with a grunt as he worked the arm on his wounded side into its sleeve.

Still, she needed to know. The fear that she had done it again—had fallen for a man who would keep secrets from her—gnawed in her gut.

"I have opened myself to you," she said, her voice low and tight. "I haven't held aught back."

"And that was yer choice." He grabbed his plaid from the floor and set about re-pleating it around his hips.

She drew back, stunned by his sudden harshness. "I would have hoped that after all we've been through, you could—"

He rounded on her. "It was cold out. Linette went to check on the animals and slipped on a patch of ice. She landed wrong and began bleeding. I rode out into the night to fetch the midwife, but by the time we got back, Linette was already verra weak."

He dropped his gaze as he fumbled with his belt. "Linette delivered the bairn, but he—it was a lad—was already dead. And then the bleeding wouldnae stop. Linette died a few hours later." When he lifted his head once more, his pale eyes flared with pain. "Is *that* what ye wanted to hear?"

Tears burned in Vivienne's eyes, blurring Kieran's stony, drawn features. "I'm so, so sorry for all you lost," she murmured. "I cannot imagine what you must have endured."

"As I said, it is in the past."

Confusion at his continued iciness engulfed her. He had just spoken of a terrible loss as if it were naught. "But it clearly still pains you," she replied.

"Nay, it doesnae," he said flatly. "I fancied at the time that I loved Linette, but we were little more than bairns when we wed, and in truth I hardly kenned her."

Vivienne shook her head slowly, an inkling of under-standing beginning to dawn. Kieran was a strong, rough-edged man, but he was not made of stone. He was trying to protect himself from something. "I do not believe you."

"Oh aye?" he said acidly. "Ye would rather I tell ye that I *did* love her?"

"If it is the truth, *oui*. I will not hold your past against you, just as I hope you do not hold mine against me," she said, rising from the chair to face him. Though he towered over her, she refused to shrink away. "But I would ask that after all we've shared, you at least be honest with me. With *yourself*."

"Since ye seem to ken so much," he replied, "why dinnae ye tell me the truth, then?"

Vivienne drew in a breath. "I believe you did care for her, but losing her terrified you. What happened to Linette and your child was a freak accident. You couldn't stop it. You couldn't control it. You couldn't protect the ones you loved, and that frightened you to your core."

"What do ye want me to say, Vivienne?" He spread his arms wide, glaring hard at her. "That I loved her? Aye, mayhap I did. That it was damned excruciating to lose her and the bairn? Fine. That is why I put it—and this place—behind me."

"So you sold everything and left, as you said," she replied, willing her voice to remain calm. "You joined the Bruce's cause, but you cannot stand the thought of putting your trust in someone again. You said before that you pride yourself on never having to rely on others, because doing so will only get you hurt."

"Call me a fool, but I dinnae care to go through the trouble of losing someone again."

There it was. The truth of his sudden coldness. The reason behind all the times he'd ducked her questions or avoided addressing the growing connection between them.

"And your solution is to never let anyone into your life again," she breathed. "To keep everyone at a distance so that you won't be hurt as you were before."

He took a step closer to her, and she had to force herself to remain rooted in place. "Ye think ye have me all figured out, dinnae ye, lass? Dredging up my past doesnae mean ye ken me, though."

"I know you better than anyone has in ten years," she countered.

He crossed his arms over his chest stubbornly. Abruptly, Vivienne realized that arguing with him would get her nowhere. He was a proud, bull-headed man, and she could not get through to him simply by force of will.

But she *had* to get through the walls he'd erected. She couldn't let him seal himself away, not when she so desperately—

"I love you," she blurted.

His eyes widened and his jaw went slack.

"I love you," she repeated. "*Mon Dieu*, mayhap *I* am the fool, but I love you, Kieran."

Of course she loved him. She'd felt the seed of it in her heart long before, but the truth in the words now struck her like the pure, clear ring of a bell.

Just like him, she had been scared. Scared to trust her heart to another, to risk being hurt again.

But to her surprise, saying the words lifted a weighty burden from her, as if she were no longer trying to fight the inevitable. It was a relief not to struggle against it anymore. As if she could have ever resisted loving him—she might as well have been trying to hold back the tide or stop the sun from rising.

She stood before him, her heart laid bare, and waited. Yet to her horror, his surprise-slackened features slowly began shuttering once more.

"Nay, dinnae say that," he said, shaking his head. "Dinnae confuse things. We agreed to keep matters simple between us."

Standing before him in only her chemise, she suddenly felt far too exposed. She hurriedly scooped up her discarded dress and pulled it over her head. Once she'd covered herself, she tried to regain what was left of her dignity, but the threat of tears burned behind her eyes.

To stop from further embarrassing herself, she pressed the heels of her palms into her eyes. "As I said, I am likely a fool. But I cannot change what is in my heart."

"We never made any promises to each other," he continued, his voice hard and flat. "We are both grown. We both ken pleasure doesnae equal love. And that is all that lies between us—lust. Naught more."

He might as well have slapped her.

Behind her closed eyes, the room spun precariously. Distantly, she imagined that this must be how a tree felt when it was struck by lightning—splintered and singed to the roots.

Mon Dieu, it was happening again. It was as if she were seventeen all over again, being humiliated by the man she'd given herself to. Just as before, she had fallen in love with a man who could never love her in return.

Somehow the blow felt even lower this time, though. Guy had used her as a plaything, but as a heartbroken seventeen year old, she'd tried to comfort herself with a lie—the only thing keeping them apart was the fact that Guy had a wife.

But with Kieran, there was no hiding from the truth. His wife was long dead, yet he was just as unavailable as Guy. Some part of him had died with Linette all those years ago. He was a shell, a walking ghost, unwilling to join the living and let himself love again.

And she couldn't fight a ghost, nor could she change the past.

She dragged in a breath that burned her lungs. "I-I cannot stay here." Doing her best to scrub the tears from her eyes, she slipped past him and snatched up her boots, shoving first one foot and then the other into them.

Kieran's brows dropped. "Ye cannae leave. It is past nightfall and we are in the middle of the Highland wilds."

Vivienne grabbed her cloak from beside the door and swung it over her shoulders. "I cannot be in this place with you. I-I need to think, to clear my head."

He strode to the door and stomped into his own boots. "Yer life is still in danger. Besides, who kens what animals lurk beyond the clearing. Ye cannae go out there alone."

She fought the urge to scream at him, to burst into tears, to shout that she had been outside countless times without him in the last five days, but none of that mattered. All she knew was that she had to escape before she lost her threadbare grasp on composure and dissolved like the weak, foolish woman she'd proven to be.

"Please," she rasped. "Leave me alone. I ca-cannot breathe."

It was true. Her lungs burned, her eyes stung, and every inhale felt like hot sand in her throat.

Before her, Kieran frowned. He sniffed, his eyes going to the fire. "It isnae just ye," he said. "Something must be wrong with the chimney. It is smoky in here."

Confused, she followed his gaze to the hearth, but the fire had burned to embers and didn't seem to be putting off smoke at all. Yet now that he pointed it out, she realized her tight lungs and burning eyes weren't just caused by the ache in her heart. The cottage was filling with smoke.

Kieran strode to the hearth, examining it closer, but as his eyes traced up the length of the stone chimney, he froze.

"*Bloody hell*. It's the roof. The thatch is on fire!"

Vivienne looked up to find fingers of smoke slipping in through the thatch. In the one heartbeat it took for her brain to understand what was happening, the fingers had turned to hands of thick black fumes. The air inside the cottage was rapidly becoming hazy and hot.

"Open the door!" Kieran barked, striding toward her.

But just as she turned to reach for the handle, a heavy thunk sounded from outside. Something had just fallen against the door.

Or someone had just barricaded them inside.

Chapter Thirty-One

At the sound of a bar falling across the door from the outside, Kieran's pulse spiked sickeningly. There could be only one explanation for the roof catching fire even in these damp conditions. Someone had done it intentionally. And now that the door was barred, he knew exactly what they intended.

Vivienne turned wide, frightened eyes on him. "The window," she offered, hurrying toward it.

"Nay, lass, dinnae!"

She froze, her face drawn with confusion. "But if we stay in here—"

In two steps, he was to her. He dragged her down to the ground where the air was slightly less smoky. "Someone did this, lass," he said, his throat already growing raw. "And they are waiting outside for us, hoping to smoke us out. If we go out the window now, we'll be walking straight into their trap."

Her lips parted in shock. "De Soules's men?"

He nodded. He wouldn't know for sure until he went outside, but he had little doubt it could be any other besides that bastard's lackey. Or lackeys. That was just one of their many mounting problems—he had no idea how many men he would have to face.

"But what are we to do?" she asked. "Stay in here and let the flames take us?"

Kieran glanced at the roof. The thatch was wet enough that he only spotted the occasional orange flare of fire, but the fact was, the smoke would be what killed them—and in only a few more minutes, too. He didn't tell Vivienne that, though, for she was already frightened enough.

Bloody hell and damnation. Besides the door and the window, there was no other way out of the cottage. He couldn't simply thrust Vivienne out the window and straight into the grasp of those who would see her dead, but if they lingered much longer, it wouldn't matter, for they would be dead anyway.

At least if they went outside, he stood a chance against whoever had lit the roof on fire. Aye, even with his sword arm injured, the odds were better against an enemy he could face rather than the thick smoke.

He crawled over to the far corner of the cottage, where their saddlebags lay. His sword still protruded from one of them. He yanked it free of its scabbard, ignoring his shoulder's protests, and moved back to Vivienne's side.

"Stay behind me no matter what, ye understand?"

She nodded, smothering a cough with her hand. He

crawled closer to the window, Vivienne dragging herself after him. But just as he was about to rise and barrel from the cottage, she grabbed his arm, snagging his attention.

"My book!" she cried. Her red-rimmed eyes frantically darted to where it lay halfway across the room beside the bedstead.

"Leave it," he ordered. At the look of desolation that crossed her face, he captured her chin and forced her to look at him. "It isnae worth yer life, Vivienne."

She swallowed hard, giving her treasured book one last look before nodding again.

"Be ready," he said, tightening his grip on his sword. Drawing a deep breath of the relatively less smoky air closer to the ground, he jerked to his feet. With a powerful kick, he sent the window's shutters flying open.

He thrust his sword out first, preparing for a direct attack. But when none came, he wedged himself out the narrow gap, keeping his blade raised defensively.

The cold, fresh air outside hit him like a welcome slap. He dragged in a lungful as his boots hit the dew-damp grass beside the hut. Behind him, he heard Vivienne, too, suck in a breath as she slipped from the window and huddled at his back.

It wasn't until he knew she was safely out of the burning cottage that he truly took in the scene surrounding them.

More than a dozen men sat on horseback in an arc around the cottage, their drawn swords dully reflecting the weak flames on the thatch roof.

Kieran muttered a curse, but when his gaze landed

on none other than William de Soules himself, it turned into a feral, rage-filled growl.

"How the bloody hell did ye get free?"

De Soules, who was the only man without a sword in his hands, gave Kieran a slow, smug smile.

"Does it matter? I am here now. If ye hand over the woman without trouble, I'll give ye a swift death."

In response, Kieran spat on the ground and raised his sword.

"Kneel like the Highland dog ye are," de Soules snapped, some of his humor vanishing.

"Try and make me, ye cowardly, traitorous bastard."

With a hissed curse, de Soules motioned for his men to dismount. "Remember, take the woman alive," he said, his dark eyes flashing with hatred as his gaze landed on Vivienne. "I want her to suffer before she dies."

Kieran backed up a step, nigh pinning Vivienne against the cottage's stone side. He gripped his sword in both hands as de Soules's lackeys began advancing on him, the surge of battle lust dulling the pain in his shoulder.

With a shout, one of the men suddenly charged, his sword driving forward. Kieran blocked the blow, then thrust, quickly putting an end to him. Even as the first man fell aside, the others rushed in.

Kieran swung wide to deflect several attacks at once. But he didn't have time to strike at them himself, for their sheer numbers were enough to nearly overpower him at every moment.

While he was beating back four attackers at once,

one of the men tried to dart around him and reach for Vivienne. Kieran whirled and brought his sword down, slicing the man's hand off. The man fell, writhing and screaming as he clutched his bleeding, severed arm.

Kieran began to turn back to the others, but by spinning to stop Vivienne from being grabbed, he'd left her other side vulnerable. Another man shot forward, grabbing Vivienne's arm and yanking her from behind Kieran.

Vivienne screamed, and Kieran's mind went blank except for the overpowering, all-consuming need to save her. He turned wild, hacking and slicing at the men closing in around him like a berserker from Viking legend.

"Enough, ye incompetent fools!" de Soules shouted. "We have her."

Through the haze of battle, Kieran realized de Soules's men, whose numbers he'd severely depleted, began retreating from the deadly arc of his blade.

But Kieran didn't stop attacking until his gaze landed on de Soules, who held a dagger at Vivienne's throat. He froze, his eyes locking on the point where the blade edge pressed into the creamy, delicate skin of her neck.

"I dinnae wish to, but I will kill her here and now if ye dinnae kneel, Highlander!" de Soules cried.

Kieran barely heard him over the rush of blood in his ears. *Vivienne.* Oh God, he'd failed her.

Numbness descended over him like a cold, thick fog. He was out of options. Slowly, he sank to his knees.

Around him, de Soules's lackeys stepped cautiously

forward and dragged their wounded away from Kieran, leaving the dead. Four bodies surrounded him in the grass, and another three were badly injured.

If Kieran were alone, he would have taken his odds against the remaining five able-bodied men to reach de Soules. But de Soules was a ruthless coward. He would slit Vivienne's throat before Kieran had dispatched even one man.

"Drop yer sword," de Soules ordered as his men began to mount. Even before Kieran could comply, he pressed the blade into Vivienne's throat, making her whimper.

Kieran tossed his sword aside, spreading his arms wide. "I am unarmed and on my knees, de Soules. That is what ye wanted."

"Oh, nay," de Soules replied, his eyes blazing. "I want so much more than that." He shoved Vivienne into the arms of one of his men, a giant with dark hair and thick features. "Bevin, tie her to the saddle," he commanded. "And keep yer sword on her at all times."

As the man did his bidding, de Soules turned back to Kieran, pointing the dagger at him as he slowly stalked forward.

"What I *want* is to drink yer precious Robert the Bruce's blood, his head lying at my feet. What I *want* is to make ye and all the other members of his inner circle pay for what ye did to me—especially Jerome Munro and the English bitch Elaine. But most of all, what I want is to make Vivienne suffer the way she made me suffer."

He halted before Kieran, staring down at him with wild, dark eyes. Firelight reflected in his gaze, and Kieran could feel the growing heat of the blaze behind him. A spark must have fallen from the roof into the dry interior of the cottage, catching on the wooden table, the bedstead, the cupboards.

"Making ye sink before me like the barbarian ye are and taking yer life is only the extra gilding on top," de Soules said with a slow smile. "Ever since ye dragged me back from France to Scone and forced me to kneel before the Bruce for judgment, I have thought on this moment, MacAdams."

Cold realization seeped into Kieran's heart. There was no more time, no more options, and no more hope. He was about to die. And Vivienne would likely suffer terribly before dying, too. He could only pray that after de Soules killed him, Vivienne would find a way to escape. If de Soules intended to draw out her suffering, it meant more time for her to get free somehow.

As de Soules droned on about having his revenge at last, Kieran let his gaze slip beyond him to Vivienne. Her hands had been bound with coarse rope to one of the dead men's saddles, and the giant of a man de Soules had spoken to before had his sword trained on her.

Her wide, frightened eyes shimmered with the glow of the growing fire. Her gaze was fixed on Kieran where he knelt on his knees in the grass, her whole body straining toward him as much as she could given her bound hands and the blade pointed at her.

God help him, he loved her so much. He'd been such a fool before, wasting the precious time they'd had together trying to fight against his heart.

His worst nightmare was coming true all over again. He would lose the woman he loved, and there was naught he could do about it. Yet it was so much worse this time than it had been ten years past.

At least he'd had a year and a half of happiness with Linette. Time had dulled the memories, but he'd known peace and contentment for a short while.

With Vivienne, it could have been even more than that. The love that lay between them was deeper, richer, more intense than aught he'd ever know. But he'd made a terrible error in denying his feelings.

Damn it all, why had he pushed her away in the few remaining moments they'd had together in the cottage? She'd been right about everything—about his fear of letting himself love again, of losing someone he cared about—but he'd been too much of a coward to admit it.

He'd told himself for ten years that all he wanted was to be left alone—long enough that he'd come to believe it was true. But it was a lie. What he wanted deep in his bones was to *feel* again, to *love*—and he had, thanks to Vivienne. Even his best defenses and greatest fears couldn't keep his love for her at bay.

Yet instead of telling her all that, he'd lashed out at her to protect himself. But the result was the same—he was going to lose her anyway, just as before, only this time, she would never know what was in his heart.

"I love ye, Vivienne," he blurted.

De Soules halted abruptly in the middle of his

tirade, blinking in confusion. Vivienne's eyes rounded, then her face crumpled with emotion.

"I love ye, do ye hear me?" Kieran said again.

She nodded, tears streaming down her face. "*Oui*. I love you, too."

"Shut yer mouth," de Soules snapped, pointing the dagger at Kieran.

But now that he had spoken the words, he couldn't stop. De Soules would kill him regardless, but he needed Vivienne to know the truth.

"Never forget that, lass," he shouted. "And dinnae give up. Ye are stronger than anyone I've ever kenned. I love ye, Vivienne. I love—"

Without warning, de Soules plunged his dagger straight into Kieran's chest.

"Kieran!" Vivienne screamed. "*Non, mon Dieu, non*! Please, *non*!"

De Soules viciously yanked his dagger free, and Kieran saw his own life's blood dripping from it.

The air rushed from his lungs. He grunted and slumped forward, toppling onto the wet grass along with the bodies of the men he'd killed. He coughed, and warm blood dampened his lips.

From where he lay, he watched de Soules stride back toward his horse and mount. He took Vivienne's reins and called an order for his men to ride out.

Vivienne twisted in the saddle, fighting to keep her eyes on him, but soon she was forced to break their gaze. Her cries grew distant as the band of men were swallowed by the night-dark woods.

"I love ye," Kieran wheezed before she disappeared forever.

Chapter Thirty-Two

A few hours' ride from the cottage, de Soules ordered his men to stop to allow the horses some rest.

One of the men had gagged her not far from the cottage to keep her cries from alerting someone to their presence. Vivienne had run out of the strength to sob any more, but tears still leaked from her eyes unchecked. She sat hunched in the saddle, staring silently at her bound hands, but inside she had shattered into a thousand shards of pain.

Kieran was dead. Kieran, her love, her heart, her soul, was dead.

She felt as though a part of her had died on the ground beside him. She squeezed her eyes shut, but the image of de Soules's dagger plunging into his chest, and then him slumping forward and collapsing, kept flashing over and over in her mind's eye.

And his words of love for her had been on his lips as

he'd died. A fresh wave of anguish slammed into her, and she moaned against her gag.

Her very bones reverberated with gratitude that she'd gotten to hear his declaration of love before his death, but a wild, broken part of her wanted to scream for all that had been lost between them. How could a love like theirs be ended so cruelly and abruptly? If there was any goodness left in the world, they should have had more time together, more happiness. Instead he had been stolen from her thanks to the petty vengeance of a would-be traitor.

Her living nightmare was interrupted when hands closed around her, freeing her wrists and dragging her from the saddle. She staggered when her feet hit the ground, held up only by the grip on her elbow.

She opened her eyes to find the giant who had bound her hands back at the cottage looming over her.

"Let her relieve herself, Bevin," de Soules said as he dismounted nearby. "But dinnae let her out of yer sight."

Bevin nodded, then pulled her off into the surrounding woods. It was humiliating to have to squat and empty her bladder mere feet from him, but her body needed relief. At least her skirts kept those beady eyes of his from seeing aught.

But when she rose on wobbling legs, instead of taking her back to the others, Bevin stood rooted, his heavy brows lowered and his lips parting. "Ye are a bonny one, arenae ye?"

He took a step closer. Though the gag was still in her mouth, the desperate urge to scream rose in her throat.

He reached out and pinched a lock of her unbound hair, letting it slide between his dirt- and blood-covered thumb and forefinger. Vivienne swatted his hand aside, and in return, the brute backhanded her across the face.

She was thrown to her knees with a muffled cry. Stars danced before her eyes, and her face throbbed painfully.

"Bevin!" Suddenly de Soules was charging toward them, the dagger that he'd used to kill Kieran in his hand.

So this was to be it. She would die here in these darkened, unnamed woods. At least the blade that had pierced Kieran's heart would be used to take her life as well.

To her shock, instead of setting upon her, de Soules unceremoniously slashed Bevin across the face with the dagger. "Ye fool," he hissed.

Bevin grunted and clutched his cheek, which streamed with blood. "Sire, I didnae mean any har—"

De Soules raised the blade again, and Bevin flinched back, falling silent. Though Bevin could have easily overpowered de Soules, who stood a head and shoulders shorter than the giant and had a much smaller build, de Soules seemed to have some power over the brute that made him obedient.

"Oh, I ken what ye were about, ye animal." De Soules pointed at Vivienne, who remained huddled on the ground. "Trying to do what ye did to that bonny wee cousin of yers again, werenae ye. But this one is *mine*."

De Soules crouched before her, gently grazing the tip of the dagger against her aching cheek. "I will be the one to mar this bonny skin, to make her beg for my mercy."

Vivienne's stomach lurched and she feared she would vomit against the gag, but she managed to swallow down her sickness.

"Do ye hear that?" de Soules shouted to the other men, who were milling about their horses. "She is mine. None of ye are to touch her."

At their grunts and mumbles of assent, de Soules gripped Vivienne's elbow and dragged her to her feet, pulling her back toward her horse. He shoved her up into the saddle and re-bound her hands. As he and the others mounted, Bevin emerged from the woods with his head lowered like a dog that had been kicked.

De Soules took her reins and the whole party set out again. Though the shroud of devastation threatened to smother her once more, she fought not to surrender to it completely.

Kieran's words rang through her mind over and over. *I love ye. Never forget that, lass.*

No matter how little time she had left on this earth, she never would.

And dinnae give up. Ye are stronger than anyone I've ever kenned.

Vivienne feared she wasn't nearly strong enough, but Kieran had believed in her. She would not disrespect his memory by crumbling now. *Oui*, she was still alive. De Soules seemed bent on taking her somewhere before the torture truly began, and he wouldn't let his men hurt her before then.

Which meant she still had time to fight for herself—
as Kieran would have wanted.

KIERAN DIDN'T KNOW how long he'd lain on the wet
grass, his breaths coming short and blood oozing from
his chest. Everything had gone quiet except for the roar
of the blazing cottage.

For a time, the fire had burned bright and hot,
sending orange flames and black smoke into the night
sky. But now the blaze had died down.

The shutters on the window had burned, as had the
door, leaving only the hut's stone skeleton. The roof had
collapsed inward a while back. From his position on the
ground, he could see through the empty doorway to the
charred remains of what had once been his home.

Naught was left. The wooden horse he'd carved for
his unborn bairn. Vivienne's book and her bottle of
violet oil. The table. The bedstead. All the memories
he'd made with Linette, and then Vivienne. It had all
burned away.

It was fitting. Linette was gone, as was his son. And
Vivienne. Nay, he told himself resolutely, she was still
alive. He had to believe she would escape somehow. It
was *he* who would be gone shortly, not Vivienne. Just like
the cottage and all that had been inside.

He coughed wetly, feeling blood on his lips. His chest
ached as if someone had dropped a boulder on it, and
he couldn't seem to draw enough air.

Yet through the haze in his mind, he knew that if de Soules had struck his heart, he would be dead by now. His pulse, which he could feel in his tongue and throat and even faintly in his fingertips, was weak but still steady.

Mayhap de Soules's dagger had only hit one of his lungs, then. Based on his years serving the Bruce on the battlefield, Kieran knew it would be a far slower death.

Woozy with blood loss, his mind drifted back to those battles. He'd once seen a man take a lance to the chest, draining the air from his lungs. But then a healer had sealed the hole and the man had left the battlefield on his own two feet.

A seed of an idea, too small to be called hope yet, planted itself in the back of Kieran's blurry mind. With a grunt of pain, he lifted his arm from beside him and placed his hand over the wound in his chest. To his shock, when he pushed down, instead of making his lungs feel even smaller and more compressed, he was able to pull in a slightly bigger gasp of air.

Hope now surged within him. He reached down to the hem of his kilt and tore away a piece of wool. He balled it up and pressed it into the wound, then ripped off another strip of plaid. With a good deal of effort and pain, he managed to fit the strip around his chest. He tied the ends together, pulling them as tight as he possibly could to hold the ball of wool in place.

When he was finished, he had to lie still for a long time, coughing blood and wheezing for air. His vision swam and spots floated before his eyes as he fought to catch his breath. After the worst of it passed, he discovered his efforts had paid off. Just as when he'd pushed on the wound with his hand, the ball of cloth and bandage around his chest allowed him to suck in just a wee bit more air than before.

Though he wanted to shout with the victory, he'd likely only bought himself a few hours before death came calling once more. He could wait and hope that someone would find him before that happened, but he knew this corner of the Highlands all too well. He was far too isolated out here to place his faith in a serendipitous passer-by.

And he sure as hell wasn't going to just lie there and wait to die. Nay, as long as he had but one breath left, he would use it to fight for Vivienne.

There was only one option, then—he had to act.

With a groan, he rolled over onto his stomach, catching himself on his elbows to avoid putting weight on his chest. He began dragging himself across the grass toward the barn.

If de Soules and his lackeys had been smart, they would have snuck to the barn before attacking the cottage and turned Kieran's horse loose. But he had a suspicion that de Soules had been so focused on getting Vivienne into his clutches that he hadn't been so careful.

He had to rest and catch his breath a dozen times, but at last he reached the barn. When he drew back the door, he was met with the sight of the trusty silver stallion, ears alert and eyes on Kieran. Breathing a prayer of thanks, Kieran pulled himself inside and toward the stallion.

Using the sides of the stall, he dragged himself upright, but he knew by the wild spinning of his head and the nausea that rose in the back of his throat that he wouldn't have the strength to saddle the horse. Instead, he let the worst of the dizziness subside and then swung himself straight onto the stallion's back.

The animal shifted beneath him as he settled into place, but he didn't fight Kieran, proving his steadfastness once again.

Tapping his heels into the horse's flanks, Kieran guided them out of the barn. He spared one last look at the burned cottage, but he couldn't linger over old memories any longer. He'd lost too much already by binding himself with the shackles of the past. He only had the future now—and Vivienne was his future.

He angled the horse southward, the same direction de Soules and his men had taken, but Kieran was in no state to track them, nor would he be good for much besides keeling over into unconsciousness even if he did catch up to them.

Nay, he knew what he had to do. Scone was only a two days' ride from here if he pushed himself and the horse to hell and back. He knew the stallion was strong enough to endure it. He could only pray that he would be, too.

Chapter Thirty-Three

Kieran slumped over the stallion's neck, swaying with its gait. Each hoof-fall sent agony surging through him, but somehow he managed to keep his seat atop the animal's back.

He lifted his head, squinting against the light even though the sun was tucked behind thick gray clouds. Through the haze enveloping him, he recognized his surroundings. Thank God in heaven, he was close.

He guided the stallion out of the denser woods and down a narrow trail that led to Scone. As he rode, his mind churned with thoughts of Vivienne. It didn't matter if he lived or died, as long as he reached Scone in time to tell the others what had happened. He prayed she was still alive and unharmed, trusting in the belief deep in his heart that she was.

When the trees thinned and the wooden palisades appeared before him, he nudged the stallion faster for the last few strides, clinging on to consciousness with all his strength.

As he drew up to the palisades, one of the guards must have recognized him.

"MacAdams, ye've returned," the man began. Then his eyes widened as he took in the full sight of him. He muttered an oath, then shouted, "Toby, fetch the King and the others in the Corps. Open the gate!"

Without stopping to dismount or even acknowledge the guards, Kieran rode through the still-opening wooden gate and into the courtyard before the palace. He slowed his horse and attempted to slide from his back, but it turned into an uncontrolled fall.

Luckily, two of the guards had followed beside him and caught him before he hit the ground. Still, he nearly knocked them both down with his large frame. As they struggled to get him on his feet, the King and several of the Corps members burst from the great hall.

"Good God," the Bruce breathed, rushing toward Kieran. "What happened, man?"

"William de Soules took Vivienne," Kieran ground out. Distantly, he registered the King and the others' stunned faces before him. "I am going to get her back," he went on, blackness creeping in at the edges of his vision. "And I need yer help."

With that, the last of his strength failed and dark unconsciousness swallowed him whole.

KIERAN SLOWLY EMERGED FROM A DEEP, dreamless

slumber. He was lying on his back on a soft bed. His limbs were heavy and warm, and his head felt stuffed with wool, as if he'd drank too much good whisky.

Reluctantly, he cracked his eyes open. A woman stood over him, her golden hair held back from her face. He squinted against the bright light in the chamber.

"V…Vivienne?"

The woman started in surprise at the low rumble of his voice, but then placed a hand on his arm and squeezed lightly. "Nay," she said kindly in an English accent. She turned to someone else in the chamber. "Fetch the others and tell them he's awake."

As the fog in his brain continued to clear, one recollection after another began to hit him. Vivienne had been taken. De Soules had her. And Kieran was supposed to be dead. The dull pain in his chest was a reminder that he wasn't, though. He'd made it to Scone.

"Ye are—"

"Jossalyn Sinclair," the woman replied. "One of the King's healers."

"And the wife of Garrick Sinclair." Though Kieran hadn't met him yet, he knew Garrick was a fellow member of the Corps and one of the Bruce's most trusted warriors.

"Aye," she replied with a soft smile.

"What…happened?" He remembered riding into the palace courtyard, throwing the last of his foolish pride to the wind, and asking the King and Corps for help, but after that, it was all darkness.

"You are lucky I was nearby," Jossalyn replied. "I do not always stay at the King's side, but I was only an hour's ride away in Perth. If I hadn't reached you as quickly as I did, you might not be alive."

"And what did ye do to me?"

A faint smile curved Jossalyn's lips, as if she were pleased at the chance to explain her methods. "Your bandage likely saved your life long enough for you to get here. In fact, the initial puncture wound had already begun closing enough for you to draw air into that lung. But it was filled with blood. I made a cut on your side and placed a reed into the lung, then sucked out the blood and sealed you up again."

Hell and damnation. He was lucky indeed.

"Your shoulder looked to be nearly healed as well," she went on. "So I removed the stitches—and finely done they were, too."

The memory of Vivienne, frightened but bravely facing the task, made his heart twist painfully. He had to reach her somehow, had to find her and keep her from harm.

He tried to sit up, but Jossalyn placed a hand on his arm, managing to hold him down with the extremely slight strength she must possess in her petite body.

"Nay, Kieran, do not rise," she chided. "You still need a great deal of time to heal. It has only been two days since you arrived, and—"

"*What?*" he barked. "I have been out for *two days?*"

Just as he attempted to throw himself from the bed again, the chamber door opened and the King strode in, with Mairin, Niall, Will, and Jerome behind him.

Will and Jerome moved swiftly to the bed, forcing Kieran back down.

"Easy," Jerome said. "Ye should be thanking Jossalyn, no' biting her head off."

"I had to give you a sleeping draught so that you would not stir or wake as I worked on you," Jossalyn said, her brows drawing together over her green eyes. "And I thought it best to keep you under so that you could heal undisturbed."

Though it was futile, Kieran struggled against Will and Jerome's hold. "Then Vivienne has been in de Soules's clutches for *four days*." Pain tugged at the wound on his chest, but it was naught compared to the agony in his heart.

"Calm yerself, man," the King said evenly, but his face was a knot of worry behind his beard. "Ye cannae help the lass by riling yerself up and undoing Jossalyn's work. Tell us what happened."

Kieran squeezed his eyes shut for a long moment. When he opened them, Will and Jerome warily released him and stepped back.

"We were attacked a half-day's ride from Scone," he began. "No' by de Soules himself, but by his lackeys. They were aiming for Vivienne, but they only hit me."

He nodded toward the freshly-healed pink scar on his shoulder, then continued. "We abandoned her horse and managed to lose them—or so I thought. I took her to an old plot of land in the Highlands once owned by my family, and long forgotten by even my clan. All was well until four days past, when de Soules and a small army arrived."

"How many men did de Soules have?" the Bruce asked.

"A dozen before they attacked me. And afterwards, five unharmed and three injured, no' counting de Soules."

The Bruce's eyes flashed with respect, and he nodded to Kieran before sobering once more. "And they made off with Lady Vivienne?"

"Aye," Kieran rasped, his rage rising once more. "De Soules put a dagger through my chest before riding south with her. I didnae have a way of kenning where he was taking her, so I threw myself on a horse and rode here." He turned a hard gaze on the Bruce. "How the bloody hell did de Soules get free in the first place?"

The King rubbed a hand over his eyes and let a long breath go. "A few days after ye departed for the Highlands, de Soules was set to be relocated to Dumbarton. As I told ye before ye left, I'd hoped to tuck him away someplace more remote to draw attention away from him and his cause. He was transported in chains with a guard of six men—more than enough to subdue him if necessary. But en route, the convoy was ambushed."

The Bruce muttered a curse, shaking his head. "Ten men sprang upon them, catching them off-guard. They slaughtered my men and freed de Soules, then rode north. Luckily one soldier survived and managed to get back to Scone to report what had happened."

"Hell and damnation," Kieran hissed, the pieces shifting into place in his mind. "The men who attacked us outside Scone must have still been on our trail. De Soules and the others must have met up with them in the Highlands and hunted us down."

"Aye, that would explain how they found ye," the

Bruce replied. "Once I learned of de Soules's escape, I sent Colin, Garrick, and two score more soldiers to try to track him and his cronies down. But it seems they will be riding all the way to the Highlands for naught."

The King swore again. "Sabine is working with her network of spies and messengers—with Elaine's help—to learn aught else she can," he continued, "but so far all we ken is that de Soules rode south from the Highlands. Which means he could be nigh anywhere else in Scotland."

"Before ye stripped him of his title and lands, de Soules had an estate at Liddesdale in Dumfriesshire," Will offered, his features drawn into a frown. "And his family owns Hermitage Castle in the Lowlands."

"But would the man really go somewhere so obvious?" Niall asked quietly. "He is on the run and surely knows we will be hunting him. I doubt he would risk returning to one of his old haunts."

The English lad made a good point, but Kieran was losing his battle to remain calm. "Damn it all, he has Vivienne," he growled. "He vowed to make her pay for the suffering she caused him. We cannae waste time wandering to every bloody corner of Scotland looking for her."

Just then, Mairin, who had remained quiet and watchful as always, stepped forward. "De Soules clearly had help," she began, her voice tight as if she wasn't used to speaking. "He managed to arrange an attack in Paris, and another just outside Scone. And he must have had a hand in organizing his escape. But he has been locked away in the dungeon this whole time."

Niall turned keen blue eyes on her. "What are you thinking, Mairin?"

She darted a glance at him before looking away. "Someone has likely been paying him visits."

The Bruce's features hardened. "I'll have the guards questioned."

Mairin held up a slim hand. "Aye, do, but mayhap first we should ask the only other inhabitant of the dungeon what she kens—Agnes of Strathearn."

The King's lips parted on a stunned exhale, and the other men all muttered curses. Kieran jerked upright in the bed.

"Bring her here," he rumbled.

Niall ducked out of the room and said a quick word to one of the guards positioned outside the door. The guard must have understood the urgency of the situation, for in no time, there was a rap on the door.

Niall opened it to admit two hulking guards flanking the much smaller, wide-eyed former Countess of Strathearn.

Agnes had once been a grand lady, swathed in fine silks and lavished with all the luxuries of a Lowland noble. Now she stood before them in a simple, ill-fitting wool gown, dirt under her nails and her face drawn as if the events of the last year had aged her a decade.

"Agnes," the Bruce said coolly.

The woman instantly lowered into a curtsy so deep that she was nearly huddled on the floor. "Sire," she said in a small, pleading voice. "I hope I havenae done aught to offend ye in any wa—"

"Nay," the Bruce cut in. "But we have some questions for ye about what ye may have overheard in yer cell."

Agnes looked up with dark, obsequious eyes. "Aye, Sire, I am yer humble servant."

Kieran nearly snorted. The woman had been imprisoned because she'd participated in de Soules's conspiracy to dethrone the Bruce. She was only alive now because she had confessed instantly upon being caught and had turned over the names of all the others she'd known had been involved.

But he had to admit, though he'd spoken against the Bruce leaving any of the conspirators alive, Kieran was now glad Agnes was at their disposal—and grateful that the woman clearly wished to prove herself useful and compliant, if only to gain a sliver more of the Bruce's mercy.

He pushed himself up to sitting in the bed, ignoring the discomfort in his chest.

"Yer cell shared a wall with de Soules's, did it no'?" he began.

Agnes nodded eagerly.

"Do ye ken that he escaped while being transported to Dumbarton?"

The woman's eyes rounded.

Kieran leveled her with a hard look. "Someone was visiting him, isnae that right?" he demanded. "He was plotting something even from his cell. Speak, Agnes, or God help me, all the leniency the King has shown ye will be wiped away."

The threat landed true. Agnes blanched and suddenly began to babble. "It was Bevin," she blurted.

"The big brute who worked in the stables. De Soules had something on him—something about his cousin, I dinnae ken—so Bevin did his bidding. At first he only visited to report to de Soules what went on above-ground, the state of the palace and such. But one night I overheard them speaking of a man named St. Giles—a Frenchman sent to kill that lady."

Hot anticipation surged in Kieran's veins. "What else?" he snapped.

"After St. Giles's failure, de Soules ordered Bevin to hire men to attack ye and the woman outside of Scone," she went on, nodding toward Kieran. "A few days later —the night before de Soules was taken away from his cell—Bevin returned and said the attack had failed. De Soules told Bevin to gather all those still loyal to him and set upon his convoy to Dumbarton."

The Bruce stiffened at that. "And how many was that?"

Agnes shook her head, her gaze darting between the King and Kieran. "None, Sire. Bevin said he'd tried to rustle up all their allies, but none would step forward. So de Soules told him to spend coin to hire however many he could."

The Bruce let out a breath, his gaze flicking to the others. "It is a small victory in light of the circum-stances, but now we ken that de Soules is on his own without a friend left in Scotland."

Though the Bruce was right, that knowledge was little comfort to Kieran given the fact that Vivienne was still in the madman's clutches. "What else, Agnes?"

"De Soules said that after Bevin and the hired men

set him free, they were to ride north—to find ye and the woman. And…and that is all."

"Bloody hell and damnation." Kieran pounded his fist against the bed so hard that the wooden frame shook. "He didnae say aught else—aught about where he would go after he got the woman?"

Agnes's brows drew together, her eyes fluttering rapidly over the floor. "He mentioned…"

"Speak!" Kieran roared, making Agnes, as well as Jossalyn, who still stood beside the bed, jump with fright.

"He told Bevin that if aught went wrong with the attack on the convoy or if they became separated, to meet him on the isle of Ailsa Craig," Agnes cried hurriedly.

The air seemed to whoosh from the room as everyone froze.

"That is all I ken, I swear," Agnes whispered.

"Thank ye for yer cooperation," the Bruce said, waving distractedly at the guards to take Agnes away. "I may see fit to reward ye if yer words prove useful."

Agnes was led out of the room, curtsying and praising the King's mercy repeatedly until the door closed behind her.

When the Bruce turned back to the others, his dark eyes were flinty.

"I should never have let that weasel de Soules live," he hissed through clenched teeth. "Martyr or nay, I should have put his head on a pike atop the palisades to show the world the fate of traitors against Scotland."

The Bruce drew in a fortifying breath, smoothing a hand over his beard. "I cannae change the past, but I damn well intend to bring the might of the entire Scottish army down on the bastard's head."

"Nay," Kieran replied. "An army will be far too slow. And he'd see them coming with plenty of time to finish Vivienne off." The words made bile rise in the back of his throat, but he forced it down. He needed to think clearly, not lose himself in his rage and fear once more.

"What are ye suggesting, then?" the King asked. "At best, the island is a several-hours' sail from Girvan, which is a two-day ride from here."

"We can make it in a day and a half," Kieran bit out.

"*We?*" The Bruce fixed him with a sharp stare. "It is obvious that yer concern for the lass goes beyond yer duty as her protector, Kieran."

"I love her," Kieran said baldly.

"Be that as it may, ye are in no condition to—"

"I am going."

The Bruce worked his jaw for a moment, but he couldn't quite seem to form a response to Kieran's blunt declaration. In the ensuing silence, Jossalyn stepped forward tentatively.

"You need to rest and heal, Kieran," she said softly. "You shouldn't be riding, let alone wielding a sword."

"I am going," he repeated stubbornly. "It isnae up for debate. If I remain here, I will tear the palace apart stewing over Vivienne's wellbeing."

"I am going, too," Mairin said abruptly, lifting her chin.

"Mairin, nay," Niall said softly, his worried gaze fixing on the lass. "It is too dangerous."

"I have been training in the Highlands just like ye, English," she snapped, her dove-gray eyes flashing. "I am a member of the Corps, arenae I? Besides, I cannae sit idly by while that bastard hurts a woman."

"I won't let you go without someone to watch your back," Niall replied. "I'll go, too."

"As will I," Will said, crossing his arms over his chest.

Jerome turned to the King. "Someone ought to stay close to ye, Robert," he said. "Though I hope ye and the others find de Soules on Ailsa Craig, Kieran, the King is still one of his main targets."

"Aye," the Bruce replied with a nod of assent to Jerome. "Ye'll stay, Jerome. And when they return to Scone, Colin and Garrick will remain by my side as well." He turned to Kieran. "Ye'll have my fastest horses and all the coin ye need to reach Ailsa Craig. I only wish I could take that bloody traitorous bastard's head myself."

Kieran rose slowly from the bed, his limbs stiff and his chest aching, but his blood fired with determination. "Oh, ye'll have his head, I vow it." He turned to the others. "I only have one request."

Will assessed him with his good eye. "What is that?"

"De Soules is mine."

Chapter Thirty-Four

Over the last five days, Vivienne had done her best to slow de Soules and his men down. She begged and pleaded nearly every hour for them to stop so that she could relieve her bladder.

After the first day, the men were grumbling about foolish women and their problems, but fearing de Soules's wrath if he believed they were mistreating her, they stopped more often than not, and left her alone as well.

The problem was, slowing them down wasn't enough. *Oui*, she was buying herself more time, but she held no hope that anyone was looking for her. Who—besides Kieran—would even know she'd been taken? And Kieran lay in the Highlands, cold and still, exposed to the elements, his life drained away.

She could not let herself dwell on that, though, else she break down once more. Nay, she needed to be strong for him. But she also needed to do more than simply bide her time.

So when the briny scent of the sea reached her as they rode southwest on the fifth day, she knew she had to act.

As dusk began to fall, de Soules drew them to a halt in a dense patch of woods. They stood on a rise overlooking a small village set along the sea.

"Ye, and ye," he said, pointing to two of his men. "Move closer to the village. When it grows dark, see about liberating a birlinn for us."

Even as she pretended to ignore his orders, Vivienne's mind churned. They were traveling by water now? Her stomach lurched at the thought, but she managed to hold on to the meager contents of her stomach. This would be her best—and possibly last, depending on where they were headed—chance to escape.

She forced herself to remain docile and submissive as Bevin undid the bindings on her hands, as he always did, and led her away to relieve herself. With her hands free, she pulled away the gag, but let him guide her to a nearby shrub.

After de Soules had lashed out at him for touching her, Bevin was now in the habit of turning partially away and standing several paces back while she saw to her needs.

She pretended to lower herself, but the moment he shifted his gaze away, she straightened and bolted. Lifting her skirts to avoid getting them tangled in her legs, she ran down the slope toward the village, hoping that someone would come to her aid.

"Help!" she screamed. "Help me, plea—"

Suddenly it felt as though a boulder had crashed into her back, driving her into the muddy and leaf-strewn forest floor. All the wind rushed from her lungs at the contact, making stars dance before her eyes as she wheezed for breath.

Rough hands rolled her over, and she found herself staring up at Bevin's coarse face.

He jammed the gag back into her mouth and tightened the strip of cloth around her head roughly. Then he hoisted her up and tossed her over his shoulder like little more than a sack of barley.

"Foolish bitch," she heard de Soules hiss as Bevin strode back to the others.

To the chuckles of the other men, Bevin dumped her unceremoniously on the ground once more and began binding her again, but this time he tied her hands behind her back, then bound her feet and secured her wrists to her ankles.

She lay there helplessly as she was trussed up like a lamb to the slaughter, silent tears streaming down her face.

She had failed. But as dusk deepened to night and the men continued to wait in the woods, she forced herself to hold on to hope. She was still alive, she reminded herself. Her heart still beat, powered by the memory of Kieran's love and his faith in her.

And because of that, she could never give up.

By the time Bevin lifted her from the birlinn and onto the dark, rocky shore of some unknown island, Vivienne felt wrung out and limper than a rag doll.

When the two lackeys de Soules had sent to the village had returned with confirmation that they'd secured a boat, Bevin had thrown her over his shoulder once more. They'd abandoned the horses, stalking toward the water under cover of night. She'd been tossed into the bottom of the birlinn, the soft rocking of the harbor instantly making her sick.

And when they'd hoisted the sail and reached open water, she'd retched until there was naught left in her stomach but bile, and then retched some more. Luckily, at her first heave, de Soules had removed her gag, else she would have choked on her own vomit. But *non*, he still wanted her to suffer more than that.

Blessedly, the journey had only lasted a few hours, and the ground felt solid under her feet once Bevin lifted her from the birlinn and cut the bindings on her ankles. He allowed her to walk but held her tightly by the elbow as the others dragged the small wooden birlinn onto the beach and into a small alcove in the island's steep, rocky cliff sides.

"Give her to me," de Soules snapped, grabbing Vivienne's arm.

As he pulled her away from the beach, she tried to get her bearings. She hadn't seen their approach to the island, for her head had been lowered over the side of the birlinn the entire voyage, but now she squinted through the dark to get a sense of their surroundings.

The rocky beach onto which they'd landed seemed to be the only entry point onto the island, for the rest of the island's sides were sheer, tall cliffs rising up from the water. She could make out the faint tinge of greenery well above them on the dome-like top of the island, but she saw no way—other than to climb straight up the rocky cliff-faces—to reach it.

De Soules continued striding across the pebbly beach straight for one of those rock faces. It wasn't until they had nearly run into it that Vivienne realized the stone opened up into a cave.

He dragged her through the cave's mouth and deep into its dripping, dark recesses. At last, he released her, shoving her to the ground, and she heard him fumbling with two flint stones.

A spark caught and struggled to light an already-laid fire. De Soules must have been here before, for he seemed to be familiar with the island and knew the cave well enough to navigate it even in the dark.

"Is this where you plotted your rebellion?" she ventured, watching his face in the weak, flickering light.

He glanced at her. "Clever whore. Aye, it was one of many locations," he commented. "But no' a soul who came here with me before is still alive, so dinnae imagine that anyone is coming for ye."

Despite her determination to remain brave, she couldn't suppress a shudder. There was still hope, she reminded herself. There was always hope as long as she remained alive.

But as de Soules slowly rose to his feet and stalked toward her, panic seared through the last of her courage.

He was no longer the quiet, obsequious man she'd first met all those months ago at the French court. Of course, his outward sycophancy and courtly manners had all been a lie, meant to lull those around him into thinking he posed no threat, but even after he'd been found out for a traitor, he hadn't borne the wild, feral look in his eyes that he had now.

In the five days she'd spent with him, he'd possessed knife-sharp focus at times, but at others it seemed his mind was hazy. She'd heard him mumbling to himself more than once, his words running in circles and his thoughts seemingly scattered.

Perhaps his time in Scone's dungeon had not only stripped him of his fine clothing, titles, and polished mannerisms, but had also chewed away at his sanity. *Non*, it likely wasn't just imprisonment that had warped him, but also his obsession with revenge.

Whatever the case, she was alone with him now, at his mercy—and he'd already made it clear that he planned to show her none.

"There is no one to hear ye scream anymore, bitch," he said, sinking on his haunches before her. "Except me, and I've been looking forward to the sound for a long while."

She sucked in a breath, trying to scoot back from him. "You are mad."

"Nay," he replied, "Just giving ye a taste of what ye did to me."

"All I did was dose you with a draught to lay you low, to force you to remain close to the garderobe," she said. "I never tortured you."

"Ye humiliated me!" he hissed, his control slipping. He drew a breath to calm himself. "And for that, ye'll pay."

He reached for her, but to her surprise, he merely caressed her cheek with his grimy fingers. She flinched back, but there was nowhere to go with the cold, wet cave wall behind her. Abruptly, he drew his hand back and slapped her hard across the face.

She gasped and sputtered, stunned.

"Och, I think ye can do better than that," he said with a grin. "I said I want to hear ye *scream*."

He drew back his hand again, this time balling it into a fist. Her mind scrambled wildly for some way to stop him, delay him—anything.

"You know that Bevin touched me again, don't you?" she blurted.

His fist halted halfway to her face. "What?"

She'd seen the way de Soules interacted with the others. He hardly spoke to the other men and didn't even seem to know their names, except for Bevin. It had made her surmise that the remaining men meant nothing to de Soules. They were likely only hired mercenaries.

But Bevin was different. Though the brute did de Soules's bidding, and he seemed to be the man's only true ally, de Soules didn't fully trust him. Based on how de Soules had reacted to Bevin hitting her before, there was a chance that the wedge between them could be exploited. Words began pouring from her.

"Before, when I tried to escape," she continued hurriedly. "When he tackled me, he grabbed my breast. Then he bent one of my fingers back so hard that I feared he'd break it and made me promise not to tell you."

In the low light of the fire, de Soules's dark eyes flared with rage. "I told him no' to touch what is mine," he breathed.

Oui, he was unhinged, but Vivienne just might be able to use that to save herself from his torment—for a time, anyway.

"That is why he told me not to tell you," she repeated.

De Soules suddenly jerked to his feet and stormed out of the cave. From Bevin's confused shout and then his grunts of pain, she knew de Soules had set upon him.

A long while later, de Soules stumbled into the light of the fire. His knuckles were rubbed raw and he was so exhausted that he staggered like a drunkard. He slumped down before the fire, breathing hard.

Slowly, the other men began filtering cautiously into the cave. They kept their distance from de Soules, eyeing him warily and muttering about needing more coin if they were expected to stay here indefinitely. Bevin slunk in after them, his face a swollen, bloody mess.

De Soules seemed oblivious to them all. He sat hunched over the fire, staring into the flames. After a while, he lay down on the cave floor, pulling his cloak around him, and fell asleep.

It seemed she had earned herself a few hours of peace. Vivienne leaned back against the cave wall, succumbing to exhaustion with a prayer of thanks on her lips.

Chapter Thirty-Five

"It is time."

Will nodded to Kieran in response and began lowering the sail on their small birlinn.

They'd agreed that once they'd crossed roughly half the distance from Girvan to Ailsa Craig, they would drop the white canvas sail to avoid being spotted from the island. Even though it was well past midnight, Kieran had feared the sail would glow pale blue in the moonlight. As it was, their only advantage was the element of surprise, which they could not risk wasting.

Just as Kieran had told the King they could, they'd made the ride from Scone to Girvan in only a little more than a day and a half. Still, that meant it had been six days since Vivienne had been taken from the cottage.

Six long, dark days. Kieran had nigh driven himself mad with thoughts of all that could have happened to Vivienne in that time. It was only thanks to Will, Niall, and Mairin that he'd maintained his threadbare hold on sanity.

Will didn't waste words on empty reassurances. Instead, he reminded Kieran in a bluntly logical way that de Soules had wanted Vivienne to suffer, which meant she was more than likely still alive. Oddly, it was a comfort.

Niall had been the one amongst them whose energy never flagged. Though he was the youngest man in the Corps, and English, Kieran realized he'd misjudged him. The lad was steadfast and even-keeled beyond his years. What was more, he seemed nearly as determined as Kieran himself to reach Vivienne. There was no doubt he was fiercely loyal and protective.

For her part, Mairin was mostly quiet, but just as they'd been departing Scone, she'd fixed Kieran with those wary gray eyes and said, "She is a strong one. I kenned it as soon as I met her." Then dropping her gaze, she'd murmured, "Ye'd be surprised just how much a lass can endure when she has to."

Kieran only knew the vaguest of details about Mairin—that her brothers Logan and Reid were both members of the Corps, that some event in her past had made her skittish and guarded—but he sensed that despite her youth, she knew a thing or two about strength herself. He'd clung to her words as they'd ridden like hell across Scotland.

Once they'd reached the wee town of Girvan, his hopes were bolstered further when they'd set about securing their birlinn for the crossing to Ailsa Craig. Even though dusk had settled over the town, the small harbor had been abuzz with the news that one of the fishermen's birlinns had been stolen the night before.

It only confirmed what Kieran knew in his gut—de Soules and his men had passed through on their way to Ailsa Craig. With Vivienne in tow, he prayed.

The King had given Kieran and the others more coin than they could have spent in a year to make their trek easier, so Kieran had not only paid handsomely for the use of another birlinn, but had also repaid the man whose boat had been stolen by de Soules.

And now they were nearly to the island. Without the sail hoisted, they would have to row the rest of the way. Though the wound on his chest was tight and achy from the hard treatment it had received in the last few days, Kieran relished the opportunity to throw his strength against the waves separating him from Vivienne.

Will took up the other oar, and they rowed in silence for a while before Niall forced Kieran to rest and took over his oar.

"Mayhap now is a good time to discuss our plan," Mairin ventured as Kieran caught his breath.

Will and Niall looked at each other, then Kieran.

"Save Vivienne," Kieran ground out. "That is the plan." He would hack through every last man himself in order to reach Vivienne.

Will, who had the mind of a strategist, cocked the light brown brow over his eyepatch. "Ye said de Soules had at least five able-bodied men, and mayhap some of the wounded have recovered as well. That would make it nearly two to one."

"Aye, but we are Highlanders." Kieran glanced at Niall, who wore a frown. "Well, no' counting the lad."

He'd never seen any of them fight, but he couldn't be questioning their abilities now, not when he'd finally set aside his pride and acknowledged just how badly he needed their help.

"We all earned our spot in the Corps one way or another," Kieran added, meeting each of their eyes in turn.

"Fair enough," Will replied. "Still, we'd best circle around the island a wee bit so as no' to be caught off-guard if de Soules's men are about. And we ought to stick together."

They all nodded in agreement.

"We can sort out the rest when we see what we find on the island," Kieran said.

Just then, an enormous, shadowed blob loomed up from the ink-dark waters before them. *Ailsa Craig.* Its sides were sheer, but the top of the isle was rounded, like a domed loaf of bread taken out of a pan.

Will lifted a hand from his oar to point off to the left, silently indicating that they make landfall there. As they drew nearer, Kieran saw the wisdom in the man's decision. The eastern shore of the island, which they'd been approaching head-on, was the obvious choice for a landing. In the moonlight, Kieran could make out a sandy, flat beach that extended toward the water from the otherwise steep cliff sides.

Will and Niall guided them around the beach to a rockier, sheltered cove. When they'd rowed as close as they could, Kieran jumped out into the cold, knee-deep water and hauled the birlinn partway onto the rocks.

Once the boat was secure, Will and Niall both hoisted themselves over the birlinn's side into the shallow water, but when Mairin moved to do the same, Niall plucked her up into his arms without a word.

Mairin gasped and likely would have bent Niall's ear —either with words or with her hand—had the need for silence not been so great. For his part, Niall simply carried her to the dry rocks higher up on the shoreline before setting her down.

With a nod to each other, they all drew their swords, except for Mairin, who left the short sword on her hip in its sheath and instead took up the bow she had slung across her body. Kieran would have marveled at the way the wee lass bristled with weapons if he didn't need to stay focused on the task at hand.

Dinnae think of Vivienne. He forced himself to concentrate only on the fighting about to take place, else his fears for her would spiral out of control.

He motioned the others forward, and they began creeping toward the beach behind the cover of the large rocks at the base of the island.

As they drew closer, a flicker of light and the rumble of distant voices reached them. They rounded a rock outcropping that opened onto the beach, and Kieran threw up a fist to halt the others.

"…stop us?" a man said, his voice filled with anger.

"Aye, are we to sit on this bloody island forever?" another demanded. "No' without another payment, we arenae."

Several others shouted in agreement.

"Silence!"

Kieran's skin pricked and his hands tightened around his sword. That was William de Soules's voice.

Cautiously, he leaned out from behind the rock outcropping until he could see the beach. A birlinn rested on the sand nearby, and beyond that, at the base of the sheer rock cliffs, a group of men stood together.

Or rather, a group stood squared off with two men —de Soules and the giant he'd called Bevin.

The mercenaries—Kieran recognized them as the men who'd attacked the cottage—shouted de Soules down, threatening to take the birlinn and leave him stranded unless he produced more coin.

Bloody hell, they'd walked in on an insurrection. Kieran's mind raced. He hadn't heard or seen a sign of Vivienne yet, but if de Soules's men were turning against him, they could use that to their advantage. There was no better time to strike than now.

He turned to the others, and judging from the way their eyes shone with anticipation in the moonlight, they'd come to the same conclusion.

"Ready?" he murmured.

At their nods, he lifted his sword and stepped from the cover of the rocks.

Chapter Thirty-Six

F rom her spot huddled deep in the belly of the cave, Vivienne could barely make out the men's shouts, but she could hear enough to know that her attempt to sow discord had taken root.

De Soules had woken late that morning all too eager to begin torturing her in earnest. But after only a few kicks and punches, he'd grown weary again. His time in Scone's dungeon had clearly sapped him of not only his wits, but also his strength.

When he'd left the cave for fresh air, she'd begun speaking to one of the mercenaries charged with watching her in de Soules's absence. De Soules no longer trusted Bevin for the task. Yet by setting one of the hired men on her, he'd unwittingly given her another opportunity to plant the seeds of discontent among his men.

In less than an hour and with a few select insinuations about the men's pay and how long they were expected to stay on the island, the man had been grumbling about this mad mission.

It seemed the men were primed like dry kindling to be resentful. Apparently de Soules was overdue in paying them, and he hadn't even brought proper supplies to the island for an indefinite stay—yet another sign that the plotting, meticulous man de Soules had once been was no more.

Though de Soules had found the energy to slap and kick her a few more times, most of his day had been spent attempting to rein in his men. And an hour past, the shouting had finally erupted, with the mercenaries threatening to take the birlinn and abandon de Soules on the island. If the matter escalated far enough, Vivienne would offer the mercenaries riches beyond their wildest dreams to take her with them.

But suddenly the shouts outside the cave's mouth changed from angry to shocked. A heartbeat later, the clang of metal on metal crashed through the air.

Her heart leapt into her throat. Had the mercenaries attacked de Soules and Bevin? If so, they might leave in the birlinn as soon as the giant and the madman were overpowered—without Vivienne.

She strained against the ropes binding her, but they held her wrists and ankles fast. De Soules had retied her feet to her hands to keep her immobile, but he'd left her ungagged, so she screamed at the top of her lungs. "Take me with you! I can pay!" she shouted, praying one of the mercenaries would hear her over the din of battle raging outside.

Suddenly de Soules himself burst into the circle of light cast by the weak fire. He had his sword drawn, his eyes wide and fixed on the mouth of the cave.

"Nay," he breathed. "Nay, I killed ye."

Just then, a large form moved in the shadows. For a moment, Vivienne thought it was Bevin, but she could make out a plaid swishing around the man's legs.

Non. It couldn't be.

The form took another step forward, and suddenly Kieran stood in the light.

"It seems ye didnae," he replied.

At the sound of his low, gruff voice, she began shaking. Was this real? A dream? Had de Soules killed her at last and she had been reunited with her love?

A sob broke from her throat. His clear blue eyes darted to where she lay on the cave floor.

"*Vivienne.*"

He turned back to de Soules, his lips drawing back from his teeth in a snarl. "Ye'll pay dearly for hurting her."

De Soules held up his sword as if he were warding off a ghost. "Nay, nay," he kept repeating, backing up until he bumped into one of the cave's walls.

With a roar, Kieran lunged forward. De Soules barely managed to deflect Kieran's sword, scuttling off to the side. Blade raised, Kieran advanced like a wraith come to drag de Soules to hell where he belonged.

"I should take yer head for being a spineless traitor," Kieran rasped, swinging at de Soules again. De Soules blocked the blow but was thrown backward several feet by the force of it. "But I willnae."

De Soules's brown eyes widened as he continued to back away.

"Nay," Kieran went on. "Instead I'll take it for laying a finger on Vivienne."

With another bellow, he charged forward. De Soules tried to parry Kieran's blade, but Kieran drove forward with such power that de Soules couldn't deflect his attack. Their blades hissed against each other, then suddenly de Soules jerked and shrieked.

He looked down with stunned eyes to find Kieran's sword lodged in his chest. Air whistled past his lips in a slow rasp. His legs buckled beneath him and he crumpled to the cave floor.

Kieran yanked his blade free, but he stood over de Soules until the last of the man's breath wheezed away. De Soules went still, his eyes wide and glassy as they stared at nothing in death.

As if waking from a dream, Kieran lifted his head and his eyes locked with hers. Suddenly he was by her side, sliding onto his knees next to her. He dropped his sword and yanked his dagger from his boot, then began sawing frantically at her bindings.

"My God," he breathed. "Vivienne. Are ye all right? Did he hurt ye?"

No doubt she was a frightful sight. De Soules had indeed relished slapping her face and kicking the rest of her. She was certain bruises covered her skin beneath her dress, and her cheeks and lips ached where he'd struck her. But she was alive. And so was Kieran.

"Naught that won't heal soon," she replied in a daze. "You...you are here. Alive."

Her hands and feet suddenly popped free as the ropes fell away. Kieran drew back, eyeing her as if he didn't believe she was real either.

She reached out tentatively and laid her palm against his bristled jawline. He closed his eyes, leaning into her hand.

"I thought you were dead," she whispered, her voice breaking.

"Nay, lass. I could never leave ye. I love ye too much."

Suddenly she launched herself into his arms, hard sobs racking her. He held her close, murmuring in her ear that she was safe now, that he would never let her go, that he loved her, over and over.

After a long while, she became aware that there were others in the cave with them. She lifted her head from Kieran's chest to find Will, Niall, and Mairin standing respectfully at the edge of the circle of light cast by the fire.

"How...how did you find me?" she mumbled, looking up at Kieran.

"I'll explain later," he said. He glanced at Will, a wordless question in his eyes.

"The rest of de Soules's men have been dispatched," Will said in response with a curt nod. "It was damn good timing to come upon them feuding amongst themselves."

"It worked," Vivienne breathed. Not in the way she'd planned, but her efforts hadn't been for naught.

Kieran searched her with his gaze, his brows drawn.

"Are ye saying…that *ye* had a hand in that business outside, lass?"

She ducked her head. "I thought to plant the seeds of discontent between de Soules and his hired men in the hopes that the mercenaries might take me with them if they abandoned de Soules."

Across the cave, Niall whistled softly, and Will's eye widened. Mairin gave her a nod, a rare smile tipping up one side of her mouth.

"Ye are so damn brave and clever, lass," Kieran murmured, respect filling his voice.

He helped her to her feet slowly and guided her toward the cave's opening. They were forced to pass de Soules's lifeless body on the way.

She made herself look at him, to seal the image of him in her mind so that she would never forget he was dead. She wouldn't allow him to haunt her from beyond the grave.

Some small, angry part of her wanted to spit on his body, but she resisted. Just because he'd treated her cruelly, as if she were an animal, didn't mean she would stoop to his level by acting like one.

When they reached the others, Kieran halted.

"Take her to the birlinn," he said grimly.

Her gaze snapped to him. "Aren't you coming?"

His big hand made gentle, reassuring circles on her back. "Aye, in a moment." Yet his hand fell away and his features hardened. "But first, I have a promise to keep."

He stalked back to where he'd dropped his sword and scooped it up, then moved to stand over de Soules. When he pulled out a canvas bag that had been tucked into his belt, she realized what he was about.

The others guided her out of the cave and onto the night-dark beach, which was littered with the bodies of de Soules's mercenaries. Her gaze landed on Bevin, who lay wide-eyed, an arrow protruding from his chest and a slash across his throat.

"Dinnae look," Mairin said quietly, taking Vivienne's arm and pulling her away. Vivienne let her, grateful for the younger woman's kind, gentle touch.

When they reached a small birlinn tucked between the rocks past the beach, Will and Niall helped Mairin and Vivienne in, then began pushing the boat into the water. A moment later, Kieran appeared, discreetly tucking the canvas bag, now heavy with something Vivienne didn't want to consider, away in the ship's stern.

She hardly noticed the sway of the boat as the men launched themselves into it and they took to the open water, so riveted by the sight of Kieran was she.

"I still do not understand how you survived the stab de Soules gave you," she murmured, glancing at his chest.

He took her hand and placed it over his heart. She could tell by the way he flinched slightly at even the light touch that he still needed time to heal, but his eyes were soft and full of love as he gazed down at her.

"I told ye, lass. I couldnae let ye go. My heart hasnae had near enough of ye."

She smiled, warmth and happiness swelling within her for the first time in what felt like ages. "I love you, Kieran."

"I love ye, too, Vivienne," he replied. His mouth broke into a gently teasing grin, which broadened into a full smile. "What's more, I dinnae mind ye overmuch, either."

Chapter Thirty-Seven

K ieran counted himself the luckiest man that ever lived when a little over a sennight later, he got to walk into Scone Palace's great hall with Vivienne on his arm.

Their arrival provoked a wild riot of cheers from the host of bedecked guests inside.

Vivienne's eyes widened at their warm reception. "This is rather too much," she murmured, "given that we are meant to be celebrating Elaine and Jerome's wedding."

For her part, Elaine didn't seem to mind that her wedding feast had been turned into a celebration of Vivienne's safe return and the obliteration of William de Soules and all he stood for. The Englishwoman rose from her and Jerome's seat of honor beside the King at the high table, then lifted her green silk skirts and raced toward Vivienne.

When Elaine reached her, she took Vivienne into a warm embrace.

"Easy," Kieran said with a frown. "She is still healing."

"You don't frighten me, Kieran MacAdams," Elaine retorted, though she did ease her grasp on Vivienne before stepping back.

"Look at you, *mon amie*," Vivienne said, her eyes shining as she took in Elaine's gown and hair, which was done up in what appeared to Kieran like a complicated labyrinth of plaits and loose copper waves. "You are the most beautiful bride I have ever seen."

Elaine laughed, her eyes filling with tears. "I am just grateful that you are here to share this day with me."

Just then, those gathered for the feast began to part as the King stepped from the dais and strode toward them.

When he reached Vivienne, he bowed deeply from the waist.

"*Non, Majesté*, you cannot—" Vivienne began, her cheeks flushing at the King's show of respect.

The Bruce straightened, his dark eyes dancing with mirth. "Ye cannae order me no' to show my gratitude to ye, Lady Vivienne," he said. "I *am* still a King, after all."

Vivienne's blush deepened, but she tilted her head graciously. "Very well, *Majesté*, but you cannot expect me to ever get used to a King bowing to me."

"Fair enough," he replied with a smile. But then he sobered, lifting her hand with both of his. "Truly, milady, I owe ye a debt I can never repay—and I ken my apologies will never be enough."

"*Non, Majesté*," Vivienne replied solemnly, "I believe you have actually given me my life's greatest gift." She lifted her eyes to Kieran, and his chest filled with so much love that it felt as though it would burst.

The Bruce patted her hand before releasing it, then shot Kieran a conspiratorial look. Kieran gave the King a firm shake of the head, silently warning him to hold his tongue.

He'd spoken with the Bruce not long ago, and they'd devised a plan that he hoped would be perfect, but he'd made the King swear to keep his lips sealed until Kieran had a chance to speak with Vivienne about it.

"All the same," the King said, clearing his throat, "I am glad to have de Soules's head on a pike atop the palisades. Forgive me, Lady Elaine, Lady Vivienne, for such talk at a wedding feast, but I cannae deny it."

Jerome joined them, slipping an arm around his bride's waist. "It is a symbol to all that his is the fate of a traitor to Scotland," he said quietly.

"Aye, and based on what Agnes said, and all that Sabine could learn through her network of eyes and ears, no one is interested in joining him on the palisades," the Bruce said. "With the head of the serpent removed, the body crumples." He drew in a breath, straightening. "But enough of such talk. This is a joyous occasion. Lady Vivienne is safely returned, and another member of my Bodyguard Corps is happily married."

The King smiled at Jerome and Elaine, but then his gaze flicked knowingly once more to Kieran.

Hell and damnation, he was going to have to get

Vivienne out of there before the Bruce let something slip.

As Jerome, Elaine, and the King made their way back to the high table, Kieran took Vivienne's hand and looped it through his arm. He began threading them through the nobles gathered for the feast, not slowing or even politely acknowledging those who bowed, curtsied, or offered them a word of congratulations.

"Kieran, what on earth——"

At last, he reached a quiet corner of the hall and pulled her to a halt.

"Marry me."

Vivienne's midnight blue eyes widened. *"Pardon?"*

Bloody hell, this wasn't going as he'd planned. He frowned. He'd prepared everything in his mind, but now that he was gazing down at her, her dark eyes depthless and those petal-pink lips parted in surprise, all his thoughts scattered like leaves in a windstorm.

"I am a hazelnut tree," he tried again, grasping for the right words.

She blinked slowly. "You are?"

"Aye, and ye are honeysuckle. Like in the *Chevrefoil*, ye ken."

Realization flickered across her features, and then her breath caught in her throat.

Aye, that was more like it. Now he was back on the right track.

He took her hand and drew her closer until the rest of the hall fell away and it was just the two of them, staring into each other's eyes.

"Ye have become so entwined with my heart that if I

lost ye, I'd die," he murmured. He paused, carefully saying the next words in his head before repeating them aloud to make sure he got them just right. "*Ni moi sans vous, ni vous sans moi*. Neither me without ye, nor ye without me."

Now tears had gathered in her eyes, making them shimmer like pools of sapphire.

"Marry me," he said again, tenderly brushing away a tear that had escaped down her cheek. "And let me work every day to give ye a life like in one of yer treasured love stories."

"*Oui*," she said, her voice low and tight with emotion.

He pulled her up into his arms in a tight embrace, barely remembering to be gentle with her bruised body or his own still-healing chest wound.

But when he set her on her feet and pulled back, her brows were drawn with worry.

"What is wrong, love?"

She shook her head a little. "It is just…I understand that your place is here in Scotland by your King's side. But I wonder what has become of my position at court, or how I might look in on my father when we are a five-days' sail away." At the mention of sailing, she blanched and shuddered slightly.

A slow smile spread across Kieran's face. She glanced up at him and frowned.

"What is it?"

"What if I told ye I have a solution to all that?"

Her brows furrowed deeper. "You do?"

"I spoke with the Bruce earlier," Kieran said. "I

explained matters with yer father, and also the importance of maintaining the alliance between Scotland and France."

"Oh?"

"The Bruce thinks it prudent to send an emissary to France to ensure that relations continue smoothly." Kieran tilted his head. "He believes I would be a good fit for the job—though why a brute like me should be an ambassador I dinnae ken."

At that, she smiled, and he went on. "King Philip doesnae seem to mind my manners—or lack thereof—though, so neither does the Bruce. It would mean that I'd sometimes have to travel to Scotland, but also that I would visit the French court—with ye, if ye wanted to spend time with the Queen and the ladies-in-waiting."

"That is wonderful," she beamed. But then she caught her lip between her teeth. "Where would we live, though? Paris? Scone?"

"Well," he said slowly, savoring what he was about to tell her. "The Bruce recognizes that Paris is a long way from Scotland. He suggested that it might be better to place an ambassador somewhere in the middle—a few days' ocean crossing from Scone, aye, but mayhap a few days' ride from the French court as well, so that either place could be reached quickly if need be. A place like…Picardy."

Vivienne let out a stunned breath. "You can't mean…my father's estate?"

"Aye," he replied, grinning.

She flung her arms around his neck, her shoulders shaking with either laughter or tears, he wasn't sure which. Abruptly, she drew back, fixing him with a searching gaze. "And this is what *you* want? To live in a crumbling keep on a dilapidated farm?"

"Wherever ye are is my home, Vivienne," he said, cupping her face in his hand. "But, aye, I am genuinely looking forward to a quieter life. Of course, I'll still be one of the Bruce's warriors, but I am a farmer by blood and birth, too. It would be an honor to help yer father bring his estate back to life."

"And…and you won't mind being away from the Highlands?"

Unspoken in her words was a deeper question, about the pain from his past, of losing Linette and his bairn, of losing his home.

He stilled, moved that Vivienne cared for him so deeply that her happiness wasn't complete unless his own was, too. His heart was so full with love for her that it ached.

"I ran from my past for a long while, thinking that if I sealed my heart away, it couldnae ever be hurt again," he said quietly. "But I'm no' running anymore. And I dinnae want to be alone anymore, either. I still have my memories, where the past can live in peace, but now I want what I didnae let myself hope for in all these years. I want a family. And bairns. But most of all, I want ye, Vivienne."

She nodded, tears streaming down her face. "I want all that, too. And I want *you*, Kieran. Forever."

He kissed her then, tasting the sweet saltiness of her tears, drinking her in, his love, his heart, forevermore.

When he pulled away at last, they were both left panting.

"I'll keep my family's plot of land," he said quietly. "No' to farm, nor to linger in the past, but mayhap our bairns will want it someday. And mayhap when the time is right, I'll take ye back there as well."

He affectionately tucked a lock of flaxen hair that had come loose during their kiss behind her ear. "I'd like to show ye the Highlands, lass. But properly, no' when we are running for our lives."

She laughed, and it was the sweetest sound he'd ever heard. "*Oui*, I'd like that, too. But I cannot promise that I will be eager to cross the North Sea very often." Her eyes widened as a realization struck her. "I suppose I will have to make the crossing at least one more time if we are to return to my father's estate."

She went white as snow and swallowed hard. Though he knew it would earn him a tart word later, Kieran couldn't help but laugh.

"Dinnae fash, lass," he said. "I'll bring plenty of good Highland whisky with us. And of course we can always employ my *other* failsafe cure for seasickness again…" Just to get a rise out of her, Kieran gave her a wink.

At the bonny blush and slow smile spreading across her face, he only laughed harder.

Epilogue

February, 1321
Three months later
Picardy, France

"Monsieur MacAdams?"

"Aye, that's me."

Vivienne paused in her recitation of *Roman de la Rose*, another of her father's favorite poems, and glanced up.

Snow flurries swirled into the keep around Kieran's booted ankles. Just outside the open door stood a young messenger lad, the hood of his cloak drawn up against the cold.

"Deliveries from the King of Scotland," the lad said, pulling a sack from beneath his cloak. "And from King Philip's court." He produced another, smaller sack from his other side.

"*Mon Dieu*, what is all that?" Vivienne said, setting aside the book and rising.

"I dinnae ken, though I have a suspicion," Kieran replied, hefting each sack experimentally. He turned to the messenger. "Come in out of the cold, lad, and have something warm to eat and drink."

The lad nodded eagerly and stepped inside.

"*Oui*, come in," Vivienne's father called from his seat before the fire. "And tell us the news from court."

Vivienne set off for the kitchen, but Claudette rose from her seat beside Vivienne's father and caught her arm gently.

"Allow me."

Vivienne took the chastising edge off her words with a soft smile. "Claudette, you are not the chatelaine anymore, nor a servant."

And Vivienne couldn't be happier about it. When she and Kieran had arrived at the estate a few months past, her father and Claudette had taken her aside with somber, worried faces. She'd feared terrible news, only to learn that the two had fallen in love several years ago.

They had kept it from her, they'd explained, because they did not wish for Vivienne to worry that after all her hard work to find a suitable caretaker for her father, Claudette would prove to be a charlatan attempting to take advantage of Lambert. Nor had they wanted to disrespect the memory of Vivienne's mother, despite the fact that it had been nearly a decade since her passing.

To their surprise, Vivienne had flung herself into both of their arms, happy tears streaming down her face. She'd reassured them that their happiness meant the world to her, and that she could imagine no greater joy than to see them joined in love.

But even a month after the two had said their vows before God, Claudette, who had grown used to looking after Lambert, occasionally forgot that she was no longer a caretaker, but a member of the family.

Claudette's mouth curved in a smile that matched Vivienne's, lifting her dark eyebrows. "*Oui*, but I can tell you are eager to follow your husband to the solar to see what is in those packages."

Kieran cocked his head in invitation. "Care to join me, wife?"

Claudette squeezed her arm warmly. "Go on. I'll see to the lad."

"Thank you," Vivienne said, eagerly falling in behind Kieran as he mounted the stairs toward the solar. Curiosity niggled at her about the deliveries from both Scotland and the French court. Hopefully all was well with both.

When they reached the solar, Vivienne took up one of the upholstered chairs while Kieran dropped the parcels on the oak desk and moved to sit in the chair behind it.

He began with the satchel from the Bruce. He pulled out a small stack of folded missives, then a rectangular package wrapped in oiled canvas. Setting the package aside, he began to open and read the missives.

Most he passed along to her after quickly scanning them. One was a personal note from Elaine congratulating Lambert and Claudette on their nuptials, which Vivienne had written to her about. To Vivienne's joy, Elaine and Jerome had been able to visit France to attend Vivienne and Kieran's wedding not long after their own. Still, that had been nearly three months ago, and she missed her spirited, kind-hearted English friend.

The other missives regarded smaller matters in Scotland, including the Bruce's departure from Scone for the winter season. He'd returned to Cardross, where he was having an estate built for his wife and family.

But one missive, which bore the seal of the King himself, gave Kieran pause.

"The Bruce sends his felicitations," he said, scanning the missive. "And news of England."

Vivienne's brows drew together. "Oh?"

"It seems that tensions in England are escalating into an all-out civil war," he commented. "Which is good news from the Bruce's perspective, as it is keeping the English out of Scotland's hair. Apparently he is considering involving the Corps to further aggravate the strain between King Edward II and his nobles. The more trouble the English face internally, the less harm they can do to Scotland."

"Would you be called to England, then?" Vivienne said, worry knotting her stomach.

"Nay, nay," he replied quickly. "The Bruce still wants me here. But he writes that he may call upon other members of the Corps."

Vivienne considered that. "Will, Niall, and Mairin all seemed to impress the King with their role in hunting down de Soules."

"Aye," Kieran said, rubbing his palm along the faint shadow of growth on his jaw. "I was mistaken about the lot of them at first. I'm glad they proved me wrong for hesitating to trust them initially."

He handed her the missive, which she scanned quickly, but her gaze kept tugging to the wrapped parcel on the desk. "And what do you suppose that is?"

"Let's see what arrived from court first," he said, a strange, knowing twitch pulling at the corners of his mouth.

Before she could question his odd behavior, he pulled open the other sack and removed a small, square box with a missive tied to it with ribbon.

"This looks to be for ye," he said, passing her the little package.

Recognizing the Queen's seal on the front of the missive, Vivienne excitedly untied the ribbon. But she held off on breaking the seal on the parchment, and instead opened the little wooden box first.

Inside, she found a bundle of fluffy white wool— wrapped around a delicate stained glass vial. With an exclamation of excitement, Vivienne lifted the vial free of the wool and removed the cork stopper.

The delicate scent of violets drifted up from the oil inside.

"Oh," she gasped. "How did she know?"

Kieran grinned. "A wee birdie may have written to the Queen to inform her that her favorite former lady-in-waiting lost the oil she so dearly treasured."

Vivienne excitedly dabbed the stopper on her wrists and neck, tears stinging her eyes. "Thank you."

"What did she write to ye?"

Carefully setting the glass vial aside, Vivienne broke the wax seal and began reading the Queen's missive.

"She wishes for me to visit court soon," she said over the parchment.

"If the snow doesnae begin to stick, mayhap we could go within the sennight. The Bruce will want me to keep King Philip abreast of his intentions regarding the English civil war."

Vivienne nodded, but as she continued to read the Queen's note, her heart sank. "She writes specifically that she wants me to sit and read to her and the other ladies—from her favorite story, *The Song of Roland*."

She hadn't let herself dwell on the loss of that most dear book in the fire. She'd come away with her life, after all, and so had Kieran, which was all that truly mattered. Still, sadness washed over her to think of it.

"I will have to select some other story to read, if the Queen will allow it," she said, trying to keep the disappointment from her voice.

Kieran frowned, but his pale blue eyes danced with something Vivienne couldn't quite put her finger on.

"Och, well, it would be a shame to deny a Queen." Slowly, he reached for the rectangular package on the desk and handed it to her. "Mayhap this will help."

Vivienne's heart suddenly leapt into her throat. What on earth was Kieran up to?

With trembling fingers, she unwrapped the oil parchment. What she found inside stole her breath.

It was the finest book she'd ever seen. The cover was made of leather dyed dark blue and embossed with a border of flowers and leaves. In the center were the words—

"*The Song of Roland*." Her head jerked up and she fixed Kieran with a wide-eyed stare. "How did you…"

Her voice failed as emotion tightened her throat and blurred her vision.

Through her tears, she saw the slow, soft smile spreading across Kieran's rugged features.

"I thought ye ought to have a new copy."

She lifted the book, tracing the embossed lettering, painted gold, with one shaking hand.

"The flowers and such were yer father's idea," Kieran commented. "When the plan occurred to me, I went to him first. He helped make all the decisions. But I picked the blue for the cover—I ken ye favor the color."

With an overwhelmed nod, she let her fingertips glide along the rich gilding on the edges of the parchment, then carefully cracked the book. Each page was a small work of art, every letter hand-painted with skillful, precise flourishes.

"This was meant to be a wedding gift, but apparently scribes cannae be rushed over such things," Kieran said with a shrug.

"This…this is…" She looked up. Another thought occurred to her through her shock. "This must have cost a small fortune!"

Kieran cocked an amused brow. "Aye, well, in that regard I cannae claim all the credit. When the Bruce learned what I was about, he insisted on paying for it as a token of his gratitude to ye."

Vivienne returned her gaze to the book in her hands. Though the expense of such an item would be staggering, the thought and love behind it meant so much more to her that the coin used to buy it.

"I ken it isnae the same as having the one yer father gave ye," Kieran said quietly. "But——"

"It is perfect."

A smile lifted the corners of his mouth. "Do ye like it, then?"

Vivienne rose, setting the book on the desk and moving around to Kieran. Tears streamed unchecked down her cheeks now. "I love it. I love *you*."

He pulled her into his lap, his eyes shining with love. "I promised to give ye the kind of life ye read about in stories. And this is only the beginning."

The End

Author's Note

As always, it is one of my great joys in writing historical romance to combine a fictional romantic storyline with real historical details. Plus, it's such a treat to share not only a thrilling, passionate, and emotional love story with you, lovely readers, but to give you a glimpse at my research into the history surrounding this book as well.

If you've read the previous book in the Highland Bodyguards series, *Surrender to the Scot* (Book 7), then you'll already be familiar with the history behind my portrayal of King Philip V of France and his royal court in Paris. But the Queen, Joan II of Burgundy, only received a passing mention in that book. It was a delight to get to showcase her a bit more in this story.

Philip was considered an intelligent, sensitive, and politically adept King. For her part, Joan was thought to be loyal and steadfast, and the two appeared to be very much in love. Philip wrote Joan love letters, and gave her generous gifts of land, money, and jewels. What was more, he protected these gifts—and by extension Joan—by specifically structuring them in such a way that they could not be revoked even in the case of his death and the crowning of a new monarch.

There is a long history of ladies-in-waiting serving in royal courts around the world, including in the medieval French court. Joan would have had her pick of ladies, women she deemed proper models for behavior at court, but also whom she enjoyed spending time with in the privacy of her own chambers. Because of their close relationship with the Queen, ladies-in-waiting were elevated above servants, and were tasked with things like helping the Queen dress, arranging her hair, and keeping her company with activities like embroidery and reading. While Vivienne is a fictional creation, her role at court was a real and important one.

Speaking of reading, all the medieval stories I mention in the book, including *The Song of Roland*, *Tristan and Iseult*, and *Roman de la Rose*, were popular tales during this time. Though books would have been rare and expensive, these tales of courtly love, battles, and chivalric knights spread like wildfire throughout Europe and the British Isles.

The Song of Roland was written in the eleventh century, and was very popular from twelfth through the fifteenth centuries. It was based on a battle in 778 during Charlemagne's reign, and featured the heroic sacrifice of Roland to save his compatriots if not himself. *Tristan and Iseult* (or Isolde, depending on the version), is the Welsh tale of ill-fated lovers forced apart by their circumstances. The story of Tristan using the hazelnut tree and the honeysuckle to signal Iseult comes from the *Chevrefoil*, the French name for this portion of the epic poem. And *Roman de la Rose*, written in the 1200s, is another sweeping poem that ruminates on love as a courtier woos his lady in a walled garden. As a lady-in-waiting at the French court, Vivienne and her real-life counterparts likely would have had access to and been familiar with these tales of chivalric love.

In *Surrender to the Scot*, I fictionalized the idea that William de Soules, a real historical figure who was behind the "de Soules Conspiracy" against Robert the Bruce, visited the French court as part of the Bruce's envoy to deliver his Declaration of Arbroath to the Pope, which asserted Scotland's independence from England. Therefore the idea that he was drugged and detained at court until the conspiracy was uncovered is also fictitious, but the actual history behind de Soules's fate is so fascinating that it almost seems like fiction!

As I mentioned in my author's note in *Surrender*, de Soules was a Lowland noble who believed he'd been overlooked when the Bruce began redistributing lands and titles he'd reclaimed from the English. De Soules gathered several other nobles (including Countess Agnes of Strathearn, and Sirs David de Brechin, John Logie, Gilbert Malherbe, and Richard Broun, among others) and began plotting a coup to remove the Bruce from the Scottish throne, replacing him with Edward Balliol, the son of Scotland's one-time King John Balliol, who was considered a puppet of the English.

Luckily for the Scots, de Soules's plot was uncovered. Upon being found out, Countess Agnes immediately confessed to her part and turned over the names of several of the other conspirators. This earned her a stay of execution from the King at the so-called "Black Parliament," where the Bruce passed down judgment on those who'd conspired against him.

Though all the other conspirators were given a traitor's death, the Bruce spared de Soules's life as well. This may have been because de Soules, like the countess, confessed and flipped on his allies. Or it may have been, as I portray in this story, that the Bruce feared making a martyr of de Soules, thus risking adding fuel to the fire if any of de Soules's allies remained at large.

In any case, de Soules was imprisoned at Scone, but was later moved to Dumbarton Castle's dungeon to serve out the rest of his life. And here is where things get interesting. Some sources say he died within a year of arriving at Dumbarton under "mysterious circumstances."

However, other accounts note that a "Lord William de Soules" was among the dead on the English side of the Battle of Boroughbridge between the English and the Scots in 1322. Some have speculated that perhaps de Soules somehow escaped Dumbarton's dungeon and fled to England in search of those more sympathetic to his cause to oust the Bruce. Playing on that juicy tidbit, I fictionalized the idea that de Soules escaped on his way to Dumbarton. In any case, de Soules died somewhere between 1320 and 1322, though the exact circumstances remain murky.

Ailsa Craig, where I had de Soules take Vivienne, is a real island off the western coast of Scotland. Its unusual sheer sides, composed of granite columns, and its domed top are a result of the fact that it is an ancient plug on a now-extinct volcano. It has been used as a landmark for sailors traveling between Ireland and Scotland, alerting them that the Scottish (or Irish, depending on which direction you're traveling) mainland wasn't much farther. It came to be known colloquially as "Paddy's Milestone" because of this.

The island has seen an exciting and rich history. It sheltered Highland pirates and smugglers (a story for another day!), was the site of a sixteenth-century castle, was invaded by Spain so that it could serve as a safe haven for Catholics fleeing the Scottish Reformation, and more. Now it is a protected bird sanctuary. Fun fact —it's also the location where stones for the sport of curling are quarried. Every stone ever used in Olympic curling competitions has come from Ailsa Craig!

And my last historical note must come with a caveat. I'm no doctor, but I did greatly enjoy learning about medieval solutions to collapsed and punctured lungs. The idea of sealing or draining a lung that had been punctured or filled with blood dates back to antiquity. In ideal conditions, a puncture wound might be washed with wine or oil, then covered with a dressing of cloth (like a linen patch) and an herb plaster to fight infection.

If blood filled the lung, it would have to be removed with a tube or reed (like I had Jossalyn use on Kieran). The first overt mention of this technique in the medieval era appears in Wolfram von Eschenbach's *Parzival*, which was written in the early 1200s. Eschenbach describes the comments by a knight named Gawan who witnessed a fellow knight, Uriens, receive a lance blow to the chest during a joust:

> *There lay a man pierced through,*
> *with his blood rushing inward…*
> *"I could keep this knight from dying*
> *and I feel sure I could save him*
> *if I had a reed,*
> *You would soon see him and hear*
> *him in health, because*
> *he is not mortally wounded.*
> *The blood is only pressing on his heart."*
> *He grasped a branch of the linden tree,*
> *slipped the bark off like a tube –*
> *he was no fool in the matter of wounds –*
> *and inserted it into the body through the wound.*
> *Then he bade the woman suck on it*
> *until blood flowed toward her.*
> *The hero's strength revived so that he could speak*
>   *and talk again.*

Uriens is said to have stood up under his own power and walked away from a wound that would have otherwise killed him in minutes.

Of course, it's probably unlikely that Kieran would have survived for two days riding on horseback with only a wool bandage to seal the puncture wound and one lung filling with blood, but this is romantic fiction, after all. A larger-than-life hero like Kieran wouldn't let something like a medical impossibility stand in the way of reaching his heroine.

Thank you for journeying back in time with me to medieval France and Scotland, and look for more riveting history and unforgettable romance in the ninth book in the Highland Bodyguards series, Niall and Mairin's story, coming late 2018!

Make sure to sign up for my newsletter to hear about all my sales, giveaways, and new releases. Plus, get exclusive content like stories, excerpts, cover reveals, and more.

Sign up at www.EmmaPrinceBooks.com

Thank You!

Thank you for taking the time to read *Her Wild Highlander* (Highland Bodyguards, Book 8)!

And thank you in advance for sharing your enjoyment of this book (or my other books) with fellow readers by leaving a review on Amazon. Long or short, detailed or to the point, I read all reviews and greatly appreciate you for writing one!

I love connecting with readers! Sign up for my newsletter and be the first to hear about my latest book news, flash sales, giveaways, and more—signing up is free and easy at www.EmmaPrinceBooks.com.

You also can join me on Twitter at @EmmaPrinceBooks. Or keep up on Facebook at https://www.facebook.com/EmmaPrinceBooks.

TEASERS FOR EMMA
PRINCE'S BOOKS

Highland Bodyguards Series:

Read Elaine and Jerome's story, and meet Vivienne and Kieran for the first time, in *Surrender to the Scot* (**Highland Bodyguards, Book 7**). Available now on Amazon.

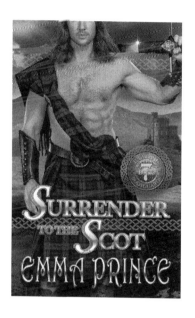

A dangerous mission. A deadly conspiracy. A daring love.

Jerome Munro has been battling a shameful truth all his life—he is the son of a traitor. So when Robert the Bruce orders him to deliver a bold declaration asserting Scotland's independence, Jerome knows it's his best chance to prove his allegiance. When he travels to the Borderlands to gather support for the King, he finds himself entranced by a copper-haired English lass whose determination to serve the Bruce kindles an unexpected attraction. Fearing his desire for Elaine will disrupt his assignment, Jerome fights against the heat between them, but when fate throws them together on a dangerous mission, he must choose between love and loyalty.

Elaine longs for much more than the sheltered life of an English lady. The darkly handsome Highland warrior who arrives at her Borderland home provides the perfect opportunity for her to show that she's more than a silly, spoiled girl. She convinces Jerome to let her return to the Bruce's court with him, but when she accidentally uncovers a plot against the King, she realizes she and Jerome are the only ones who can save Scotland's hard-earned freedom. As the threat spirals out of control, can they unravel the mystery and protect their growing love?

The Lady's Protector, the thrilling start to the Highland Bodyguards series, is available now on Amazon!

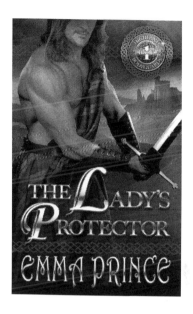

***The Battle of Bannockburn may be over, but the
war is far from won.***

Her Protector...

Ansel Sutherland is charged with a mission from King
Robert the Bruce to protect the illegitimate son of a
powerful English Earl. Though Ansel bristles at aiding
an Englishman, the nature of the war for Scottish independence is changing, and he is honor-bound to serve as
a bodyguard. He arrives in England to fulfill his assignment, only to meet the beautiful but secretive Lady
Isolda, who refuses to tell him where his ward is. When a

mysterious attacker threatens Isolda's life, Ansel realizes he is the only thing standing between her and deadly peril.

His Lady…

Lady Isolda harbors dark secrets—secrets she refuses to reveal to the rugged Highland rogue who arrives at her castle demanding answers. But Ansel's dark eyes cut through all her defenses, threatening to undo her resolve. To protect her past, she cannot submit to the white-hot desire that burns between them. As the threat to her life spirals out of control, she has no choice but to trust Ansel to whisk her to safety deep in the heart of the Highlands…

The Sinclair Brothers Trilogy:

Go back to where it all began—with Robert and Alwin's story in ***Highlander's Ransom***, Book One of the Sinclair Brothers Trilogy. Available now on Amazon!

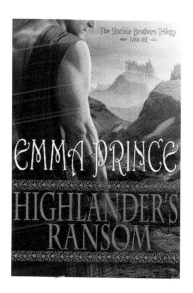

He was out for revenge...

Laird Robert Sinclair will stop at nothing to exact revenge on Lord Raef Warren, the English scoundrel who brought war to his doorstep and razed his lands and people. Leaving his clan in the Highlands to conduct covert attacks in the Borderlands, Robert lives to be a thorn in Warren's side. So when he finds a beautiful English lass on her way to marry Warren, he whisks her away to the Highlands with a plan to ransom her back to her dastardly fiancé.

She would not be controlled...

Lady Alwin Hewett had no idea when she left her father's manor to marry a man she'd never met that she would instead be kidnapped by a Highland rogue out for vengeance. But she refuses to be a pawn in any man's game. So when she learns that Robert has had them secretly wed, she will stop at nothing to regain her freedom. But her heart may have other plans...

Viking Lore Series:

Step into the lush, daring world of the Vikings with
Enthralled (**Viking Lore, Book 1**)!

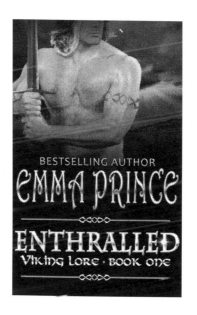

He is bound by honor…

Eirik is eager to plunder the treasures of the fabled lands
to the west in order to secure the future of his village.
The one thing he swears never to do is claim possession
over another human being. But when he journeys across
the North Sea to raid the holy houses of Northumbria,
he encounters a dark-haired beauty, Laurel, who stirs
him like no other. When his cruel cousin tries to take
Laurel for himself, Eirik breaks his oath in an attempt to
protect her. He claims her as his thrall. But can he claim

her heart, or will Laurel fall prey to the devious schemes of his enemies?

She has the heart of a warrior...

Life as an orphan at Whitby Abbey hasn't been easy, but Laurel refuses to be bested by the backbreaking work and lecherous advances she must endure. When Viking raiders storm the abbey and take her captive, her strength may finally fail her—especially when she must face her fear of water at every turn. But under Eirik's gentle protection, she discovers a deeper bravery within herself—and a yearning for her golden-haired captor that she shouldn't harbor. Torn between securing her freedom or giving herself to her Viking master, will fate decide for her—and rip them apart forever?

About the Author

Emma Prince is the Bestselling and Amazon All-Star Author of steamy historical romances jam-packed with adventure, conflict, and of course love!

Emma grew up in drizzly Seattle, but traded her rain boots for sunglasses when she and her husband moved to the eastern slopes of the Sierra Nevada. Emma spent several years in academia, both as a graduate student and an instructor of college-level English and Humanities courses. She always savored her "fun books"—normally historical romances—on breaks or vacations. But as she began looking for the next chapter in her life, she wondered if perhaps her passion could turn into a career. Ever since then, she's been reading and writing books that celebrate happily ever afters!

Visit Emma's website, www.EmmaPrinceBooks.com, for updates on new books, future projects, her newsletter sign-up, book extras, and more!

You can follow Emma on Twitter at: @EmmaPrinceBooks.

Or join her on Facebook at: www.facebook.com/EmmaPrinceBooks.

74364909R00224

Made in the USA
Middletown, DE
23 May 2018